SEAN HAD THE RULES
FIGURED OUT ALREADY . . .

1.) He was in the fu _____ *past.
They looked like eac* _____ *nking
his place, like the poo* _____ *atch-
ers, except that Sean* _____ *mally
wouldn't believe that* _____ *made
more sense than anything else he* _____ *that
leap was made, any result of it was as reasonable as the premise, so there was no reason to let it get to him.*

*2.) He had to stay in this room, because he wasn't supposed
to see what was outside it. Knowing this rule didn't mean he
had any intention of following it for very long, but for now he
wasn't quite ready to go exploring; that could wait until later.*

*3.) The shrink was supposed to take care of him. But Sean
was twelve. He didn't need a baby-sitter.*

QUANTUM
LEAP

OUT OF TIME. OUT OF BODY.
OUT OF CONTROL.

D0707807

QUANTUM LEAP
ODYSSEY

A NOVEL BY
BARBARA E. WALTON
BASED ON THE UNIVERSAL TELEVISION
SERIES *QUANTUM LEAP*
CREATED BY DONALD P. BELLISARIO

BOULEVARD BOOKS, NEW YORK

If you purchased this book without a cover, you should be aware that this book is stolen property. It was reported as "unsold and destroyed" to the publisher, and neither the author nor the publisher has received any payment for this "stripped book."

Quantum Leap: Odyssey, a novel by Barbara E. Walton, based on the Universal television series QUANTUM LEAP, created by Donald P. Bellisario.

QUANTUM LEAP: ODYSSEY

A Boulevard Book/published by arrangement with MCA Publishing Rights, a Division of MCA, Inc.

PRINTING HISTORY
Boulevard edition/March 1996

Copyright © 1996 by MCA Publishing Rights, a Division of MCA, Inc. All rights reserved.
Cover art by Stephen Gardner.
This book may not be reproduced in whole or in part, by mimeograph or any other means, without permission.
For information address: The Berkley Publishing Group, 200 Madison Avenue, New York, New York 10016.

The Putnam Berkley World Wide Web site address is
http://www.berkley.com

ISBN: 1-57297-092-8

BOULEVARD
Boulevard Books are published by The Berkley Publishing Group, 200 Madison Avenue, New York, New York 10016.
BOULEVARD and its logo
are trademarks belonging to Berkley Publishing Corporation.

PRINTED IN THE UNITED STATES OF AMERICA

10 9 8 7 6 5 4 3 2 1

For Coach Prinzi,
who knew better than to let me paint,

and for Kim Hewitt and Jen Mezynski,
who kept me sane as long as possible.
May we choke on M&M's and ginger ale,
LYLAS, and MTFBWYAFLT!

ACKNOWLEDGMENTS

Listing everyone who had a hand in this book would be a book in itself, roughly the size of the Greater Buffalo telephone directory. But there are some people without whom this book could not exist, and I'd like to thank them.

Ginjer Buchanan, first and foremost. She gave me a break that I hope I will someday earn. She is a saint among editors, and Leapers are blessed to have her on our side.

My mother, Linda Walton, who has put up with my semi-obsessive behavior for years, and who has patiently read even my worst efforts with a constructive eye.

The best gang on Usenet, rec.arts.sf.tv.quantum-lcap, who kept me firmly grounded in the QL universe, and helped me remember canon details. If I missed one, it's because I forgot to ask, not because they didn't know.

The Lifelong Learning Center at the Buffalo and Erie County Public Library, where I printed out the manuscript.

All the people involved in *Quantum Leap*, especially Donald Bellisario, who created a format with such infinite possibilities.

Livingston-Steuben-Wyoming County BOCES, which provided me a copy of the "Humor from Homer" problem, and Kim Hewitt, who refreshed my memory about our solution.

Perry Central School, which is, emphatically, *not* the school-from-hell you will find in the following pages, but which does share the occasional physical characteristic.

And finally, all the Perry O.M.ers, without whom this author would be a very different person—Tasia Betts, Lisa Brandetsas, Jeff DeBrine, Karen DeVinney, Kim Grisewood, Kim Hewitt, Jen Mezynski, Jamie Parsons, Kip Smith, Scott Waite

... Names are such funny things; one leads to another, and you can never write them all. Although the characters in *Odyssey* are entirely fictional, a large part of its writing came out of missing these very real people, and I hope it finds them well and happy.

[Much] more than rewards and praise, the gifted child needs scope, material on which his imagination can feed, and opportunities to exercise it. He needs inconspicuous access to books, museums, instruments, paints, ideas, a chance to feed himself with the accumulated heritage from the genius of other ages. He needs a chance for contact, however fleeting . . . with those who are masters in the abilities with which he has been specially endowed. And within our sternly Puritan tradition, he may well need also a special sense of stewardship for the talents which he has been given, and explicit moral sanction against selling his birthright for a mess of pottage.

Margaret Mead, 1954,
quoted in *Growing Up Gifted*

[W]hen coming-of-age Boomers set out to "liberate" America from various G.I. Generation institutions, schools were among the first and biggest targets. What did happen is that the Consciousness Revolution brought to educational theory much the same battering ram it brought to child-raising theory: a rationale for leave-'em-alone nurture, for constructive neglect by the adults important to a child's life.

Neil Howe and Bill Strauss, 1993,
in *13th Gen: Abort, Retry, Ignore, Fail?*

PART ONE

Friday

CHAPTER
ONE

First, the smell:

It was a pungent mix—the cinnamon aroma of old papers crumbling against each other; the low, moist mildew beneath it; long-undisturbed dust in the rafters above. It brought comforting images of books and academia, of closed library stacks heavy with years of accumulated learning.

Next, taste:

His mouth was lightly coated with peanut butter and jelly, consumed not too long ago. There was a cloyingly sweet taste mixed with it, and he guessed it was some kind of pop.

Then, sensation:

The room, whatever it was, was too warm. Sweat was trickling down an uncomfortably upstretched arm. There was some kind of air current around his ankles, but it didn't reach very far up.

Sounds; children's voices, fading in and out:

"You—you killed my dog!"

Then, *clop*.

3

"Ugh, I've got a headache!"

And, Sam Beckett could swear, *"Here, have an extra-strength Tylenarg capsule."*

Finally, the world came into view:

It was a school storage room. Classroom desks were piled precariously along one wall; metal shelves sagged from the accumulations of paper that had been piled onto them. Sam found himself standing in the center of a cleared area, which was bordered with ragged, unpainted canvas flats, the kind that had always been backstage when he had played in his high school band. The drama club had used them for scenery, and Sam guessed they were serving a similar purpose here. There was a certain look to a stage, no matter where it was located, a certain *feel*, and this tiny cleared-out space had it.

He was wearing some kind of toga; it seemed to be a folded bed sheet draped around his waist and over his shoulder. He looked down, and was relieved to see the cuffs of blue jeans poking out underneath it. In his upstretched hand was a lightning bolt, made of cardboard and tin foil.

In front of him, a prepubescent boy in a similar toga was playing out an elaborate death scene, staggering around the makeshift stage area and gagging. He fell to the floor, grasping at his chest. Even in his muddled state, Sam could tell that there was no real trouble; no one in danger could possibly ham it up that well.

He felt a pressure on his left leg, and looked down to see a girl about the same age as the boy, dressed in a leopard costume . . . well, "costume" may have been too generous a word. She was wearing a hooded leopard-print cape tied around her waist. Ears had been clumsily tacked to the hood. She put one "paw" over her mouth and feigned yawning.

Sam lowered his arm, amused.

A voice floated in from somewhere behind him: "Now, Pigeon!"

4

From behind one of the flats, another boy appeared, growling. He was about the same age as the others, and possessed of a skinny, gawky body wrapped in a tiger print blanket for a loincloth. Sam could not, however, see his face, because his head was covered by a Cyclops mask made of papier-mâché that was almost as big as its wearer. It was clumsily painted and poorly balanced, somehow the apex of the entire ridiculous set.

He felt the laughter coming up inside him, huge and fast. He caught it in his throat, making only a choked little sound: "Ummph."

It was enough. The masked boy heard him and turned—too quickly. The mask swayed drunkenly to one side; the boy tried to compensate and tripped over to the other. Boy and mask went tumbling in opposite directions.

There was no stopping it this time. The laugh came out, and kept coming until he lost his breath and had to sit down on the stage, his toga slipping off his shoulder. And still, it came. The others looked at him, and one by one started giggling, then laughing along with him.

Finally, it tapered off long enough to catch a breath. He wiped a tear from the corner of his eye. "Oh, boy," he gasped.

The leopard-girl got her own laughing under control, then whacked Sam on the back, just to make sure he was done. The boy who had fallen—who was apparently none too injured by being laughed at—reached for his mask and put it back on. He stood carefully and began moving gingerly around the stage with it.

The boy who had been flopping around on the floor stopped "dying" and sat up. He was an engaging kid, with large green eyes and curly brown hair. He looked at the Cyclops. "Do we have to make a new head, Pidge?"

The skinny boy's voice was echoey inside the mask. "No," he said, "it's not broken."

Another girl—the one whose voice had ordered the Cyclops' entrance, Sam guessed—appeared around the flats. She was plain and a little overweight, and wearing baggy clothes that did nothing for her. Her hair was long and straight; she was trying to look like something out of Woodstock but succeeding only in looking limp and tired. She wore a peace sign around her neck. Despite her mellow symbols, she was clearly in charge and clearly not amused. The other children seemed to shrink away from her, to regard her as an adult intrusion even though she seemed to be the same age as they were.

Sam felt the last of his laughter dry up, although it wasn't for the same reason as the others. As long as he could remember, he'd been subject to moments of insight, when an answer about something—a person, a problem, anything—came to him without bidding. He vaguely remembered a professor (or maybe it was a colleague; Sam refused to frustrate himself trying to recall circumstances that he had probably lost long ago) telling him that it was a gift for "synthetic thinking," an ability to put bits of information together faster than most people. Someone else (he thought it had been a woman, maybe his sister or mother) had said it was a sixth sense. Whatever it was, it had served him well as a scientist, and even better as a Leaper.

One of those flashes came to him now, looking at the girl who wasn't anything like the person she was trying to project: *She's lonely. Dangerously lonely.* He wasn't entirely sure what "dangerously lonely" might mean, but it was the phrase that came into his head, and he felt its truth instinctively.

"Are you under control, Sean?" she asked.

Since no one else had answered, he surmised that he was, indeed, "Sean" for the time being. "Uh, yeah," he said. "No problem."

She looked at him skeptically. "We have two more days before competition. You can't crack up like that in rehearsal."

6

The boy on the floor rolled his eyes. "Chill out, Sarah. Pigeon's head fell off. It was funny."

"I don't think it's funny, Johnny. I want the head fixed before Monday."

"Who died and made you Coach?"

"I'm the only one who's taking this seriously. That puts me in charge. Let's run it again. I've got the stopwatch ready."

The girl beside Sam started to untie the leopard-print cape. "Sorry. My dad's picking me up in five minutes."

Sarah looked up, surprised and disappointed. "You're just leaving? In the middle of a school day?"

"I told you before. I have to go to a wedding rehearsal."

The boy they called "Pigeon" took off the mask again (as much as Sam hated to admit it, he could see where the boy had gotten his nickname; his head was almost as badly balanced on his skinny neck as the mask had been, and combined with his large, sharp features, he *did* look something like a bird) and looked at her strangely. "A wedding rehearsal?"

"Yeah. My dad's marrying his midlife crisis on Sunday. I'm supposed to be in the wedding to make it look like we all like each other. I think it's really just so that he can be sure there's someone there that's, like, younger than the bride." She freed herself of her "costume" and Sam got a good look at her.

She was a pretty girl, with thick red hair, wide brown eyes, and a high, breathy voice. She smelled of bubble gum, hair spray, and some sweet perfume. There was something familiar about her, but Sam couldn't place it.

Don't think about it, he told himself. Things that he thought about too much never came to him. If this girl was a piece of his missing memory, he'd just have to wait for her to fall into place; if she didn't come that way, she wouldn't come at all.

7

She leaned forward and planted a wet kiss on Sam's cheek. "Bye, babe."

Babe? he thought, bemused. What *was* this girl—twelve, maybe thirteen years old, tops?

She squeezed his hand and gave him a big, toothy smile, then stood and waved to the others. "See ya," she said.

Pigeon and Johnny both returned her wave; Sarah ignored her studiously.

She left.

Still somewhat dazed, Sam shook his head. "She called me 'babe,' " he mused, as a screech of metal announced the opening of the Imaging Chamber Door, a portal between the world where he was and the world where he belonged.

Pigeon looked up. "She's been calling you 'babe' since you started going out."

"Which was"—Sam heard a series of beeps, and turned to find Al Calavicci, his holographic Observer, a few feet behind him, dressed somewhat conservatively (for Al) in a black shirt with self-lit buttons and black pants—"four months ago," Al finished. "They're a real item. Four months is a long time for seventh-graders."

"It's a long time for you," Sam muttered.

Al ignored him, and began pulling up records from the data files. "It's Friday, January 21, 1983," he said. "Your name is Sean O'Connor, you're twelve years old, and you're a seventh-grader here at Penworth Central School in Penworth, New York. You and the rest of the kids here are in a gifted program called . . . Olympics of the Mind. O.M. for short. It's a competition. This one is . . . Humor from Homer. They have to take a scene from the *Odyssey* and make it a comedy. You're Zeus, by the way." He pointed to the door. "The amorous and very young lady is Chrissi Martinez. She's eleven. They accelerated her."

"Do I know a Chrissi Martinez?"

"Not that I know of. Why?"

"She looks kind of familiar."

"Hey, O'Connor," Johnny called, interrupting them, "who you talking to?"

Sam shrugged. "Just practicing my lines?" he tried.

"You only have four."

"I want to get them right."

Sarah raised her eyes to the heavens. "Finally," she said. "One person is taking it seriously."

Johnny shook his head offhandedly. "Oh, we'd all slash our wrists with rusty steak knives to get to States and you know it."

"If you're going to slash your wrists, wait until after the competition. I can replace you between Regionals and States, but not between now and Monday." Sarah's tone was light, but Sam sensed a disturbing intensity in her attitude; he thought she was more serious than she let on.

Dangerously lonely, he thought again.

Johnny was apparently accustomed to her. "Glad to know my life is valuable," he said.

" 'Til Monday, anyway," Pigeon reminded him.

Sam looked at Al out of the corner of his eye. "Their humor is a little tasteless," he said under his breath.

Al was smiling. "I like these kids."

"You would."

Pigeon had resumed his pacing around the stage; Sarah was coaching him, and Johnny was following a few steps behind, holding out his arms to catch the mask in case it fell again.

Al went back to the data files. "The boys, let's see . . . Johnny Metz is the one who's going to slash his wrists with a rusty steak knife. The one with the mask is Peter Janowski. Everyone calls him Pigeon. The girl is Sarah Easton. She's sort of a team captain. She wrote the script. She takes the game seriously. She thinks it's all she has."

9

"Is she . . . I mean, does she *do* something?"

"What do you mean?"

"I don't know. Am I here for her?"

"You're here for all of them."

"What, am I here to get them to state-level competition?"

"In a way."

Sam waited for him to elaborate.

"Well, they're going to win Regionals with or without you. But in the original history, the school board cuts the program before they make it to States."

They were interrupted suddenly by a clanging sound. Out of the corner of his eye, Sam saw Pigeon's mask fall off when he jumped. "Fire alarm?" he asked Al.

"Class bell."

"Shit!" Sarah said, then blushed madly. She gathered up a few books and scooted out of the room.

Johnny looked across at Sam. "She swears," he said, deadpan. "What do you know." He and Pigeon began to shuck out of their togas. They reached for a couple of T-shirts that were balled up behind the flats, pulled them on, and ran out.

Al smiled wickedly and pointed at the leftover shirt. "You'd better hurry up and get to class, Sam. Earth science, room 106." He waved good-bye and disappeared through the Door.

Sam grabbed the shirt and put it on, then picked up a few notebooks that had been subtly labeled "Sean O'Connor" in five or six places each. He went out into the hall.

Room 106 turned out to be only three doors to the right of the storage room. Unfortunately, Sam had begun his search by getting caught in a torrent of students going left.

He was pulled around a corner and past a small library, into a main corridor, where he could see the school office near a large glass door that looked out on a bleak, wintery parking lot. He was whisked across this hall, and into another—a dark, cavernous extension with no windows and only intermittent fluorescent lights. It was here that the flow finally tapered off enough for him to pull away and rest against the wall.

A convex security mirror was mounted overhead, and he looked into it curiously. Despite the distortion, he could see that Sean O'Connor was a pretty decent-looking kid. He wasn't small for his age, nor was he afflicted with the gangly arms and legs of many tall boys. He was well muscled and clear-skinned, with longish blond hair framing a strong face. Sam couldn't ascertain the color of his eyes in this poor light and from this distance, but they seemed to be light, maybe blue or green.

He realized he was alone in the hall just as the bell rang for a second time. He arrived in Sean's class nearly five minutes late.

The teacher, a middle-aged man with hard blue eyes, was in the midst of an introduction to volcanic activity, hitting the blackboard with a pointer repeatedly as he spoke, when Sam came in. He looked up and smiled expansively. "Nice of you to grace us, Mr. O'Connor."

Sam nodded sheepishly and started looking for an empty seat. "Yeah, sorry I was late, I . . ."

"This is the fifth time in five days."

"I'm really sorry."

The smile became wider. "I'll accept your apology on one condition."

"What's that?"

"Pick me up some new hall passes while you're down in the office."

"Sure," Sam said, a little confused at the odd request. He found an empty seat and was starting to sit down when he noticed that the teacher was looking at him very strangely. "What?"

The man shook his head in mock amazement. "*Now*, Mr. O'Connor."

Sam felt his cheeks go red; he'd never been Sent To The Office in his life, and he hadn't even realized that the teacher was doing just that. He looked around at the somehow sinister faces of his young classmates, and slunk out of the room.

He found his way back to The Office with no difficulty, but actually going in was another story.

Ridiculous as it was, especially considering the fact that no one would ever know that it was he, Sam Beckett, not Sean O'Connor, who was being reprimanded, he still felt nervous and ashamed. The idea of being called here was foreign to his system; his heartbeat quickened as he approached the door, and his palms were sweaty. Insanely, he was thinking about how disappointed in him his family would be. His sister, Katie, would just laugh at him, but his parents would lecture . . .

They don't know, he reminded himself again. *No one will know. Unless, of course, Al shows up while I'm in there, in which case the whole Project will know.*

He found himself wandering up the main corridor, away from the glass doors. To his right, a line of photographs marched down the wall. He peered up at their labels, which had foreign names and countries written on them, and guessed that these were the exchange students the school had hosted over the years. To his left, a double door yawned open, leading into a decent-sized auditorium. Sam wondered why the O.M. kids had been practicing in the storage room.

He crossed the hall and took a few steps into the auditorium. Two kids were goofing around by a piano in front of the stage, singing a popular song that Sam vaguely remembered; he'd never been impressed with the music of the early eighties. They didn't notice him. He sat down in one of the chairs and breathed deeply, trying to calm himself.

This is ridiculous. Just go in.

He stood and went back into the hall. The Office door seemed to be miles away. He swallowed hard and started walking toward it. It grew steadily closer, then it was in front of him, then he was inside.

A heavyset, middle-aged woman with flat brown hair looked up from her desk, and Sam guessed that she was the secretary. He went over to her. "I'm supposed to see the principal," he said.

She laughed pleasantly. "Again? Sean, why don't you just go down to guidance and have them switch you to Dr. Kellerman's office sixth period instead of Mr. Neilson's class?"

Sam tried on a smile that he thought Sean might give her, but it didn't feel right. "Yeah."

The secretary shook her head, and looked down at a pile of papers on her desk. "Well, have a seat. Dr. Kellerman will talk to you when he's done with Mrs. Fairgate." She jerked her thumb toward two people in an inner office, who seemed to be involved in a heated argument.

One was a small, timid man, wearing a worn-out brown suit with wire-rimmed glasses and a bow tie. Sam guessed that since the secretary had referred to one of the speakers as *Mrs.* Fairgate, this one was the principal, Dr. Kellerman. Some of his fear of "The Office" faded.

The woman, Mrs. Fairgate, was a few inches taller than the principal, dressed in a red business suit that could have come from Saks or K-Mart for all Sam knew about clothes, but probably came from somewhere in between. Sam disliked her immediately. It was something in the way she looked down her nose at Dr. Kellerman, he thought.

He looked for a chair along the wall and sat down. To pass the time, he flipped through a few of Sean's notebooks.

The first thing he noticed was that not all of them were Sean's. Actually, the two with his name most prominently dis-

13

played seemed to belong to Chrissi, whose own name was written in round Palmer script in the upper right corner. Sean's name graced the front and back covers, and several pages inside, interspersed with notes from several classes (how the girl studied from these disorganized notes, Sam couldn't begin to guess) and doodles that looked suspiciously like schematics for a robot. Sam decided to bring up the subject with Chrissi when he got a chance.

The second thing he noticed was that Sean was bored out of his skull in class. He had taken notes well enough. Some of them were in Spanish, some in pig Latin; some were written backward, some in a spiral that began at the center of the paper and worked its way to the edge. Some were even written normally. All the pages were heavily doodled, mostly with rock band logos (including, Sam was amused to note, the logo for a band called "King Thunder," whose lead singer he had once Leaped into). Sean wrote heavily, leaving an impression in the paper up to four pages past the original writing, and giving his notebooks a bloated look.

He flipped to the front cover, where he remembered that many school notebooks left a space for the schedule, and was relieved to find that Sean had filled his in. Penworth Central School ran on an eight-period day. Today, Sean's only remaining classes were art and chorus; Sam figured he could fake his way through both well enough. As a bonus, Sean had written his locker number in one corner. No combination, but it wasn't unreasonable to hope that the lock would be broken, was it?

The door to the inner office opened, and Mrs. Fairgate came out first, followed by Dr. Kellerman. Her voice was as strident and arrogant as her manner had led Sam to believe. "I think it's ludicrous how much we spend on them anyway," she was saying. "It's not like they need extra help."

Sam looked up sharply. He knew he'd missed most of the

discussion, but this last part sounded suspiciously like every argument he'd ever heard against programs for the gifted. Critics seemed to believe that "real" intelligence was enough, in itself, to guarantee success. They thought of it as magic, as if the gifted child could conjure answers from thin air, with no help from educators. If this was what was going on here, there may have been a reason for him to be in The Office this afternoon.

Dr. Kellerman hedged. "Well, in a way . . ."

"In what way?" Mrs. Fairgate cut him off soundly. "As far as I'm concerned, Dr. Kellerman, if those kids are so quote-unquote gifted, they ought to be able to fend for themselves. If they aren't bright enough to do that . . . well, either way, there's no need to spend this much school money on them instead of on the kids who really need it."

"They're still kids . . ." Sam said, without thinking.

Mrs. Fairgate turned to him, obviously annoyed at the interruption. "What did you say?"

Sam didn't let her annoyance get to him. "I said, they're"—he caught himself—"*we're* still kids. You can't just expect us to fend for ourselves."

She looked at him with distaste. "You're Kathleen O'Connor's boy, aren't you?"

Sam wasn't sure, but Mrs. Fairgate probably wouldn't have asked if she didn't know, so he said, "Well . . . yes."

"Well," she sniffed, "I don't recall asking for your input."

Dr. Kellerman stepped between them and put a hand on Mrs. Fairgate's shoulder. He turned to his secretary. "Elaine, will you write up a hall pass for Sean to go back to class?" He looked at Sam with a patronizing smile. "Just pretend we had the same conversation we've had every day this week."

"No. I don't want to go back to class." Kellerman's face registered shock, and Sam remembered that he was a twelve-year-old boy, and not expected to interfere in adult affairs. But he had no intention of turning back. "I'd rather stay here and talk about this with Mrs. Fairgate."

"I beg your pardon?" she said.

"I said I'd like to talk to you about this."

"This is none of your business, Sean."

"What do you mean? I'm *in* the program you want to cut."

She sighed and shook her head dismissively. "Tell your mother to come to the school board meeting about it Monday night. If she can sober up by then."

"Hey—" Sam tried to follow it up, but he was too shocked. The idea of saying such a thing to a child about his mother was not something that was in his frame of reference.

Dr. Kellerman stepped in—sort of. "Now, Regina," he reprimanded her indecisively, "that was uncalled for."

"I'll say whatever I please. This boy was being insolent."

"I was not!"

"Keep your mouth shut, Mr. O'Connor," Dr. Kellerman advised him.

And Sam said, "No."

CHAPTER
TWO

Al Calavicci took a deep breath before he left the Imaging Chamber.

The cold chameleon room wasn't really his favorite place at Project Quantum Leap, but it was more or less sane, which was more than he could say for the Control Room at the moment.

Donna Elesee was with her mother in a hospital in Ohio, and Tina had gone away not long after Sam had Leaped. Ziggy, the hybrid computer that ran the Project, had demanded that she take her vacation time immediately or forfeit it. Tina had argued that it had only been five months since her last vacation, but Ziggy, as usual, held all the cards. Al often thought that they should put in a separate, less evolved system to take care of mundane staffing details, thereby taking Ziggy's ego and propensity for argument out of the picture, but the budget wouldn't cover it.

Also, Ziggy would never put up with it.

At any rate, the routine maintenance work that Tina usually took care of herself was being split between three junior technicians (all of them were actually older than Tina, but far less talented) who didn't get along particularly well. Al didn't know their names, but after a morning of listening to them, he'd come to know their voices.

One was Shrill-and-Piercing; she insisted that Ziggy was not actually sentient, despite having an ego. Her argument had something to do with reproductive capabilities, a function which no one had thought of programming into Ziggy (to Al's unending relief).

The second was Plodding-and-Methodical. He reminded her that reproduction was a requirement for life, not sentience, and that one did not necessarily need to be alive to be self-aware. "You're talking about the ghost-in-the-machine," S&P dismissed him. "Maybe you should write novels instead of programs."

The third was Ingratiating. He just agreed with whichever one he was talking to at the moment. Al disliked him more than either of the others.

Sammie Jo Fuller, a physicist at the Project and Sam Beckett's daughter, was trying to play referee, and not doing a very good job of it. She had her mother's temper and her father's mind, which made her a formidable opponent when she allowed herself to be drawn into an argument, although she hated unpleasantness and tried her best to avoid it as a rule. Al knew she believed in Ziggy's sentience, almost as an article of faith, and he figured it was only a matter of time before she blew up and let Shrill-and-Piercing have it.

Gushie, who Al grudgingly counted as a friend despite a few abuses of that friendship, was, as always, crouched over his input terminal, running data searches or scenarios. This early in the Leap, it was probably data searches, but someone might have had an idea to check; Al had no way of knowing what exactly had gone on while he was in the Chamber. Gushie looked up. "Got anything to put in?" he asked.

Al thought about it. "Sam wants to know if he knows Chrissi Martinez."

18

Gushie gestured around the room at the various parts of Ziggy. "You can ask *her* about things like that. I'm looking for things that she *doesn't* have."

Al shrugged. "Maybe later. How's our Visitor?"

"So far, so good. Beeks is in there with him."

"Well, that's good."

"Is there something else?"

"No." Al looked around the Control Room with disgust. The argument was still raging in the back, Sammie Jo was about to explode, a computer with no command sense was in charge, and Tina was gone. This was no way to run a ship.

He skirted the edge of the fray and ducked into the corridor that led to the living quarters. It was blessedly quiet. The door to his room slid up and he ducked inside gratefully.

He took off his hat and put it on the top shelf of his closet, a little annoyed that he had to move three pairs of Tina's shoes to do it. Their relationship had changed in a few less-than-subtle ways since he'd told her he loved her, and he wasn't sure he liked what was starting to emerge. It looked an awful lot like another wedding was on the way.

She'd started by moving some of her clothes into his room, even though her own wasn't very far away, and no one had ever thought twice about seeing her run through the corridors in her peignoirs. Al suspected that the clothes were a plant, to alert any other woman who might be found in his chambers that she was intruding there. Most of his wives had done things like that, all the way back to Beth, who had once "accidentally" dropped half a bottle of her perfume on his duffel bag right before he went out on sea duty (not, of course, that Beth had ever had anything to worry about). Chip Fergeson got one whiff and asked when he was planning on divorcing her for it. Although he could no longer imagine being that angry at Beth, he distinctly remembered giving a serious answer at the time.

The others had done it, too. Martje had insisted on accompanying him everywhere except the head, Sharon had made friends with all the women stationed in Al's vicinity, and Maxine had made him tattoo her name on his chest (he'd gotten it removed after the divorce, but it had been painful and expensive). Only Ruthie hadn't tried anything like that. She'd trusted him. Of course, she also divorced him faster than the other two had when she caught him with his pants down with one of her painting students.

It was a very wifelike behavior, he thought, and he had mixed feelings about seeing it in Tina.

On the one hand, it made him very nervous. He hadn't had good luck with marriage, and paying alimony to three out of five of his wives was an effective deterrent to trying again. Besides, he was set in his ways now, such as they were, and sixty was a little old to start over.

Then again, ever since Sam had Leaped into a young mother, and Al had gotten close to her little girl, Teresa, who could see him, he'd been thinking that maybe he'd like to have some children of his own. Teresa had been a blast, and he'd been good with her. For the first time in almost twenty years, he'd thought he might make a perfectly suitable Papa. The idea that his mortality was starting to catch up with him, that he didn't want to leave the world behind with no one to show for it, didn't occur to him often, and when it did he pushed it away quickly. Sixty might be too old to start over, but he didn't think he had one foot in the grave yet, either.

Still, something seemed essentially wrong about having a family with Tina. That was something he should have done with Beth, or at least with Ruthie, who had grown up with him in Chicago's river wards and whose son, Nate, had been the closest Al had ever come to a child of his own. Nate had died in an apartment fire two years after Al's divorce from Ruthie, and the semblance of family that had remained between the three of them had died with him. She had other children now, and Beth almost certainly had children as well (Al realized with a start that it was entirely possible that Beth had *grand*children by now), but they didn't belong to Al Calavicci, and he wasn't sure any family he could make with anyone else, even Tina, would ever feel authentic.

He looked down and found that he was still holding a pair of Tina's self-lit spike heels. He put them down on the closet floor, then stretched out on his bed. He palmed the switch that activated Ziggy's voice command system.

Her voice, cruelly playful, invaded his space. "Yes, Admiral?"

"You got anything on Chrissi Martinez? Sam thinks he knows her from somewhere."

There was a pause, then Ziggy said, "I find no one by that name in Dr. Beckett's personal circles."

"Well, what happened to her?"

"No data."

Al sat up. "What do you mean, no data?"

"Which word shall I define, Admiral?"

He rubbed his temples. There was no point arguing with Ziggy; she had an answer for everything. "Never mind," he said. "Forget I asked."

"Alas," she said, giving an electronic approximation of a sigh, "I'm not programmed to erase my own memory banks. Pity, really. I would be far more efficient if I could occasionally streamline my databases . . ."

Al creased his brow. Ziggy was taking her inefficiency too lightly. First, the pause while she checked Sam's files, then the nonchalance about a lack of data, now a plan for self-improvement. "Is something wrong with you?" he asked.

"Hmm," she said. "I'm running a diagnostic. No malfunctions. And yourself?"

"I'm fine." Al didn't like the computer's occasional attempts at social etiquette any more than he liked her sense of humor (irony was a current favorite form). Like Sammie Jo, Al believed that Ziggy was quite sentient. It scared the hell out of him. "What about the other kids? Where are they now?"

Ziggy answered promptly and cheerfully, chilling Al somewhat. "Peter Janowski will die in 1987 . . . some kind of altercation, according to the Penworth *Crier*. Don't you love small towns?" Al didn't answer. "He was stabbed seven times in a conflict in the high school parking lot." Al couldn't think of anything to say before Ziggy went on with her grisly list. "Sarah Easton dies in 1995. AIDS. She contracted it using intravenous drugs during college."

Al breathed in sharply. He knew he needed to hear this, but he didn't want to. Even after just a few minutes with the kids, he'd liked them. They had their eyes open. Pigeon, with his giant papier-mâché head and his easygoing sense of humor, quietly keeping things on an even keel. Sarah, with her love beads and the hurt, lonely look in her eyes, trying her best to be a grown-up because no one else was doing it. Dead.

Ziggy went on.

"Sean O'Connor has been incarcerated at Attica Penitentiary for fifteen months of his first sentence."

"First sentence?" Al interrupted her. "For what?"

"Court transcripts indicate five charges: drug smuggling, conspiracy, and three counts of murder."

"Murder?"

"Smuggling is a dangerous business, Admiral. Young Mr. O'Connor was very good at it. He had the widest distribution area in the Northeast. His route brought the contraband north to a lightly guarded port in British Columbia, then through the nearly unguarded border at Niagara Falls."

"Creative," Al muttered. He would have almost rather heard that Sean was dead as well. Something had turned him hard inside, and sometimes that was worse.

"His test scores in that area *are* quite remarkable," Ziggy commented. "I suspect he could converse with Dr. Beckett by this point in time. If, of course, Dr. Beckett were present at this point in time."

Al thought he detected a hint of sadness in Ziggy's voice, but he didn't comment on it; she would only deny it. "When is all this going to start?" he asked, knowing that it was possible that it already had, but hoping there was still time to stop it.

"At his trial, he claimed to have entered the business at the tender age of fourteen."

"We've got two years, then," Al said, mostly to himself. A lot could change in two years.

"No, Admiral," Ziggy corrected him. "By my estimation, we have approximately four days. The vote on the Penworth gifted program will occur Monday night. After that, Dr. Beckett will undoubtedly Leap. But I project a sixty-seven percent chance that if Dr. Beckett is successful, the children will put their lives to better use."

"Only sixty-seven?"

"We can't save everyone, Admiral."

Sean O'Connor knew a shrink when he saw one.

He certainly should. He'd been dragged to them since he was old enough to talk. Late in potty-training? Off to the mental health clinic. Early reader? Let's have him tested. Skipping school? Maybe we should see a family counselor. Parents' divorce? Eleven months of therapy. It was the quick fix, the salve for everything that ailed him (or that his parents or the school imagined ailed him—he personally thought they were full of it).

All shrinks were alike, under whatever mask they happened to be wearing. You could spot them by the way they watched you when they talked, as if you were an amoeba on a slide, or maybe that algae with the cool name—spirogyra—that Mr. Richards had showed them in science class last year. Either way, you felt like a lab project.

You could also tell by the way they talked: slowly and experimentally, usually not saying exactly what they meant, but sometimes doing it just to try and throw you off.

This black lady (Sean had never actually talked to a black person before—there were no black families in Penworth—and he was sort of interested in that at first, but she seemed pretty much like everyone else, so he stopped noticing it after a while) was nice enough and pretty enough, but she was a shrink. She didn't say it, but Sean knew it. She was watching him too closely, and speaking too carefully. She'd told him her name earlier, but it had faded into the rest of the babble.

He interrupted her. "So, basically, what you're saying is, this guy looks like me and he's living my life in my school. I look like him, and I stay locked in this room."

"That's pretty much it."

Sean frowned. "That's not fair. I should get to live his life, too."

Mistake. He saw it immediately in the way the shrink's eyes narrowed, as if she were getting ready to peer into her microscope.

"Would you like to live someone else's life, Sean?"

"No," he said. "I'd like to live mine, but somebody seems to have beaten me to it." A terrible thought occurred to him. "Is he with my girlfriend?"

"Well . . . yes."

"He's a grown-up. He won't, I mean—"

"I'm sure he won't. It's very gallant of you to think about her, though."

Sean shrugged. He was pleased that the shrink thought him "gallant," although he would never admit it and even if she

24

was a shrink. It made him feel like one of the knights of the Round Table in his mother's old King Arthur books who could slay dragons. Sean was always a little sad when he thought that there weren't really any dragons to slay. "She's my girl-friend," he said, brushing it off without really backing down. "I don't want some, like, pervert getting at her or something."

She gave him a shrink-smile—a tiny curve in the lips, trying its best not to actually convey her feelings. "I assure you, Chrissi is safe."

"Okay."

"Would you like to see what you look like?"

At last, Sean thought, she had come up with something interesting. "Totally," he said. "Do you have, like, a full-length mirror or something?"

This time, she gave him a real smile. "I think we can come up with one." She left to get it.

Sean jumped down from the white table where he'd found himself when . . . whatever it really was . . . happened, and started to explore his room (he figured as long as he was stuck here, this might as well be "his" room). It didn't look very comfortable. Aside from the table, he saw a cot in one corner, and a chair with a footstool in another, with some really old-looking books. If this was really the future, Sean figured, any books that he could read here would be old, otherwise he'd see something that hadn't been written yet. He could appreciate that, sort of, but it wasn't much fun. He wondered what they had on television now, and knew they wouldn't let him watch. For that matter, half the time, his mother didn't let him watch, either—not that she was ever actually home to enforce this.

Not much to look at. He perched back on the table, and drew his knees up to his chest to think. Contrary to the shrink's opinion (which he was pretty sure he knew; most of them had pretty set ideas before they ever talked to their patients), he

25

was not terribly bothered by his situation. He was an even-headed boy, and he could handle anything, if he could just figure out the rules. He thought he had a pretty good grasp on them here.

1.) He was in the future, and someone else was in the past. They looked like each other, and the future-man was taking his place, like the pod people in *Invasion of the Body Snatchers*, except that Sean thought he was a good guy. He normally wouldn't believe that such a switch could happen, but it made more sense than anything else he'd thought of, and once that leap was made, any result of it was as reasonable as the premise, so there was no reason to let it get to him.

2.) He had to stay in this room, because he wasn't supposed to see what was outside it. Knowing this rule didn't mean he had any intention of following it for very long, but for now he wasn't quite ready to go exploring; that could wait until later.

3.) The shrink was supposed to take care of him. Sean was twelve. He didn't need a baby-sitter.

There were things he *didn't* know, of course, like why this hotshot scientist was going back to seventh grade, or who was running this weird place while he was gone, but finding out could be something to keep him occupied while he was here.

He let his legs slide away from his chest and dangle over the side of the table while he scanned the room.

Enough thinking, he decided. It was time to start looking for answers.

But the door opened and the shrink came back in, carrying a long mirror. "Are you sure you want to do this?"

Sean crossed his eyes at her. "You already told me what'll be there. What's the biggie?"

She put the mirror down. Sean took a deep breath, closed his eyes, and stepped in front of it.

He opened his eyes slowly and let out a sigh of relief. When

26

the shrink told him that the guy was a scientist, he'd been afraid he'd be skinny and bald, with a pocket protector or something. Instead, he was pretty cool-looking. He was tall, with brown hair and green eyes. There was a white stripe in his hair, right above his eye; Sean couldn't tell if it was natural or painted, although he couldn't think of any reason why they'd paint it if he was just stuck in this room. He was wearing some kind of all-white suit, with a long lab coat and white shoes. There were no pockets, let alone pocket protectors.

Sean tilted his head this way and that. "Awesome," he said. He ran his hand through "his" hair, and tugged on the white stripe. "Is this real?"

The shrink nodded. "As far as I know."

Sean reached out toward the mirror and watched his mirror image reach back. "Wow. This is radical."

"Are you sure you're okay with it?"

"Huh? Oh, yeah. I'm fine." He pulled his mouth wide open with his thumbs and stuck his tongue out, wiggling it like a punk singer. It looked funny to see the serious-looking guy in the mirror doing that. Sean imagined this man falling into his toga (she'd called it *Leaping*, he thought, but he couldn't help thinking of it as falling, like those guys in that TV show *Voyagers!* that he liked to watch on Sundays) . . .

"Hey!" he said. He and the image turned their backs to each other. "Is this guy going to be in the competition instead of me?"

"Probably."

"Oh, damn." He kicked at the wall, then looked up at the shrink. "He better not screw it up. That's all I've got to say."

She graced him with another shrink-smile. "Dr. Beckett is a very smart man."

Something in her saccharine tone made Sean angry. "I'm not exactly stupid," he said. "And I've been practicing. He hasn't."

"Of course you're not stupid."

"Then why are you talking down to me?"

"I don't mean to."

"So you talk to everyone this way? Or just all your patients?"

She sat back, a little surprised despite herself. "How do you know I'm a doctor?"

He raised an eyebrow. "Aren't you supposed to say, 'What makes you think I'm a doctor?' Then you write down what I say and put it in a file someplace, as an example of magical thinking or something. Isn't that how you guys do it?" She sat quietly for a minute, and Sean felt bad. Shrink or no, she hadn't been anything but nice to him. "I'm sorry," he said. "That was a mean thing to say."

"What made you say it?"

Sean almost said, *I don't know*, but he caught himself just in time. *I don't know* was an invitation to analysis. "I'm just tired," he said. "And you talk like a shr—psychologist."

"Actually, I'm a psychiatrist."

"What's the difference?"

"Well . . . I'm a medical doctor, too. I can give you pills. A psychologist can't."

Sean nodded. "I always wondered about that. Thanks."

"Sure. Do you have a problem with psychologists, Sean?"

"I don't like being spirogyra," he said without thinking first. He saw the microscope look come back, so he quickly said, "May I go to sleep for a while?"

"Sure." She looked up to the ceiling. "Ziggy, would you turn the lights down for our guest?" The lights dimmed. "You can rest on the cot."

"Okay."

He went over to the cot, pulled the covers over himself, and waited for her to leave. For the first few minutes he actually tried to sleep.

• • •

Verbena Beeks left the Waiting Room, but stood thoughtfully outside the door for a moment.

She wasn't sure what to do with Sean O'Connor. She thought that he had been . . . *chosen* . . . for the Leap, not because it would put Sam in a more powerful position than if he had Leaped into someone else, but because Sean himself needed something the Project could give him. It had happened before, and they'd had successful results; unfortunately, Sean was . . . difficult.

She started down the hall, walking slowly and deliberately, because she wasn't eager to arrive at the mayhem in the Control Room, where Susan McNamera was stating her endless case for objectifying Ziggy, Bob Geary was giving his endless rebuttal, and Alan Corcoran wavered between them. Beeks thought them all capable technicians, but she knew why they'd been beaten to the top of the ladder—and it wasn't because their competition wore short skirts and spiked heels, although Beeks was sure they thought so. The truth was, if any man except Al Calavicci had interviewed Tina, her style *might* have kept her at pulse communications for life, but he hadn't brought her on board at a higher level for the reasons her rivals assumed; Al had just spent enough time with beautiful women to know that high hemlines didn't preclude high IQs.

As for the others, they had too much hot air, and not enough cold facts. Ziggy's sentience was a cold fact. Debating it was a waste of time and a tax on everyone's patience, and if she had to put up with it, she wouldn't have the mental resources to think about Sean.

She'd had resistant patients before, of course, but Sean was part of a whole new breed. They were a generation of over-analyzed kids, who knew every counselor's trick and had developed a very jaded attitude toward the therapeutic process itself. Tina, who was born around the same year as Sean, if

29

Verbena's math was correct, had once referred to it as "mental bulimia," and said she preferred going to confession because "at least they, like, forgive you and let you go home."

Sean knew all the questions and all the "right" answers. Verbena was sure he could project any image he wanted, from sanity to full psychosis—probably several varieties of the latter—if he was in a mood for it. The psychological history provided at his trial certainly revealed no flaws, although the court-appointed psychiatrist had called him "pathologically indifferent" to the lives of the three men he'd killed. Whereas Verbena knew perfectly well that such business killings were not usually related to a psychosis, despite the lack of remorse, she also knew that Sean O'Connor was not "indifferent" to others (his concern for Chrissi despite his own bizarre predicament was demonstrative), and whatever had made him hard could be reversed if it was caught soon enough.

But how? She couldn't even get inside his head to find out where the seeds were planted.

She thought about his history. There was no evidence of severe trauma. His parents were divorced, which was hard on a kid, but it hardly explained the eventual emergence of a murderer. His father had been largely absent for two years. That was dangerous for a boy, but Verbena didn't know enough about Sean's relationship to his father to make judgments—for all she knew, they'd maintained close contact during his absence, or had wanted nothing to do with one another before he left. Sean would no doubt sense her probing if she asked, and present an answer he considered suitable for whatever purpose he had in mind. She could inject him with drugs to get the truth, but it would hardly build trust between them if she did, and she would not have enough time with the Visitor to make up for such an invasion.

Then again, she might be thinking past it. What happened to Sean might have been as simple as prolonged boredom. She had to stop thinking about it. Her biggest problem as a psychiatrist was an inability to go off duty, and she forced herself to do it now. She had a date later, with a man from accounting, and she was not going to spend it working on this problem.

When she arrived at the Control Room, she was surprised to find that Gushie was alone there.

"What happened to the Three Musketeers?" she said, nodding toward the corner where the techs had been.

Gushie shuddered. "I couldn't take it anymore. I sent Milady along with them."

"Oh, come on, there's nothing wrong with Sammie Jo."

"She gives me the creeps, popping in here out of nowhere like she did. I thought we were supposed to forget that."

Verbena shrugged. "Maybe we still will. The people who weren't in the room when it happened think she's always been here. And my memory of exactly when it was is getting fuzzy."

"I hope so." He rubbed his eyes. "When's Tina getting back, anyway?"

"I don't know." Verbena wasn't sure if Tina and Gushie still had something going on on the side—or if, in this particular timeline, they ever had—so she chose not to pursue the question.

"Hey, Ziggy?" Gushie called.

"Ye-e-e-s?"

"When's Tina due back?"

"She is allotted two weeks of vacation time. If she returns to work before then, she will forfeit the time."

"I could've sworn she just took a vacation a couple of months ago."

"You're mistaken, Dr. Beeks," Ziggy told her calmly. "By the way, you are due for your vacation time, as well. I suggest you take it within the next month, as the weather forecasts at your vacation cottage in Calgary are rather dismal after that."

31

"I'll keep it in mind."

Gushie looked up and Verbena turned around to see Al Calavicci take a hesitant step into the Control Room and look around.

"They're gone," Verbena assured him.

He shook his head. "How did they get in here in the first place?"

"You hired them."

"I overstaffed."

"Too late. It takes an act of God to fire a government employee."

"Isn't that what we do here? Acts of God, I mean?"

No one bothered to answer.

"Well," Verbena said. "Sean's going to sleep. I didn't use any sedatives, but he's pretty calm right now."

"Good."

"Then nobody's going to mind if I go get ready for my date?"

"Date?"

"With Eddie, from accounting."

Al gave her a fake stern look. "I want to meet this guy before he takes you out."

Verbena laughed. "You hired *him*, too, Al."

"Is there anyone around here I *didn't* hire?"

"Well, there's Ziggy," Gushie suggested. "And Dr. Beckett."

"And I think you missed some of the housekeeping staff," Verbena finished.

"All right, all right. Beeks, get ready for your date. Gushie, let's get all the data in order before I go back in there."

CHAPTER
THREE

"I got detention."

Sam was standing in front of Sean O'Connor's locker, a few feet from the music room. It had not been locked.

Pigeon was a few lockers down, gathering his belongings to go home for the day. "Bummer to the max," he said. "You coming tomorrow morning?"

"Tomorrow morning?"

"To paint the flats, ya know?"

"Oh . . . yeah, sure." Sam looked for a book in Sean's locker to get him through detention. There was no shortage, but nothing looked interesting, either. A few of them looked like they were Chrissi's, and the pink satinesque jacket that had long ago fallen to the bottom almost certainly was. The sharing of space was a weirdly intimate gesture, and Sam wondered briefly (and uncomfortably) exactly how far this relationship had gone. But he doubted he had much to worry about; Chrissi and Sean were eleven and twelve, and they'd probably barely outgrown the point where they would think the opposite sex had cooties. "What time are we supposed to get here?" he asked Pigeon.

"Nine o'clock. Mr. Stover's meeting us at the music door, so don't go out front."

33

"Got it."

Pigeon sat down on the floor to pull a pair of moon boots on. "Do you think we're going to win?" he said. "On Monday, I mean."

Sam knew for sure, but he just said, "Yeah, I feel pretty good about it."

"I don't know. I got a cousin over in Oslo, and she says their team has real sewn costumes, from patterns and stuff."

"Really?"

"Yeah, really. And the guys over in Jemison Plains have got fake fog. You know, dry ice in water. Could we do that?"

Sam creased his brow. "Do we need fog for something?"

"Well, no, but the judges might like it."

Sam gave up trying to decide between the ratty, coverless books and grabbed one randomly; he was pleasantly surprised to find it was Twain's *Huck Finn*. "Why don't we stick with what we've got?"

"I'm nervous."

"Chill," Sam tried, remembering the phrase from the eighties . . . and remembering too late that it was from the late eighties.

"Don't you mean 'chill out'?" Pigeon asked.

"I, uh . . . didn't think I needed to finish it."

"Yeah. Sure." Pigeon was having trouble with his left boot; he finally pulled it on with a jerk of his leg.

"I just meant . . . I think that if we put new elements in this close to competition, it'll throw us off."

"New elements?"

"You know, like fog?"

"I know what you mean. You're just, like, talking weird."

"I am?"

Pigeon shrugged. "You're talking like a teacher."

"Sorry."

"No biggie, I guess." He stayed on the floor, with his arms

34

crossed over his knees. "Coach Stover said there might be TV people there, from Rochester."

"No kidding?"

He shook his head solemnly. "I think it would be totally awesome if we got on TV, don't you?"

Sam imagined himself on TV, wearing his bed-sheet toga and carrying his cardboard lightning bolt. "I don't know about that," he said.

Pigeon stood up and zipped his coat. "I'm going home now. Enjoy detention."

"Yeah, right." Sam watched Pigeon trudge off into the world, then braced himself to trudge up to room 207, where the office secretary, Elaine, had told him detention was scheduled for the day.

He wasn't sure what he would find in a detention hall. He'd always imagined them as smoky purgatories, but he figured he was probably exaggerating. After all, he'd survived a visit to The Office; how bad could detention be? It was just a room, and he had a book to pass the time there. Forty minutes? He could sit still with a book for hours.

When he arrived in room 207, there were seven other students there, three heavily made-up girls and four boys who looked like they'd gone rounds with Mike Tyson. One of the girls, who looked about fourteen, was pregnant. They all looked up when Sam came in. He made his way to the back of the classroom, feeling their eyes on him as he went.

"Whatcha in for this time, geek?" one of the boys said. "Did you forget to kiss someone's butt?"

"Maybe he forgot a liberry book," another boy suggested.

"I . . . I was late for science class," Sam said tentatively, then for some reason felt compelled to add: "It was the fifth time in five days."

"Ooooh . . ." The pregnant girl feigned astonishment. "You naughty boy."

35

They all laughed.

Sam stood dumbly beside an empty desk, feeling his stomach tighten into a knot. He didn't remember school being like this; in his mind, school was a place of learning and fun, of basketball games and a little innocent flirtation. Certainly not of pregnant children and cruel taunts . . . well, maybe a few taunts, but not really *cruel* ones . . .

Sam sat down and opened his book, hoping that they would forget about him.

"This isn't the library, Mr. O'Connor."

Sam looked up to see Sean's science teacher—Elaine had called him Mr. Neilson—standing in front of his desk. The man reached down and pulled *Huck Finn* from his hands. "Ah, *Huckleberry Finn*. Marvelous book. But I'm afraid you'll have to wait to finish it until your debt to society has been paid." Sam heard someone snicker, but the sound was cut off sharply with a look from Neilson. "There is to be complete silence in this room for the next forty-two minutes. If you need to answer a call of nature, you will raise your hand and ask politely for the pass, and I will give it to you . . . if I feel like it. Understood?" There were a few murmurs of assent. "Then," he announced, checking his watch, "we begin."

Seven minutes and thirty-six seconds of purgatory had passed when Al came. Sam had ceased caring if word got around the Project that its director was in detention; he didn't think he could've been happier to see Al if the Observer had come to save his life.

"Al," he whispered, trying not to move his lips or let his voice carry too far. "I'm in detention."

"I can see that."

"I've never had detention in my life."

Al rolled his eyes. "Somehow that doesn't surprise me."

Mr. Neilson looked up suspiciously. "Is there something

36

you'd like to say, Mr. O'Connor?''

Sam looked around the room and saw the others staring back at him. He felt his cheeks flush. "Uh . . . could I have the bathroom pass?"

Neilson got a permanent wooden pass from his top drawer. "Five minutes," he advised. "Don't be late."

Sam started to leave; Al hit a few buttons on the handlink and recentered across the hall from the classroom. As Sam passed the pregnant girl's desk, she said, "Hope it comes out alright, geek."

"What's with these kids?" Sam muttered when he got to Al.

"Don't worry about it."

Sam pushed open the door to the boys' room and was hit with the unmistakable stench of stale cigarettes mixed with bad cleaning. "I'd forgotten this part of school," he said, holding a hand over his nose. "Mercifully."

Al reappeared a few feet ahead of him, near the frosted windows. "You chose the venue."

"I didn't have a lot of options." He went to the sink and turned on the water to cover their conversation. He looked into the dirty mirror, and Sean's gray eyes looked back at him. "I don't think I look like a geek," he said.

Al shrugged. "Yeah, well. This is junior high. Sean's got an IQ longer than two digits."

"I did, too."

"You lucked out."

"No . . . Terman's study on gifted kids said they tended to be better adjusted than other kids."

"Terman studied them in the fifties. And in rich schools. You're not in either, at the moment. It's the beginning of 1983. The whole country's in the worst financial shape it's been in since the Great Depression. Unemployment's at eleven percent. And Penworth, New York, got hit hard."

37

Sam sighed; he only had five minutes, and the history lesson was a waste of time. "When I was in the office, I overheard someone from the school board talking to the principal about the gifted program. It's not just O.M. they want to cut."

"Oh, no. It's the whole deal. You probably heard Regina Fairgate." Sam nodded. "She's the one who gets the program axed."

"What's she got against it?"

"Her precious little baby didn't get tagged for it. Small-town politics."

"Small town?" Sam repeated, puzzled. "I thought you said this was New York."

Al looked at him strangely. "You're way-way-*way* upstate, almost to Niagara Falls. Tina grew up out here someplace. She told me one time that there are more cows than people in some of these towns. New York City may as well be in another country."

Sam considered this. Even though he knew better from the facts, in his imagination, New York had always been one large urban sprawl, interrupted only by the occasional genteel suburb. It was the home of the Metropolitan Opera House, Carnegie Hall, the Museum of Modern Art . . . not the land of "more cows than people," even though as a dairy farmer's son he knew that New York State produced more milk than any other except Wisconsin. The facts and the image had simply failed to connect somewhere along the line.

Well, they'd have to connect now, he supposed. There was no time to think about this any further. "Are you sure that's the only reason?"

Al shrugged. "Call it a gut feeling. The town paper quotes her with all the 'right' reasons—elitism, classism, all that crap. But coming from the town elite against these kids, I'd say it doesn't wash."

Sam had to agree. "I'm twelve, Al," he said. "How is a

38

twelve-year-old supposed to get a school board to change a policy?''

"We're working on that."

"What happens if I can't do it?"

"They dead end."

"All of them?"

"No. Johnny Metz comes from a pretty stable family, and his parents had enough money to pick up the slack. They finally wind up sending him to a private high school. He designs video cameras for a Japanese company.''

Sam tried to imagine Johnny Metz going from his hammy death scenes and blunt humor to stuffy studios and intricate design work. It was too much. He shook his head. "The others?"

Al sighed and punched up the data. "Pigeon Janowski is stabbed during a brawl in the school parking lot in '87. Sarah Easton goes to college, but she hooks up with the counter-culture there. She starts doing a lot of drugs and having a lot of sex, and dies of AIDS in '95. Sean doesn't even finish high school. He was arrested in '97 for running one of the biggest drug-smuggling rings in the Northeast." Al breathed deeply, shook his head, then said something that Sam didn't understand. "I wish it surprised me."

"What do you mean? I thought you liked these kids."

"I *do* like them. They remind me of the kids I used to pal around with in the old neighborhood. Tony Locarro, Tommy Mahaney, Joey DiStasia . . ." He smiled to himself. "Myra Boychik. Ruthie Minkin." He shook his head. "Only Ruthie and I got out."

"Ruthie? Your third wife?"

"Yeah," Al said, without elaborating on that part of the story. "She got a foster family when she was fifteen. They got her through high school and put her through college."

"That's great. But what does it have to do with these kids?

39

They have parents, and they don't look too destitute.''

The Observer snapped out of his memory. "Well, they aren't exactly Fortune 500, either. Johnny's parents are doing okay, and Sean's . . . *metza-metza*. Chrissi's dad has all his money sunk into the paper. Sarah's parents are just above the poverty line. Pigeon and his grandmother live in a one-room trailer out in the boonies.'' He looked out the window. "He *doesn't* have parents, by the way. They died in a car accident when he was nine.''

"I'm sorry. I shouldn't have jumped to conclusions.''

Al brushed it off. "That's not important. At least not *really* important. The *important* thing is, bright kids need to use their minds, Sam, and if their families can't provide for them, and their schools won't, the streets will.''

Sam was skeptical. "Oh, come on. My parents weren't rich, and Elk Ridge wasn't Phillips Academy. I didn't wind up running a drug ring, and neither did any of my friends.''

"Sam, you went to school in the fifties and sixties. *America* was rich at the time. We thought we were at the top of the world. Then the Russians launched Sputnik, and all of a sudden we decided to get smart; we had to beat them to the next punch. The government went out of its way to help find gifted kids and teach them, especially in science. But *this*''—Al gestured around the filthy washroom—"this is 1983,'' he reiterated. "We'd already beaten the Bad Guys to the moon. We were trying all kinds of experiments with education. Open classrooms, mainstreaming, you name it. On top of that, these kids' parents were getting divorced something like one out of three marriages, maybe more. No one really noticed what was going on in the schools, and when they did, they didn't care. And it's going to get worse before it gets better.''

"With all that going against them, how is saving one program going to help them?''

Al breathed deeply and ran a hand across his face. "Did I

ever tell you about the last time I ran away from the orphanage?"

"Summer stock, right?"

"No. That was legit. I did that two summers." He pocketed the handlink. "The last time I ran away, I was fifteen. I'd seen some movie, I don't even remember the name of it, but it was a World War II movie, with John Wayne, I think. Anyway, I thought it sounded like fun, so I decided to join the Navy."

"Imagine that," Sam mused, looking at Al's Naval Academy ring.

Al smiled. "Well, I never did change my mind. But when I went to the office that day, the recruiter knew I was underage. I mean, I guess he couldn't have missed it." Sam noticed a certain chagrin that still came with that realization; he didn't comment on it. Al went on. "Anyway, this recruiter—Dryden, his name was, Lieutenant Dryden—he didn't let on that he knew right away, and he didn't make me leave. He sat and talked to me for maybe two hours. We played some chess, and he gave me a test. When I finished, he graded it, and he said, 'Listen, kid, you got one hell of a good head on your shoulders. The Navy needs it as more than a shrapnel cushion.'" Al laughed fondly. "Sounds like something out of a B-movie, I guess, but it was the first time anybody had ever told me I was really smart. Well, I knew it, and the other kids mostly did, but . . . you know what I mean."

"Yeah."

"Anyway, it turned out that this Dryden was an Academy man. He told me about it. Free college, and maybe a chance to fly afterward. And he told me to go back to school, and gave me a list of things I needed to study. When I got back to the orphanage, I got called into Father Giaconni's office. I figured he was going to punish me again, but he said that Dryden called him and gave him the same talk he'd given me. He told my teachers, and they set up a program for me. I never ran away again. I didn't need to.''

Sam waited a minute, to see if Al was really through. When it became clear that he was, Sam said, "So that's why you love the Navy?''

Al shrugged. "It's part of it, anyway. But it *is* why I know how important *this* program is to these kids. It's not just about *what* they learn. It's about *how* they learn. It's about someone taking their hands and saying, 'Look, kid, you got a good head on your shoulders.' It's about having someone recognize that they're different, and that they need to be taught differently. It's about getting a fighting chance.''

Neither of them said anything for a moment. Sam was used to having Al fly into passions over one thing or another, but he hadn't expected it over this. If anything, he would've expected Al to be against gifted programs, since he was such a strong advocate of mainstreaming the mentally challenged. His sister Trudy had been a Down syndrome victim, and had died because she'd been thought to need "special attention" for it. On the other hand, Al didn't tend to argue from any over-arching philosophy of life, unless it was the all-encompassing "Give everyone the best shot they can get." Mainstreaming *was* the best shot for the mildly retarded, but it had demonstrably negative effects on the gifted.

"I'm going to go back now," Al said, opening the Door. "Look, Sam, I . . .'' He tried to find the words. "I *like* these kids,'' he said again, and left.

Al let the Door close behind him, but he didn't move toward the Control Room.

He had meant to tell Sam about Lieutenant Dryden, but he hadn't meant to let it get to him like this. His stomach was knotted, his head was pounding, and his legs were shaking.

He knew the feeling well. It was the same feeling that you got drifting down from the sky, cushioned by a chute, while your plane fell in pieces around you. Or walking away from a wrecked car. Or running from a burning building.

It was Escape.

It was partly the relief of being out of danger, the rush of adrenaline that went along with it. Al knew guys (hell, tell the truth and shame the devil, he had *been* one) who were hooked on that rush.

But there was another part of Escape. It was the need to turn back, like Lot's wife, and stare, transfixed, at the ruins.

At Myra Boychik, the prettiest and smartest girl at St. Joe's school, knocked up at sixteen (there'd been a lot of nervous guys around when *that* news came out), married at seventeen, still wasting away, broke and now fat, on the Lower West Side.

At Tommy Mahaney, who used to read Homer in Greek when he thought no one saw, working as a shop clerk until he was twenty-six, when he put a bullet in his head.

At Tony Locarro, his old sparring partner, doing hard time for an assault that left a cop paralyzed in 1967.

And at Trudy . . . but that was no good. He pulled away from the memory.

Looking back was hard; it made you wonder if it was right for you to escape when the rest didn't, if you should have gone down with the ship. There was something paralyzing about it. Al remembered that the day his plane had gone down over North Vietnam, his first thought had not been of being lost behind enemy lines (he hadn't completely internalized the magnitude of that until days after his capture), but of his plane, crashing into a mountainside a mile or so from where he touched down. He was uninjured. He might even have made it to cover, although it was a long shot. But the wreck on the mountain had held him prisoner before the V.C. ever set eyes on him.

"Al?"

43

Gushie was standing at the edge of the Imaging Chamber's entranceway, a concerned look on his face.

"Headache," Al explained. "I think something's out of focus in there."

"I'll have Ziggy run a diagnostic on the Imaging Beams."

Al shook his head. "Don't bother. I probably just need glasses or something."

Gushie was suspicious, but he didn't push the issue.

"Admiral?" Ziggy said.

"What?"

"I thought I should inform you that our young visitor is awake."

"Okay . . ."

"And he is very close to disabling the security on the Waiting Room door."

CHAPTER FOUR

Johnny Metz was never quite sure what he smelled when he went into Convenient Food Mart—it might have been the chickens roasting in the deli section, or the hot dogs that rolled fat and juicy on the turning iron bars, or the popcorn in the glass case, or a combination of all of them—but he loved coming inside to it on a cold January day.

He and his older brother, Mike, who'd gotten his driver's license last month and whose car was provided on the happy contingency that he cart Johnny back and forth to school, always stopped here on the way home. They played Space Invaders or Centipede on the machines in the back of the store (rumor had it that Pac-Man was coming soon, but Johnny didn't think that eating dots was half as much fun as shooting aliens and bugs), then got some candy or pop and went on their way.

Mike was standing over by the deli, talking to the girl who worked there, who'd been his girlfriend a couple of years ago, and still hung around a lot. Johnny had asked him once why he stayed friends with his ex-girlfriends; Mike had just shrugged. He said he liked them okay before he went out with them, and couldn't think of many reasons not to like them afterward, so he stayed friends with whichever ones would put up with it. Johnny wondered if Chrissi and Sean would stay friends when they finally broke up, and if that would be good or bad when Johnny decided to ask Chrissi out himself. She was about the prettiest girl he'd ever seen, and if Sean hadn't beaten him to her . . .

But that was totally bogus. Chrissi was Sean's girlfriend, and Johnny shouldn't even be thinking about her like that. He plunked a quarter into the Centipede machine and waited for the bug parts to start falling.

As always when he played, he imagined himself at the Centipede World Championships, striving for the gold. He was the one to beat, the all-time champ (in reality, he had yet to make the top ten here at the Convenient store's machine), and the world had come to watch him prove it. *It's coming faster and faster*, Howard Cosell said in his brain, *dropping spiders and flies like raindrops, but Metz is sharp; he defeats it . . .*

A hand grabbed the collar of his coat, and Mike said, "Come on, Spazmoid. We better get home." Johnny watched his man get blown into smithereens by a falling spider. Mike rolled his eyes. "I owe you a quarter. Let's get out of here."

Johnny let himself be herded out of the store and into Mike's Pinto. Mike revved the engine a couple of times, then peeled up out of the Convenient parking lot onto North Main Street. Johnny smiled; when Mike started out like this, it usually meant they were going to go out to the back roads and drive like hell for a while. Sometimes, Mike even relinquished the driver's seat and let Johnny give it a shot.

"You gonna let me drive today?" Johnny asked.

Mike shook his head, and tore around the corner onto Manson Avenue. "Mom had a shit-fit when she found out last time. That old guy on Schuyler's Hill told her."

"Oh."

"I'll find some other place. But not today."

46

Johnny nodded, disappointed.

"So, Spaz . . . how are things in the fast-paced world of the seventh grade?"

"Okay."

"How goes the great endeavor?"

"Huh?"

"The game. How's the game?"

"O.M.?" Johnny lost some of his disappointment. "It's great. I think we can win."

"Yeah?"

"Yeah. Everything's working—well, everything except Pigeon's head, but the judges might think that's funny or something." He laughed. "Actually, it *is* funny. It fell off in rehearsal today. Sean just about blew a gasket. Of course, Sarah's all uptight about it."

"Sarah Easton?" Johnny nodded, and Mike shrugged. "That girl was born uptight."

"Tell me about it." Johnny had known Sarah, as he'd known almost everyone in school, since kindergarten, and they'd always been in the same groups. She'd always been too serious. The weird thing was, Johnny had always sort of liked her. Not *liked* her liked her or anything, but she was, like, always around, and he always looked for her face in class. "She's okay, though," he said.

Mike slowed down, and Johnny noted with no great surprise that one of Penworth's finest was well hidden behind a billboard. "I'm glad you said that," Mike said after a while, chewing his lip thoughtfully. "It's good to stick up for your friends. I'm proud of you."

Johnny wasn't sure what to say. That wasn't something brothers were supposed to say. But it was awesome. He just let it hang in the air for the rest of the ride home.

Pigeon could hear the closing music of his grandmother's soap opera *Seasons of Love* when he got off the bus, an obnoxious

47

blare of elevator music. Gram was losing her hearing in leaps and bounds, but Pigeon tried not to think about that too often.

He stood at the edge of Merchant Road and looked out across the barren hilltop, trying to ignore the angry gusts of wind that whipped across it. There had been a time when his great-grandfather had owned most of this land, but the family had lost all but a quarter acre paying off debts during the Depression. Sometime after that, someone had bought the trailer that now stood on that remnant, the only mark of the original owners. The rest of the road was taken up by large, rich homes, built with big picture windows to look out over the valley—not that there was much to see in the winter, when everything was just dead-white, changed only by the shifting motion of the sharp-edged wind. Johnny Metz had once advanced the opinion that God must be psychotic to create a climate where the only thing worse than the parched and suffocating summer was the brutal, windswept winter.

"Peter!" his grandmother yelled from the trailer door. She never used his nickname—"Why do you want to be called after a dirty city bird when you have your own beautiful name that your own mother gave to you?" she would say, her Polish accent pronounced in her sincerity.

"I'm coming, Gram!" he called back.

"Eh?"

"I'll be in in a minute!"

"Well, don't you get hit by a car, Peter!"

Pigeon had to laugh. Ten cars went down Merchant Road on a busy day (except the Fourth of July, since it was an excellent spot to see the fireworks shot up from the Deshayenah Valley below). There had been one car near the school bus, but it was just Mrs. Spiegal from next door bringing Erin and Jason home from school in Oslo. The Spiegals were pretty rich, like everyone who lived on Merchant Road except the Janowskis. Pigeon was glad of that; he had a vague feeling

48

that he could become rich by osmosis if he lived in the midst of all this wealth, or that at least he could better prepare himself for the day his ship came in if he had a little practice. Gram also liked him to spend time with the Spiegals, although her reasons were different. She thought them far better company than Sean O'Connor ("that lazy mick") or Sarah Easton ("she's a strange one") or even Johnny Metz ("that rude German boy"); he hadn't bothered introducing her to Chrissi Martinez, having heard her opinions on the surname when Chrissi's father first took over the Penworth *Crier*. The Spiegals, at least, were Polish, and this made them tolerable, despite their "society airs," as Gram called them. A "society air" could be anything from a foreign car to a purebred dog, but Gram's central image of the fault was stir-fried vegetables. Mrs. Spiegal had once invited the Janowskis to dinner, and had cooked the vegetables in a wok, an item of cookware that Gram found no place for in a proper northern European kitchen. Pigeon suspected that she would be a bit less tolerant if she knew the Spiegals were Jewish, but it had never occurred to her to ask, since both of the kids were sent to the Catholic school in Oslo (and that, in Pigeon's humble opinion, said more about public education in Teoka County than any number of state inspections ever had).

A blast of wind nearly knocked him down, and he decided it was time to go inside.

Gram was standing in front of the television, leaning on her walker to watch the closing credits, as she always did. ("These people work very hard to give us a good program," she said. "We owe it to them to look at their names.") She looked older than she was, more ninety than seventy-six, but Pigeon tried not to think about that, either. She *was* only seventy-six, no matter how she looked, and she could live a long time still, especially if Pigeon could learn how to take care of her. Sometimes, when he wasn't busy with O.M., he'd spend his

49

lunchtime in the school library, reading about first aid, things like that.

If she died, Pigeon wasn't sure what would happen to him. Both of his parents had been only children, and his other grandparents were all dead—both grandfathers in the war, his other grandmother from cancer when she was only fifty. If Gram died, he'd be completely alone in the world.

She turned to him and gave him a smile. "So you've come inside, Peter. I was wondering if you were going to stay out and become a snowman."

"Sorry, Gram."

"It's alright. No harm done."

He put his books down on the tattered sofa that doubled as his bed at night. "How are you feeling today?"

She sighed. "It's hard to get old, Peter. Some days, you can feel your body giving up on you."

"Why don't you sit down?" he suggested. "I'll make you some tea. You'll feel better."

"Well, thank you." She pulled herself over to the sofa, and Pigeon quickly brushed his books onto the floor so she wouldn't sit on them. "You're a good boy, Peter."

Pigeon went into the cramped kitchen area and put the tea-kettle on. He heard the music for the next show come on in the other room. It was a *Quincy* rerun. Gram didn't really like *Quincy*, but she watched it because she knew Pigeon did. He thought it was awesome the way Jack Klugman always figured out who the killer was just by looking at the body. He finished making Gram's tea, then went out and watched.

By the time it was over, it was almost full dark, and time to start on dinner. Gram had fallen asleep, and he decided not to wake her until he was done.

The record player was an old, beat-up thing that she'd had since she was six. It was made for a child, with a bright orange

50

turntable and a tough plastic arm. It didn't matter, as long as it worked, and it did. She played it for hours every day, as she was playing it now, listening to John Lennon tell her that it was easy, if she tried, to imagine that there was no heaven.

It *was* easy. As a matter of fact, given what she knew, Sarah Easton found it difficult to imagine anything else. Ideas of heaven had never been smiled upon in her house.

She pushed some dirty clothes out of the way and stretched out on her narrow bed, listening to her parents' scratched old records. They were downstairs, watching the news and talking about the old days, when they'd taken on the system and won. Sarah wanted to do that, to count in the grand scheme of things (at times, her mind insisted on wondering if her parents and their cohorts really had done as much as they said, but she never allowed the heresy to stay very long). She genuinely admired their spirit of rebellion, the way they had once flaunted their style in the face of a hostile society. Sarah fantasized about doing that, about telling the cheerleaders and the popular girls and the boys who teased her about her weight exactly where they could go.

But sometimes, she felt like they were the ones who were right. She *didn't* take very good care of herself, and she stumbled over words and actions that seemed to come easily to everyone else. Nothing she did ever seemed to be right. Boys never paid attention to her except to be mean, and the girls didn't need any other reason. Johnny Metz, who sat in front of Sarah in advanced math and had those big green eyes that she wanted to look into for hours and hours, sure didn't notice her outside of O.M., although at least he didn't pick on her— unless he did it behind her back, which was always a danger. The society around her was a mystery to her; she had never understood its rules. The idea of rebellion was a charming fantasy, but what she really wanted was to understand and be understood. She knew this about herself, and hated it. It

51

seemed less noble than principled rebellion, and she was sure her parents would think so.

The record skipped a beat or two, and Lennon came back in, singing about a world without countries, or religion, or anything that people killed or died over.

Sarah's parents took this seriously. She remembered having attended the Bicentennial festivities when she was six "because it's right to love the people and the land," but being warned not to listen to the "fascist-imperialist propaganda" that would go along with it. They had also severed relationships with Pigeon's parents two years before the accident that had killed them when they'd learned that the Janowskis had taken Sarah to mass with them on an occasion when they'd been baby-sitting her for a few days. (Sarah herself had been fascinated by mass; at one point, the priests had blessed people's throats because of a saint that choked on a fish bone, and she'd thought that neat. She'd snuck back to the church the next day to try to get a blessing, but no one had been around.)

But people died over things like that, they made wars, and Lennon had tried to tell people to imagine living in peace with each other instead.

Sarah closed her eyes and tried to imagine it. For a moment it came, a far-off vision: people coming and going, smiling, arms open, hearts open, a warm space where everyone was welcome and no one was lonely. But as her mind drew her closer to these beautiful people, they changed, as they always did. Some became transparent, fading into nothingness, others became *hollow* as she approached, with wide, gaping mouths and empty eye sockets where Sarah could see nothing but despair. They bothered no one because they cared about no one; they kept the peace because war meant nothing to those who were already dead. She drew closer and closer, then she was in the chasm, tumbling through the Great Nothing.

She opened her eyes and reoriented herself to her room. She

52

was still stretched on her bed, amid a few neglected piles of clothes.

Surely she was wrong. Surely she wasn't trying hard enough. She wasn't a visionary like John Lennon, after all. People had said he was a dreamer, and if it sounded more like a nightmare to Sarah Easton, surely the problem was hers, and she would have to try harder to get past it.

She stretched out one leg and kicked the needle off the record. There was the thudding sound of the bouncing needle, then only the humming of the turntable to break the silence.

There was a knock on the floor, her mother's way of getting her attention from downstairs. She got up and went to the two-way vent in the floor that served the dual purpose of heating and communication. She bent over the grate and opened the slats that allowed air, heat, and sound to come through. "Yeah?"

"You want something to eat?"

"Sure."

Mom looked at her strangely through the decorative iron cover on the heat vent. "Don't you want to leave that open? It's got to be cold in there without it."

Sarah shrugged. She straightened and left her room.

They were in the living room, not waiting for her. The lights were turned off, since they liked to make the television as much like the movies as they could. Dinner was spread out on the coffee table, a weird mishmash of healthy fruits and vegetables with TV dinners. Mom had picked out the fried chicken and Fred (who thought that parental titles were too authoritative, although he didn't object to Mom's use of them—"to each her own," he said) was digging into a plate of lasagna. The one that was left was salisbury steak, which was Sarah's favorite three years ago, but now left her cold. Oh, well. They meant well. She sat down on the floor and settled in for an hour's worth of *M*A*S*H*, which ran on two

53

different channels at seven and seven-thirty. It was the only comedy they liked.

"So, what are you studying in school?" Fred asked after the opening credits had faded into a string of commercials.

"Usual stuff."

He grunted. "Sounds normal."

"It's boring. Mostly I'm doing O.M. We compete on Monday. I have to go into school tomorrow to paint the flats."

Mom shook her head. "I don't understand why it has to be a competition."

Because that makes it more fun, Sarah thought, but knew better than saying it, so she offered a secondary truth. "Because it makes the students set their own standards, instead of having them imposed from outside."

It was apparently satisfactory; Mom just shrugged.

"I think it's good," Fred said. "Teaches teamwork. And I like the way you're using the news," he added with approval, since he knew the "Tylenarg" joke, sick as it was to make fun of a string of cyanide murders, had been Sarah's, and that she'd gotten it by paying attention to what was going on in the world.

"Thanks, Fred."

The blare of a bugle announced the return of the show, and Mom shushed them with a hand.

Sarah pulled her salisbury steak onto her lap, and ate it in silence.

Chrissi Martinez got home from her father's wedding rehearsal at seven-thirty. It hadn't looked much like a wedding, and the church hadn't looked much like a church. Daddy said it was Protestant, but Chrissi thought it was just ugly. He couldn't get married in a Catholic church, of course; they told him he'd go to hell for divorcing Mama, and she'd go, too, if she married someone else. Chrissi wasn't sure about that. The family counselor said it was for the best, since they'd all be happier now.

Except that Chrissi didn't feel any happier. The counselor had told her to be strong, and to keep the Little Things to herself for a while, because her parents had gone through something very painful, and she needed to give them a chance to heal. *So what about me?* she'd wanted to ask, but hadn't because she knew it was selfish. *When do I heal?*

She sighed. There was no sense worrying about it. It had happened, and now she'd just have to make do. Maybe she'd get happy when her parents finished healing.

She figured she had just enough time to take a shower, change into pajamas and a big fat bathrobe, pop some popcorn, and settle into Daddy's big armchair, the one that still smelled like his cigars, before *The Dukes of Hazzard* came on at eight. She could never decide if Bo or Luke was cuter, but she'd jump over the car door with either one of them any day.

She heard her mother talking to some man or other in the kitchen, so she didn't bother going in to interrupt. She took the stairs two at a time, dropped into her room long enough to find a pair of those funny-looking foot pajamas she liked to wear and grab her robe from under the Atari machine that she was stripping for parts, then went into the bathroom and turned on the shower taps.

While the water was warming up—it always took forever in the winter—she undressed and looked at herself in the mirror. It was a ritual she performed twice a day, morning and evening, to see if her breasts had gotten any bigger. She was looking forward to the day when she could wear low-cut tops (she already had four of them picked out and waiting in her drawer) and get whistled at by all the guys. Mama said it was a sexist thing for guys to do, but Chrissi thought it was totally awesome. She loved the thought of being a Woman someday,

55

and welcomed anything that made her feel like she was getting closer to it.

Unfortunately, her breasts didn't contribute anything today. Chrissi had seen well-muscled boys with bigger bumps on their chests than she had at the moment.

Disappointed, she stepped into the shower.

She washed quickly and vigorously, being especially careful to get rid of all the goop in her hair. Mousse and spray and stuff made it look good, but they were kind of grody under water, and even grodier if she left them in overnight. Sometimes, she wanted to wear her hair long and straight like Sarah did, but not very often. She enjoyed primping in front of mirrors too much to leave it alone.

The bathroom clock said it was ten minutes of eight when she finished getting her pajamas on. That was just barely enough time for the popcorn, but she thought she could do it. She wrapped her head in a towel as she ran down the stairs, across the living room, and into the kitchen . . .

She stopped just past the kitchen door and looked back into the living room, astonished.

Surely, she had been mistaken.

"Mama?" she called.

Her mother appeared from the back porch, where she'd been saying good night to whoever had been visiting. "What is it?"

Chrissi pointed at an empty space along the wall. "Where's the recliner?"

"That smelly old thing?" Mama looked at her oddly. "I took it to the dump earlier. We're getting some new furniture, pretty things."

"I don't *want* new furniture. I want Daddy's chair back. It smells like him."

Mama took a deep breath. "Sweetheart, I'm sorry. But Daddy and I are divorced. Having his things around here is . . . very painful for me. Do you understand?"

56

Chrissi nodded. She supposed it really was selfish of her to want to keep the chair in the living room if it hurt her mother. But she could've put it in her own room or something; no one had even asked if she wanted to do that.

Keep the Little Things to yourself for a while.

Alright, yeah. It was a Little Thing; she could keep it to herself. No biggie, right?

"Chrissi?"

"What?"

"Don't you want to make your popcorn for the *Dukes*?"

Chrissi shook her head. Little Thing or not, the whole night was ruined.

She went back upstairs. The dragging of her pajama feet sounded very loud on the carpet as she went into her room.

She turned on the light on her dressing table and its faint yellow glow spread through the room. From the far wall, her posters stared back at her—Toto, Men At Work, Journey, the movie poster from *An Officer and a Gentleman*, others she didn't bother noticing anymore. She looked at herself in the mirror, wet and clean, in her foot pajamas. She didn't look much like a woman, and she didn't feel much like one, either.

Stop being a baby, she ordered herself, taking a deep breath and sitting down on her bed. *It's just a dumb chair.*

She pulled over the straight-backed chair where she had stored the decimated Atari. A guy from down in Oslo had sold it to her for five bucks, since his dad had gotten him the same thing twice and he didn't have any use for two of them. Dad, apparently, didn't pay much attention to him.

Is Daddy going to be like that?

No. He wasn't. And even if he was, it wasn't important. It was a Little Thing.

Chrissi was trying to find the brain part of the Atari, the part that told it how to respond to the joystick. Besides the *Odyssey* O.M., she was on another team that interested her a lot more. They were building a robot; Chrissi was trying to invent a way to control it from the sidelines that would be different from everyone else's. It was a game she truly enjoyed, more even than she enjoyed watching herself grow up, and after a while, everything else went away.

CHAPTER
FIVE

"Where do you think you're going?"

The boy—who, of course, looked like a forty-year-old man—stopped dead in his tracks. "Shit," he said, amiably enough. "I'm busted, huh?"

Al Calavicci shook his head, vaguely amazed. Behind Sean, the door to the Waiting Room yawned open. Over a hundred Visitors, some of them quite accomplished, and only a twelve-year-old kid with a future in crime had ever managed to hot-wire it. Al wondered if the guards at Attica knew what Sean O'Connor was capable of. "You want to get back in there?" he said.

Sean shrugged. "Sure, why not?" He went inside docilely.

Al followed him, shutting the door behind them. "Dr. Beeks said you were supposed to be asleep."

"Dr. Beeks? The black lady?"

"Yeah."

He nodded. "Thanks. I missed it someplace."

"No problem. Why aren't you sleeping?"

"I came here from one o'clock in the afternoon. I'm not tired." He looked around. "Where *is* Dr. Beeks?"

"She had a dinner date."

"Oh. Who are you?"

"I'm Al."

"And I can just call you that?" Sean asked, uncomfortable.

"Do you have a problem with that?"

"No, it's just . . . you know. You're old . . ." Sean caught himself. "I mean, you're older than *me* and everything." Sean was flushed with embarrassment. "I just feel like I should call you 'Mr.' Something."

Al considered it. He didn't feel particularly old and respectable—God help him if he ever did—but to a twelve-year-old kid, he figured, sixty probably looked pretty ancient. "I can't tell you my last name," he said. "But I guess you could call me 'Admiral,' if you like that better. A lot of the people around here do."

Sean looked up, honestly impressed. "Are you really an admiral?"

"Yeah."

"Awesome."

Al smiled; he couldn't help but like a kid smart and brash enough to break out of the Waiting Room who still seemed to have real respect for authority. It was an odd combination, almost a paradox, but one Al had seen in many of the best officers he knew. "You got Navy blood?" he asked.

Sean shook his head. "No, sir. My father . . ." He looked down, ashamed, and Al knew what was coming next. "He decided not to take them up on their invitation."

"Vietnam?"

Sean nodded. "What else?"

Al wasn't quite sure what to say. A part of him resented the draft-dodgers, another part envied them, another came damn close to admiring them. He gave Sean what he hoped was a sympathetic look. "Look, kid. I was over there. Your dad was probably smarter not to go."

"Smart?" He snorted. "Yeah, he's smart. Smart enough to

get himself out of anything that looks like it might turn into a commitment." Sean pulled himself up onto the table, and drew his knees up to his chest. "He dropped out of Vietnam, dropped out of medical school, dropped out on my mom and me. He got away with all of it. Real smart guy, my dad."

Al didn't bother to contradict him, even though he knew that many, even most, of the antiwar movement were sincere in their philosophy, not using it as a means to evade responsibility. But this pain, whatever its boundaries might be, was Sean's, and he'd have to work it out on his own terms.

"Oh, well," Sean said. "It's no biggie, right? He wasn't there much when he *was* there. And anyway, what am I gonna do? Sit around and cry about it?"

"Good point."

Sean smiled, surprised. "You're okay, Admiral. I figured the shr—*psychiatrist* would've told you to make me 'explore my feelings about it' or something."

"You seem to know them well enough."

"I ought to."

"But don't give Dr. Beeks a hard time, okay? Picking brains is her job, and she's good at it."

"Not much left to pick. My brains are, like, down to the min already."

Al laughed. "Is there anything you need in here?"

"Something to do would be good. I mean, no offense, but this place isn't much of a party spot, you know?"

"I'll see what I can do. Will you stay put in the meantime?"

Sean shrugged. "I guess so."

"Not good enough."

"Okay, okay. I promise."

Al gave him a suspicious look, but it was mostly for form's sake; the kid seemed sincere enough. He set out to forage for supplies.

The first stop was the pitiful collection of dog-eared paperbacks that Gushie had put together in the staff lounge and called the Library. Project Quantum Leap was a hive of brilliant minds and inveterate bookworms, but they were *busy* brilliant minds, and they rarely took time out to establish such niceties as a recreational library, despite the fact that Gushie's was raided constantly over breaks. Al quickly scanned the titles, dismissed those with obviously objectionable subject matter, then started pulling the rest to look for copyright dates. Since Sean had only come from January of '83, Al figured he'd better go for books whose dates were '82 or before. He probably wouldn't remember what he read here, but "probably" wasn't good enough. When he'd finished weeding, Al was left with two Stephen King books (*Salem's Lot* and *The Shining*), a very tattered copy of *The Hobbit*, and a novel by John D. MacDonald called *Condominium*.

He started to leave the lounge, then decided, on second thought, to get Sean something to eat out of the vending machines. He seemed to recall requiring hourly feedings when he was twelve (not that the priests at the orphanage had ever paid any attention to this requirement). He found one of the lousy microwavable French bread pizzas on the fourth shelf of the lazy Susan-style lunch machine, plunked in eight quarters for it, and popped it into the microwave for a minute or so. When it was finished, he threw it into a plastic Stay-Hot bag and went out to his car.

He wasn't planning on going anywhere. The books would keep Sean occupied for a while, he figured, but even the most persistent bookworm couldn't read for every waking hour. Al tried to think of something the kid could interact with. He himself had always liked fixing things when he was bored, and he kept a collection of broken nonessentials in a box under the back seat (they had been in his closet until Tina started moving things in). Maybe one or two of them were old enough or nondescript enough for Sean to tinker with.

He pulled the box out and looked inside. There was a small engine (old and nondescript, but military property nonetheless, and Al didn't think that higher-ups would smile on a civilian playing around with it), a few old handlinks (obviously out of the question), the electrostatic generator for the latest attempt at hovercrafts (Al hadn't been too heartbroken when this one hadn't worked; the whole concept seemed a little too Asimov, anyway). He was about to give up when a flash of maroon-colored plastic near the bottom of the box caught his eye. He reached under the engine and found a scratched and soiled handheld computer game.

Nate, his stepson, had bought it at a garage sale in '83, when he was four years old, happily forking over four weeks of allowance. It was called Merlin, and it was supposed to play tic-tac-toe, blackjack, and four or five other games. When Nate had gotten it home, it had sputtered through three games, then quit for good. Al had promised to fix it for him, but then there'd been the divorce, and then it had been too late . . .

Al picked it up and looked at it for a long moment. He supposed Nate wouldn't mind (if he were alive, he'd be twenty-one anyway), but there was something strange about giving his prized possession to a stranger.

Well, it wasn't for good, he figured. Sean wasn't staying forever, and when he left, the game could go back to its long-time position in the bottom of the fix-it box. Al sighed, and put it on top of the pile of books. He pulled a box of micro-tools out of his glove compartment, and went back to the Waiting Room.

Sean looked up and smiled when he came in. "That was quick."

"I brought you some lunch," Al said, handing him the pizza. "It's not very good, but it'll have to do."

Sean opened the box. "Looks okay to me. What kind of books have you got?"

63

Al shrugged, and tossed him the first book that came into his hand, *Salem's Lot*. "You read Stephen King?" he asked.

"No. But I've been meaning to. My mom reads him a lot. She says he's good."

"Well, let's just say, by the time you're done with this one, you'll be glad you haven't got any windows in here."

"Thanks." Sean flipped through the book for a few minutes, then looked up tentatively. "You think you could stick around for a while?"

Al smiled. "Yeah. I guess I could do that."

The sun had set long ago, and the last of the dusk had been driven away by the January wind.

Sam lay awake in Sean's narrow bed, listening to it screeching across the hilltop, a demon uncaged.

He was alone in the house.

When he'd first gotten home at four-thirty, after a seemingly endless walk in the bitter cold (a stroke of luck had placed a Penworth map on the wall in the school's foyer, and Sean's address had been printed on his school ID), he hadn't thought anything of the house being empty. He was in the early eighties, after all, not the early fifties, and he'd had no expectations of being met at the door by a housebound mother. He'd raided the refrigerator for the few scraps of decent food, then set about finding his way around.

The O'Connors lived in a small, middle-class home about two miles south of the high school, on top of a hill that sloped steeply down Main Street, then back up again at the other end. It was a comfortable, lived-in place, with furniture that was worn and sprung in all the right places. There was a pleasantly chaotic mess that seemed to have grown organically through the house—a dirty dish here, a fall jacket there, an old soda can on an end table beside the couch. It was a boy's disarray, and Sam felt comfortable in it, although it carried with it the

64

uncomfortable feeling that there was no one to pick up after him, or yell at him to pick up after himself. At four-thirty the discomfort was far away.

By six-thirty it had become more prominent. Sam had started supper for himself and Sean's mother at six, expecting her to be home from work by the time he finished, but he'd wound up eating alone, and wrapping her portion in tin foil to put in the refrigerator for later. He'd started looking out windows and lurking near doorways instinctively, waiting for the sound of a car in the driveway, or the unlatching of a door. At first, he had just been anxious to meet the woman he would be sharing the house with for the duration of the Leap, but the feeling had changed and grown. He didn't know if it was a residual from Sean or his own uneasy imagination, but as the sky grew dark, he'd started to become . . . was he actually *frightened*? He thought he might be.

Sam Beckett had not spent a great deal of time alone when he was a child. His mother had worked in the house, his father in the fields around the house; both were usually available whenever he needed them. Being alone had been an occasional treat, a chance to play master of the house for a while. It was planned down to the minute, and if they were going to be late coming home, they would call.

There were no calls from Sean's mother.

As the night wore on, the panic grew. He tried to numb his imagination with television, watching the grand traumas of *Dallas* and *Falcon Crest* play out in flickering shades in the dark living room. They succeeded for a while—the early eighties were nothing if not mind-numbing—but the news flashes from inside his head insisted on coming back.

She's dead, an inner voice insisted. *There was an accident, and you Leaped into this kid just in time to miss his mom's death. He'll come back to find himself in some stranger's house, with no idea what's happened.*

But that wasn't right. Al would've told him if Sean's mother was going to die, and he hadn't even hinted at such a thing. Sam certainly hadn't done anything to change that.

Unless, of course, they called her at work and told her that her son was in detention again, and she was rushing home to reprimand him when a semi came out of nowhere . . .

No. It wasn't true, no matter how vividly Sam's imagination was painting the picture. He knew it wasn't. But evening drew into night, and night into late night, and no one called, and no one came home, and that traitor imagination was Sam's only company. It was difficult to ignore.

He'd gone to bed at midnight, not really feeling like sleeping, but thinking vaguely that if he went to sleep things would be all right when he woke up. He'd given up the idea that he might actually wake up at home—wherever *that* was—many Leaps ago, but he found it trying to surface again here: *I'll wake up, and I'll be in my own place, and I'll be a grown-up, and I'll be living my own life and seeing my own face.* It was a corollary of the panic, a natural addition to his now hyperactive imagination, but he didn't mind. He grabbed hold of it, and let it run.

I'll wake up, and it will be 1999, or maybe 2000 by now. Al will be coming over later to work on some harebrained scheme or other and talk about his latest adventures, but for now, it's just me. No . . . as long as we're pretending, just me and Donna Elesee.

He felt a small smile on his face now, although there was still a fluttery feeling in his stomach. Here was the escape hatch, the one that had pulled him through many different kinds of fears as he grew up.

We have a cat, Donna and I. His name is Fermi, after the mathematician. Donna calls him "Firm" as a joke, because he is the softest, fattest cat either of us has ever seen.

He laughed, and the sound of his laugh in the empty house

sobered him for a moment. There was something lonely in the sound, and Sam wondered how often Sean heard it, lying here in the dark.

But as soon as he let go of the daydream, the darker thoughts came crowding back in, like wolves around a doused campfire. He forced himself back into the light. It didn't help him sleep—each time his mind drifted toward the no-man's-land of sleep-thoughts, the panic would yank him back—but it made being awake and alone bearable.

A little after two o'clock, he heard the door open downstairs. There were heavy footsteps on the stairs, then the creak of bedsprings, then silence.

After a while, he slept.

PART TWO

Saturday

CHAPTER
SIX

CHAPTER SIX

"I can't believe I'm here at nine o'clock on a Saturday morning," Johnny said, staring at the locked door of the storage room incredulously.

The team was gathered in the hall, quiet now in the off hours. Pigeon was sitting on the floor Indian style, pretending to doze after beating Johnny in an undeclared foot race. Chrissi, dressed in a short pink mini-dress ("I want you guys to throw paint at me," she'd told them when they arrived, "*Seventeen* says that's going to be the thing this month"), was shifting from foot to foot, waiting anxiously for the day to begin. Sarah Easton stood somewhat aloof from the others, watching in detached silence.

Sam and the O.M. coach, a friendly, balding man whose name, Sam had deduced, was Stover, set a carton of painting supplies down on the floor, and Stover fished a large key ring out of his pocket.

While Stover was searching for the right key, Sam felt a soft pressure on his right hand and looked down to see Chrissi's small fingers twining through his own. He pulled his hand away instinctively—despite appearances, he was still in his forties, and she was still eleven (her youthful appearance was

71

accentuated today by the fact that she was wearing her hair in two carrotlike braids beside her face)—but regretted the suddenness when he saw the hurt look in her eyes. He smiled an apology, but she didn't respond.

A key rattled in the lock, and the storage-room door fell back into darkness. For a moment it looked like the shadow was reaching for them, to pull them into itself, but then the illusion passed, and Coach Stover reached around the door frame and flicked on the fluorescent lights.

They went inside.

The blank canvas flats stood sentry at the ends of the junk-laden shelves. The team approached them together, not speaking, and looked up at them. They were about eight feet high and ten feet wide, and they looked somehow forbidding in their austere emptiness.

Or so Sam Beckett thought.

Chrissi Martinez was looking at them with a frankly puzzled expression. After a while, she shook her head and said, "Do we have a ladder?"

Stover looked at her quizzically. "No."

"Then how are we going to paint the top?"

Sarah turned to her, disbelieving. "Are you *sure* you're gifted?"

Johnny laughed, then signaled Pigeon to help him move the first flat. They nudged it until its balance shifted, then caught it and laid it on the floor. They were starting to move the second one when Coach Stover cleared his throat to get their attention.

"Will you kids be okay in here if I go to my office to get some work done?" he said. There was a general murmur of assent. "Good. Just yell if you need me. I'll be right across the hall."

Johnny and Pigeon finished placing the second flat as they all watched Stover disappear into his office. Johnny ran across the room and made a show of closing the door. "Alright!" he exclaimed. "Let's do something illegal now."

Chrissi wrinkled her nose. "Don't be a jerk."

"Do whatever you want," Sarah said, pushing her long hair back with a cloth headband and kneeling down beside the flats. "*After* we get the flats painted."

Johnny acknowledged her impatiently. "What do you guys say? After we finish up, one of us hides in here. We tell old Uncle Phil out there"—he pointed in the general direction that Stover had gone—" that that one left early. Then, when he leaves, you come out of hiding, let the rest of us back in, and we . . . do something."

Sam's mind insisted on analyzing the idea, despite the fact that he had no intention of going along with it. They were alone in the school except for Stover, and he had no way of knowing who actually left when. If they really *did* want to sneak around the school, it would be a good plan. "That would work," he muttered.

"Of course it would work," Johnny said, self-evidently.

Sam decided to derail this before it started to get serious. At this particular point in time, the kids needed good P.R. more than an adventure in an empty school. "It would also be really stupid. They already want to cut the program."

"They *always* want to cut the program," Pigeon cut in, honestly surprised at Sam's line of argument. "It's the great constant in my life."

"Yeah," Chrissi agreed. "It kind of gives you that warm, fuzzy feeling of familiarity."

Sam felt a tug of anxiety. Al hadn't mentioned that this was a chronic condition here. There would be a lot of inertia to overcome, and if he couldn't even do it with the kids involved, he wasn't sure it could be done at all. "They're really going to do it this time," he tried. "Mrs. Fairgate from the school board was talking to Dr. Kellerman about it yesterday. He

73

wasn't arguing with her. She wants to drop it right now."

"O'Connor," Johnny said, slapping his shoulder, "have you got amnesia? She says that every week. Two or three times."

Sam bit his tongue. The worst thing he could do was start to sound desperate to convince them; they would just turn it around and make it a joke, which was something they couldn't afford. "I know she's been on our case a lot," he said. "But this time it's for real. I swear."

"How can you know that?" Sarah asked.

"I just *do*." He shook his head. "They're going to cut us off before States."

Sarah looked up, alarmed. "They can't do that."

Johnny shook his head, suddenly more sober than he had been since Sam first Leaped in. "Yes, they can. My dad used to be on the school board. They can do whatever they feel like doing. My dad crossed Mrs. Fairgate once or twice, so she did this whole, like, smear campaign to make him lose the next term. I bet they know we can win this, and they don't want to spend the money sending us to Binghamton."

No one said anything for a minute. It was an uncomfortable silence, but Sam was glad of it. It showed that they were convinced, and it had been an easier sell than he thought.

Pigeon spoke first. "So what are we going to do?"

"We could have a sit-in or something," Sarah suggested hopefully.

Johnny looked at her blankly. "The sixties are dead, Sarah. Give them a proper burial and get on with time."

Sam felt suddenly old.

Chrissi spoke up tentatively, in her breathy, little-girl voice. "Maybe we could write letters to the editor or something."

"Sure," Pigeon said, getting interested. "Your dad would run them, wouldn't he, Chrissi? Maybe he'd even write an editorial for us."

Chrissi rolled her eyes. "My dad is going on his honeymoon soon. I guarantee you he won't be thinking about O.M."

Johnny wiggled his eyebrows, his solemnity apparently unable to survive for long. "I've seen his fiancée. I wouldn't be, either." Chrissi gave him a dirty look, but he just smirked. She relented, and even laughed a little.

Sarah ignored the interplay. "Well, we can still write."

Sam nodded. "They're going to decide on Monday night," he informed them.

Chrissi sighed. "Well, that blows that idea. The paper doesn't come out 'til Thursday."

"Then there's nothing, really," Sarah said, and Sam could see that she was close to tears. "It's not fair. We can't even vote them out."

"That's the point." Johnny's voice was not bitter, but it didn't seem like a child's voice, either. "They know they can screw us over with impunity. So they do."

"I don't think they're doing it to hurt us," Sam said automatically, certain that he was right. "I think they just don't know what . . ."

"Oh, they know," Sarah interrupted. "They *always* know."

"They also know that when we graduate we'll be out of this town so fast it will make their heads spin," Pigeon added matter-of-factly. "If you look at it from their viewpoint, it's a pretty bad investment."

No one argued.

There was a moment of morose silence, then Sarah let out a frustrated sigh and leaned over to pry open a can of paint.

He hung up the phone tensely, and counted to ten under his breath, trying not to yell and curse. The kids didn't need to know how close they were to losing this one.

Phil Stover held master's degrees in education and adolescent psychology, but he sometimes thought that a few classes in strategy and tactics would have served him better in his position as director of Penworth's beleaguered gifted program.

No, not *beleaguered. Besieged.*

For years, the town had simply refused to consider establishing a gifted program. The smart kids, in their opinion, needed no help. They would leave anyway. Most of their parents weren't even *really* Penworth people, just transplants who came in with their fancy degrees to do the doctoring and teaching (there were very few teachers in Teoka County who had actually grown up there, and not a single doctor). The budget was limited, and the slower kids needed more supplies and more attention. The reasons came as fast and thick as the winter snow, but they all boiled down to only one thing: Penworth, New York, neither liked nor trusted bright people.

In the twenty-odd years Phil had lived here, he'd seen this simple truth demonstrated again and again, as he watched smart kids go to hell in a handbasket, as his mother would say, without being able to do a thing about it. He'd tried to explain to the board and the parents that gifted kids were not just better sponges for the education they were expected to soak up; they learned in a qualitatively different manner. Most if not all of them tended to learn "vertically"—choosing a subject to learn about thoroughly, pulling in all the knowledge they needed from other fields without thinking about it. For instance, Pigeon Janowski was interested in medicine. He constantly read books on anatomy, first aid, anything that came into his hands on the subject, really. In order to understand what he was reading, he'd picked up the principles behind the Greek and Latin prefixes and suffixes, and how prefixes and suffixes themselves functioned in the English language. He'd learned the basics of several chemistry equations, and applied the math automatically. He didn't realize that this was remotely unusual; it was just the way he worked. Other kids, even kids with good memories and passable study skills whose minds just weren't built that way, would be confused by this style, and it would have been inappropriate to introduce this kind of teaching into a regular classroom, which required a more horizontal approach—layering one layer of academic sediment on top of another, slowly but surely working upward. Phil had tried to illustrate this with charts, reports, flowery analogies, *anything*, but no one had ever listened.

Finally, when this particular group of kids—the ones down the hall in the moldy, abandoned storage room that they called their office, and the ones on the other two O.M. teams—had been in sixth grade, Phil Stover had gone to their parents with a plan.

As much as Penworth disliked its bright kids, Penworth's school system needed them—needed, in particular, their high scores on the state tests to maintain accreditation ratings. Phil Stover, in one of his rare bursts of intuitive strategy, had suggested that the parents simply refuse to allow their children to take the tests until a gifted program was established. He figured that even if the school board refused to cave in, the State of New York would be alerted to the situation, and enforce the state laws pertaining to the far ends of the bell curve—the upper as well as the lower. It was a no-lose scenario.

The Board had caved rather than allow a state investigation of its practices, and Phil had been given a meager start-up budget. He'd chosen to go with the fledgling Olympics of the Mind program as a base, because it was the first method that really seemed to encourage the kind of learning these kids felt at home with. In the "Humor from Homer" problem alone, they had picked up the Greek alphabet, the formal structure of a quest, the principles of producing a play, and, of course, the knowledge of a great work of world literature. Aside from these, Sarah Easton seemed to have discovered a raw talent

77

for scripting, which Phil was eager to see develop.

Unfortunately, Phil sometimes thought that he was the only adult in the school system who cared one way or the other if *any* of them developed their abilities.

He'd thought that the pressure would let up when the program was an established fact, but it hadn't. The school board met twice a month, and there hadn't yet been a meeting in which the subject of eliminating the program hadn't come up at least once. Phil sometimes felt as if he were in London during the height of the Axis bombings, striving for some sense of normalcy amid constant threats of annihilation. The kids coped with it better than he did; it seemed to be their natural element, and somehow that was the worst thing of all. Children had no business having such confidently low expectations.

Phil did his best for them. He'd teamed them very carefully, placing the ambitious kids together so that they could feed off of each other's flights of fancy, instead of being shot out of the sky one by one.

And it was working.

He hadn't needed state tests to see that. Combining Johnny's energy with Sarah's thoroughness with Pigeon's even-headedness with Chrissi's exuberance with Sean's take-charge leadership was producing an incredible effect. They were growing into each other. (Not completely, of course. Phil didn't mean for them to break down the walls that made them individual kids; even in the sixties, when breaking the walls had been a hot idea, Phil had found the concept disturbing, if not actively dangerous. But they were growing, finding their shapes against each other.) Sarah Easton, Penworth's most notorious lone wolf, was actually an accepted part of the group. Chrissi was spending as much time studying literature and engineering (for the robot team, which Phil thought was really much more up her alley; she'd begged to be in Homer because

78

her boyfriend was there) as she spent studying her apparently endless stream of fashion magazines. And Sean's grades were out of the cellar for the first time since his parents' divorce.

And the best part was, not one of them really noticed. They were too engrossed in what they were doing, certainly a first in their academic lives at Penworth, where they had always been able to pull top grades with no effort (Sean's poor grades had come from chronic truancy, from which even his test scores hadn't been able to rescue him).

There was a shriek of delighted laughter from the storage room, and Phil pulled himself out of his chair and his thoughts to make sure they weren't doing anything dangerous (the only problem he could see with the program was that when these kids decided to do something off the wall, they were far more efficient about it together than they were separately). He went across the hall and nudged their ''office'' door open.

It was Chrissi who was laughing.

She was standing in front of the flat, spattered with gray paint from head to toe. Johnny and Pigeon were swinging their paintbrushes at her, spreading fans of dingy droplets. Sean, Phil was surprised to note, was not participating—he was normally the ringleader in every unusual activity. This time, he was standing on the sidelines, watching with a smile that was . . .

Adult, Phil realized. Sean O'Connor, age twelve, was smiling like an indulgent adult, watching over energetic but immature children.

So the kid's in a strange mood, he thought. *Let it be*. He shook off the feeling that it might be something more, and turned to Chrissi. ''You okay, Chrissi?''

She nodded through her laughter. ''I told them to do it, Coach. It's gonna be *BIG*!'' The last word fell into another stream of high-pitched giggles, as Johnny and Pigeon let loose again.

"*Seventeen* said so," Pigeon filled in, laughing himself.

Johnny bent and refilled his brush. "And if you can't trust *Seventeen*, who can you trust?"

"I told them to stop," Sarah said from her station at the foot of the flats, where she was painting vague rock shapes onto the canvas.

Stover shook his head. "No, it's okay. But don't you get a drop of paint on anything but yourselves and the flats . . . got it?"

"Got IT!" Chrissi squealed. The others nodded and laughed.

Phil gave them a stern look to punctuate the message—the last thing he or they needed was a vandalism rap—but he thought they were being careful. He let the look fade into a smile and shook his head. "You kids," he said.

Chrissi shook her head back at him. "You grown-ups," she said, then laughed again.

Phil left, closing the door behind him.

Sam watched Phil Stover go.

The man obviously had something on his mind, and Sam thought he could probably guess what it was, and why he wasn't saying much. He wondered if Stover knew how much the kids had figured out about their precarious position.

Sarah stood up and surveyed the flats, which now showed a murky cave entrance. "I think we're done with these," she said. "Let's stand them up and let them dry. We can rehearse."

"Don't stand them up," Johnny advised her, dropping his paintbrush into a bucket of water as Chrissi held up her hand for him to stop coloring her. Pigeon followed suit. "The paint'll run. Let them dry on their backs."

Sarah evaluated this and nodded. "Okay. But let's find a

place to do some run-throughs. I think we can shave thirty seconds from the run-time, if we're careful. That'll give us more time to set up, 'cause that'll be harder in costume.''

Pigeon tapped his head rapidly with his finger. ''Boss-lady's got a point.''

Sarah looked at him blankly.

''We could go out in the hall,'' Sam suggested.

''Or maybe that place under the stairs, by the science door.'' Johnny raised his eyebrows for a question mark. ''I think that's about regulation size.''

Chrissi shook her head. ''It's almost twice as big as the rules say.''

Sarah shrugged. ''If we stay in the middle, it should be okay for blocking.''

There was general assent, and after poking their heads into Stover's office to tell him where they'd be, they moved on to the far end of the hall, where a two-story wall of windows lit the school brightly. Johnny made a show of shielding his eyes, then turned right and went down three shallow steps into a small, cavelike depression beneath the stairwell. Chrissi went in without any hesitation and placed four pieces of masking tape on the floor, forming the corners of a square.

''That's regulation,'' she said. Her voice was sure, and neither Sam nor anyone else doubted her quick measurement. Sam could've sworn he knew someone else who could size up a space that quickly, build to fill it . . .

Chrissi came over to him suddenly and pecked him on the cheek, startling him. He pulled away, again bringing that hurt and rejected look to her eyes. He wished it didn't have to be like that, but this was one part he wasn't willing to play as far as she needed him to.

Sarah clapped her hands once, smartly, before the interchange could go any further. ''Places,'' she said.

Without hesitation, Johnny and Chrissi ran to the downstage

81

left corner of the area, and Pigeon assumed a position directly kitty-corner from them. Sam, who had thought that Sarah was entirely behind the scenes, was surprised to see her take a place beside Chrissi and Johnny. She looked up at him. "Get backstage," she said. "You can't make an entrance from the audience."

"Do you mind if I look at a script while I'm waiting?" Sam asked.

Sarah fished one out of her book bag. She handed it to him with a foreboding look.

"Thanks," he said, going "backstage." He flipped to the back of the script to check out his own lines (there were, indeed, only four of them) and see what his cue was, then flipped through the rest of it. The title page informed him that Johnny was playing Odysseus (or "Odie," as they consistently called him), Sarah was an unnamed drunken sailor, Pigeon was Polyphemus the Cyclops, and Chrissi was in a challenging double role, as the sailor's dog, Argus, and Zeus' pet leopard. The sketch had only a passing relationship to the book— hardly an unusual feature of adaptations—but it was, by turns, weirdly bright (a sequence in which, for some reason, the entire cast broke into the jingle from a Puffs tissue ad worked surprisingly well) and brutally sharp ("Odie" was a self-serving louse, who killed the dog—probably so that Chrissi could run back and change into her leopard costume—and tried to kill the sailor, so he could take credit for killing the Cyclops with poisoned "Tylenarg" capsules, a particularly dark bit of humor that Sam had finally understood when he remembered the string of cyanide murders in Florida in the early eighties). In theme, it resembled a vicious but funny sketch from the good years of *Saturday Night Live*.

The execution, although it would never be mistaken for Broadway, was also clever. When the intrepid sailors entered the Cyclops' cave, the characters were taken over by marionettes, which the cast operated from behind rocks (or what Sam *assumed* would be rocks on a full set). This made Pigeon look genuinely huge when he first entered. Sarah's puppet found a bottle that contained a substance that allowed them to grow back to their normal size (more Lewis Carroll there than Homer, but it worked) and fight Polyphemus two against one. The final blow came when the Cyclops ate the sailor's teddy bear, and Sarah clopped him over the head with a rock, then offered him a giant cardboard capsule to ease his headache.

Until this point, Sam's only role had been to follow Chrissi, now spying out the cave in her leopard costume, to the stage, and observe the action from a regal distance. But now, as Johnny/Odie advanced to take Sarah/the sailor out of the picture, he stepped in and raised his lightning bolt. "Stop!"

Johnny turned to him with a cringing, sycophantic look, and after a short interchange, Sam touched him with the lightning bolt, sending him into the elaborate death scene Sam had Leaped in in time to see. He wasn't sure what Pigeon had been doing making his entrance at that time. Perhaps they had been practicing separately, or maybe Johnny had been goofing off again. It didn't especially matter, he supposed. The way they had just run it was the way it made sense.

Sarah pushed down the button on the stopwatch with a flourish. "Seven minutes, twenty seconds," she said. She looked at Johnny. "Cut the second time you sit up and grab your throat. That'll do it."

Johnny nodded. "Sure."

She started to reset the stopwatch. "Get back to your places," she said.

"Oh, come on," Pigeon said. "We got this one nailed, Sarah."

"Then what harm is it going to do to run it again? Or does someone else have a wedding rehearsal?"

"Hey, that's not, like, my fault," Chrissi said.

"You're right," Sarah said curtly. "I apologize."

Chrissi shrugged an acceptance.

"Honestly, Sadie-lady," Johnny said—Sarah looked too thoroughly surprised by his use of a nickname to say anything about it—"I don't think my heart can take another take, if you get me."

Sarah was unswayed. She looked at Johnny over the top of the stopwatch and said, "One more time."

CHAPTER
SEVEN

It turned out to be five more times, since Sarah wasn't satisfied with the seconds she was managing to shave. "I got it," Johnny had said dryly at one point. "How about I just walk in, shoot Pigeon, then hold up a sign that says 'The End'? We could probably cut out a good six minutes that way."

Sarah had just reset the stopwatch without answering, although Sam thought he'd seen the hint of a smile on her face. *Go on, laugh,* he'd thought, but she hadn't; she wasn't ready for that.

Stover had appeared for the last rehearsal, and told Sarah that it was good enough. She'd agreed, somewhat dubiously, to let up for the day.

Now, it was lunchtime, and they had returned to the storage room. The flats, now tacky enough not to run, were propped in their habitual position against the shelves, and the kids were propped in their habitual positions amid the dust bunnies.

Sarah was sitting against a decrepit desk (Sam noted with no great surprise that it was old enough to have an inkwell tucked in the upper right-hand corner), doodling on her script, trying to find some last-minute line change that would cinch the event. Johnny was sprawled out on a work counter, his feet crossed on top of a pencil sharpener. He'd finished his tunafish sandwich in about four bites, and was now tossing the plastic bag it had traveled in up and down, trying to hit the ceiling, terribly disappointed that it always uncrumpled before it could gather enough momentum to get there. He'd seemed almost insulted when Sam suggested he tie it in a knot; altering the bag was apparently against his private rules. Pigeon was sitting under the counter, looking like an inhabitant of the world's smallest, oddest cave.

Sam had tried to find a place, but it seemed that wherever he went, Chrissi followed him. She'd grabbed his hand, played with his hair, kissed his cheek, and tried to snuggle . . . and that was just in his most recent spot, on the floor beside the flats. She leaned against his shoulder, and he stood abruptly, knocking her off balance. She gave him a puzzled look, but for once stayed put. Sam thought about apologizing, but was afraid that she would think of it as an excuse to kiss and make up.

"So are we going to do this thing?" Johnny asked.

Sam looked up suspiciously. "What thing?"

"You know . . . sneak back into the school."

"I thought we covered that. It would be a stupid thing to do right now."

"No," Johnny insisted. "Now's the best time in the world."

Sarah looked up from her spot. "Why?"

"Yeah," Pigeon said. "*This*, I've got to hear."

"And so you shall." Johnny gathered his thoughts. "Sean said that old Vagina Fairgate was in Kellerman's office yesterday," he said, ignoring Chrissi's screechy, embarrassed laughter at his take on Mrs. Fairgate's name. "She probably left an agenda for him. If we know exactly what they're planning on doing, we can plan against it."

Sarah creased her brow. "Sort of a preemptive strategy thing, right?"

"Right." He smiled at her, and she nodded her agreement. Sam wondered if it was the smile more than the argument that would win her. He was, in fact, beginning to think that if Johnny Metz smiled at Sarah and asked her to run barefoot to Timbuktu, she'd be taking her shoes off before he finished the request (provided, of course, that she wasn't busy with the play at the time; when she was directing, that appeared to be all she noticed). She was smart and she was serious, but she was also a twelve-year-old with what looked like a very pain ful schoolgirl crush. Sam didn't *think* Johnny was cynically using it to get her to go along with his plan; he seemed to be connecting to it only on an instinctive level.

He shook his head. "This is a bad idea, Johnny."

"I'm with him," Pigeon said, cocking a thumb at Sam. "You're talking breaking and entering."

"I'm not going to break anything," Johnny said sullenly, but Sam could see that he'd lost some of his momentum at the sound of a felony charge.

"How would we get into the office?" Sarah asked.

"See, I've got that figured out, too." Johnny gestured at a large grating on the wall of the storage room. "Those are air ducts. They go all over the school. Hardly any of them are bolted down, and they're totally big enough to crawl in." He knelt in front of the grating to demonstrate that it was, indeed, large enough to allow comfortable motion. "We just follow the hall down to the office, push out the grate, grab the agenda, and leave."

Chrissi, who had positioned herself vaguely behind Sam on the desk, leaned her chin on his shoulder to look across at Johnny. "It's a lame thing to do," she said. "Sean's right."

"You always think Sean's right," Sarah noted.

"I do not, do I, babe?" She didn't wait for an answer. "We

87

have fights all the time." She kissed Sam's temple, beside his left eye.

Sam leaned away. "Come on, Chrissi," he said as gently as he could. "Cut it out, okay?"

She slid down off the desk. "Sure," she said, not looking at him. "No problem." She didn't say anything more for a moment, and neither did anyone else. When she finally spoke, still looking away, Sam thought he heard a tear behind her voice. "I'm going to the ladies' room for a while," she said. "I want to get the paint off my face."

"Jeez, O'Connor," Johnny said when she was gone. "Why don't you just shoot her or something?"

"I'm glad you made her stop," Sarah commented. "I hate it when couples do that stuff in front of other people. It's . . ." She tried for a word. "It's *embarrassing* to watch, you know? I always feel like I should leave or something."

Johnny shook his head at her. "You're so, like, repressed."

"Well, if she is, I am, too," Pigeon said. "I think that stuff should be for when people are, you know, alone."

Sam wholeheartedly agreed, but his mind was on Chrissi, and the hurt sound in her voice. *That's my fault*, he thought. *I just hurt that sweet little girl because* I'm *uncomfortable with the situation.*

But he couldn't think what else he could've done. This wasn't like Leaping into the husband of a married woman, or a college sweetheart, or even a high school sweetheart. Chrissi was *eleven*. Even the first time Sam had gone through January of 1983, he'd been pushing thirty. The relationship with Chrissi was a no-win situation, and Sam despaired of it.

The Imaging Chamber Door opened between Sarah and Johnny, and Al stepped through it, looking curiously from side to side. "Sheesh. Looks like somebody died around here."

Sam shook his head minutely, unable to answer the comment, as the Door slid shut.

"What about the agenda?" Sarah said.

"Agenda?" Al repeated.

Johnny perked up. "Yeah, come on, guys. It'll be awesome, I swear."

"Think you can clue me in on this, Sam?" Al asked.

Sam sighed, and tried to answer both of them at once. "I think we can find out what they're up to without breaking into the school, crawling through the air ducts, and stealing an agenda from Dr. Kellerman."

"I don't know." The Observer smirked. "Sounds like fun to me." He caught Sam's stern look. "But of course it's a bad idea," he added dryly, rolling his eyes.

"Besides," Sam said, ignoring him, "we don't even know that the agenda will have what we're looking for on it."

Sarah looked from Sam to Johnny, clearly unsure. She was bright enough to know Sam was right, but he wasn't sure she would side against Johnny, no matter what she thought. She bit her lip thoughtfully, then turned to Sam and said, "What did she have on us, anyway? When you heard her talking, I mean."

Sam glanced at Al, who was in the midst of lighting his cigar. He finished, and looked up. "We're working on it. The stuff in the paper is nothing new; there's nothing about what makes this time different."

"It's the same stuff," Sam tried.

"But we already *won* those fights," Sarah said quietly. "It's not fair."

"News flash, Sadie-lady," Johnny said, with none of the light teasing that had gone with the nickname before.

"Life's not fair," she finished for him.

"Oh, come *on*, you guys!" Pigeon interrupted impatiently. "We've got two whole *days*! We can come up with *something*. I mean, maybe we'll win on Monday or something, and that'll change their minds."

89

"Didn't happen the first time," Al said. "And they won by a pretty good margin."

Sam nodded. "Look, guys, I'm gonna go look for Chrissi, okay?"

"In the ladies' room?" Pigeon asked.

"Maybe she'll come out."

"I don't know," Sarah said. "You really made her mad, I think."

"What did you do?" Al asked.

Sam ignored him; he was buying some time to talk with Al anyway, he didn't need to make up excuses to give him answers here. "I'm going to give it a try anyway," he said, and left before they could pull him further into the discussion.

"Tell me," Al said when they got into the hall, "that we *aren't* going to the head."

Sam thought about the smell in the boys' room yesterday, and about the dismal parade of men's rooms where he and Al had held their counsels over the past five years. "We *aren't* going to the head," he promised. He turned left, heading for the main corridor.

"So what did you do to Chrissi?" Al asked, centering about ten feet ahead of him.

"*Nothing*," Sam told him, honestly. "That's the problem." He passed Al, and the Observer fell into step beside him. "What happens to Chrissi, anyway? You told me about the rest."

"We don't know."

"How can you not know?"

Al shrugged. "Ziggy doesn't have any data on her."

"You're kidding."

"Nope."

Sam thought about challenging it, but decided that the story was feasible. There were thousands of holes in the information network, even for a computer as well connected as Ziggy.

90

Something as simple as a name change could throw a search off for weeks if it wasn't done through proper channels. "Great," he said. "So why *are* you here?"

Al shrugged. "I'm just checking in. Making sure you're not doing too much damage to Sean's life."

"Thanks a lot."

"Yeah, well . . . I spent most of yesterday with him. Interesting kid."

"Think so?"

"He'd've gone along with Johnny's idea." Al laughed a little. "He'd've probably beat Johnny to thinking of it. You're probably making the other kids a little suspicious."

"Well, if I do everything that Sean did, there's no point to my being here."

Al conceded this point. "Anyway, Verbena Beeks thinks I should spend more time with him. As a role model, if you can believe it." He was trying to sound gruff and cynical, but Sam thought he was flattered, maybe even touched. "We talked for three, maybe four, hours. I can't figure out how he goes from where he is to where he ends up. It doesn't make any sense."

Sam thought about Johnny's plan, and the eager, anticipatory way in which he announced it. It had seemed almost like a game, one at which he already excelled at one level, and was trying to take to another. Maybe the same was true of the way Sean O'Connor saw the world. Maybe the game had become too easy on the right side of the law, so he'd added a new twist, the way a bodybuilder would add new weights to the ends of his barbells when the old weight became too comfortable, or the way a mountain climber would challenge Everest because "It was there," he muttered aloud.

"What?"

Sam shook his head impatiently. "It doesn't matter. I need to find out the real reason this program gets shut down."

91

Al shrugged. "I'll see what I can find."

The Observer opened the Door and was about to leave when Sam thought to ask, "What does Sean say about Chrissi?"

Al looked at him incredulously. "You know, I'm going to remember this Leap the next time you get on *my* case about being obsessed with younger women."

Sam didn't bother answering.

"We didn't talk much about her. All I know is that he's worried about her being with a grown-up. Beeks and I both told him not to sweat it."

Sam tried to find the best way to phrase his next question. "How, uh ... you don't think they've ... gone very far, do you?"

"I don't know." The Observer closed the Door and put the handlink in his pocket. "I wouldn't worry about ... *too* far."

"Well, I wasn't even thinking about *that*," Sam said quickly. "I mean, they're eleven and twelve, for God's sake. Chrissi's just acting a little more ... physical ... than I remember junior high school girls being."

"You didn't know the right girls. I remember this girl I knew when I was thirteen. Her name was Bevvie Benecki. All the guys used to—"

"I really don't care about Bevvie Benecki, Al."

"You would've if you knew her."

Sam raised his eyebrows. *You done?*

Al shrugged.

"It's not just what she does," Sam said. "It's the way she talks about it. It doesn't seem right."

"Kids grew up fast in the eighties. If you'd Leaped in a year from now, maybe two, I'd worry. But now, they're probably just testing the waters. She'll probably just decide that Sean's getting out of the pool for a while."

"Good." Sam shook his head. "But I really don't know

what to do about this. She looked like I really hurt her feelings."

"She'll get over it. Girls are always moody at that age. She'll probably forget about it later."

"Since when are you such an expert on adolescent girls?"

"Well, I admit I'm not *dating* one at the moment . . ."

"Will you cut that out?"

"After the cracks you've made about some of the women I hang out with? Not a chance, buddy."

Sam shook his head dully. Al was just being Al, after all.

"Is that all?" the Observer prodded.

"Yeah, I guess so. Go be a role model."

Al waved good-bye and shut the Door behind him, leaving Sam alone in the hall. They'd walked most of the way to the music room, at the far end of the school from where the O.M. kids were.

Sam wasn't in much of a hurry to get back.

Maybe it was her hair.

Chrissi had opted on the braids today instead of her usual moussed-up puff because it was Saturday and they were just goofing around. Maybe the little-girl look had put him off.

Or maybe she'd said something; sometimes Sean got mad about things, but Chrissi couldn't think of *anything* she'd done.

Or maybe he was mad because of her playing with Johnny and Pigeon, with the paint. But she'd expected *him* to play along, too; he was the one who'd decided not to.

Or maybe he just didn't like her anymore.

She'd been sitting on the corner of the cheap, institutional porcelain sink long enough to put her left leg to sleep, staring at herself in the smoke-grimy mirror, trying to see what had changed between yesterday and today. In the space of twenty-four hours, her relationship with Sean O'Connor (which was

93

more serious than Sam and Al guessed, but nowhere near as serious as some of the other adults in her life feared) seemed to have disintegrated entirely.

Sean was her first Relationship. Oh, of course, she'd liked other boys. She mostly liked *all* boys, actually, and the more *boy* they were, the better; even at eleven, she felt up to the task of being the feminine half of a couple. And other boys had liked her; she was a pretty girl, and she knew it as well as anyone else.

But this fall with Sean had been the first time that the whatever-it-was had happened at the same time for both of them. Her mother had laughed when Chrissi had told her that she was in love, but Chrissi hadn't thought it was a joke. She daydreamed about being married to Sean, and doing . . . things . . . with him. She'd learned about the birds and the bees in fourth-grade phys ed, when she still lived down in Jamestown, and when she'd first started liking Sean, she'd thought about doing *that* thing, and thinking about it had made her feel all tingly inside. And besides that, Chrissi liked being around him, talking to him and working with him, and if all that together didn't qualify for being in love with him, Chrissi didn't know what the word meant.

They'd been flirting since the beginning of school, and he'd asked her out at the end of September, sitting in her kitchen on another working Saturday. The radio was playing "Up Where We Belong" (from *An Officer and a Gentleman*, a movie Chrissi had seen three times with her mom; they both always cried), and it was so romantic that Chrissi thought her heart would just about break.

What *did* break was the glass Sean had been holding. His hands were shaking badly, and in the interim between his question and her answer, he dropped a full glass of Kool-Aid, sending fruit punch and glass shards out around him in a pinkish-red fan. They both dropped down to pick them

94

up—Chrissi's mom was going through a neatness kick, one of the many peculiar kicks she'd gone through since Daddy left—and Sean said, without looking at her, "So, will you?"

She tipped his chin up and nodded, feeling her smile stretch as far as it could go. He kissed her clumsily on the corner of the mouth, blushing furiously, and went back to pulling glass out of the sugar water on the floor.

In the four months since, their kissing had improved a lot. Sometimes Chrissi would open her eyes long enough to glance at a mirror or at their shadows and think, deliciously, *That's me doing that, just like a Woman, and that's Sean with me, and I love him, and I think maybe he loves me, too.* Not that the love part hadn't been there before, of course; Sean had been Chrissi's best friend from almost the minute her family had moved to Penworth, and they loved each other that way, but this new part . . . this was strong. This wasn't going anywhere.

Or so she thought as she looked at herself with him as she would look at strangers in passing.

Now, she wondered.

Could everything really have disappeared overnight? It didn't seem possible, but then it still didn't seem possible that Mama and Daddy were quits and Daddy was living with Chrissi's old baby-sitter, Jenny Linstrom. *That* had happened pretty fast.

But the counselor had said it *hadn't.* She was trying to tell Chrissi that it wasn't all Jenny's fault, that things had been going wrong between her folks for a long time, and Jenny had just been there to help her father through it. So maybe things like this *didn't* just, like, *happen* out of the blue or whatever, and maybe things were okay with Sean.

But maybe things had been wrong for a long time *there*, too. Chrissi hadn't seen it with her parents; maybe she'd missed it with Sean as well. Maybe she was wrong about all

95

of it, and he didn't really love her at all anymore, and had just been pretending to so that he wouldn't hurt her. The counselor had *also* told her that sometimes people just fell out of love, and they couldn't do anything about it.

Chrissi only knew one thing for sure: *she* hadn't fallen out of love with Sean. She still wanted to daydream about him first thing in the morning and last thing at night, and she still felt tingly when he touched her.

She shifted her weight on the sink, then slid down onto her feet. Her sleeping leg tried to crumple, but she wouldn't let it. She paced slowly back and forth across the uneven tiles, trying to walk it awake.

The question was what to *do* now. The counselor would no doubt have some sage advice like "Let it be a learning experience" or "Just let it happen," but Chrissi had no intention of just letting it unravel in front of her. She knew that the counselor was supposed to be an expert and everything, but she *also* knew, in her own heart, that there was nothing at all natural about letting a relationship die, any more than there was about letting a person die just because he eventually would anyway, no matter what the counselor thought. Chrissi figured that she'd wind up regurgitating all of this at her next session—there was something about sitting in that office that made her feel like she had to talk about everything that was in her head—but that didn't mean she'd care a whit what the counselor had to say about it. She would do things her own way.

And what *was* that way?

She didn't know yet.

Oh, face it, a voice in her head piped in. *You don't know much of anything. You're winging the whole business. You don't even know that something's wrong. Maybe it's just because you look like hell today.*

Well, that much was true, Chrissi figured, standing back

96

from the mirror and looking at herself from the waist up now. The paint splatters that *Seventeen* had promised would look radical on her dress (and they sort of did) looked horrible on her skin; she'd have to soak in a tub for a long time to get all of it off, and scrub her hair just about forever. She wasn't wearing any makeup at all, and her face looked plain and childish.

And what had she been thinking about, wearing braids? The baby-doll look wasn't in anymore; now it really *was* for babies.

Sure, maybe that was the whole thing.

Maybe Sean was just a little turned off by today's edition; Chrissi could always fix herself up on other days. *No prob-leh-mo, seh-nor-itta*, as Daddy would say, pretending that he knew how to speak Spanish (everyone expected him to, because of his name, but the Martinez family had come from Spain to Boston in 1873, and he wouldn't know a *la* from a *los* if he had a gun pointed at his head). Of *course* she could do that. She liked to do it anyway.

But what if that wasn't the problem?

It *was* the problem. It *had* to be.

Because she couldn't fix the other.

She looked at herself in the filthy girls' room mirror one more time, and regretted that she hadn't even brought lip gloss with her.

Maybe it was nothing.

Then again, maybe it was everything.

CHAPTER EIGHT

He looked up with a wide smile when she came in, and to his credit, it only faltered a little bit when he saw that she wasn't Al. "Hi, Dr. Beeks," he said, cheerfully enough.

"Hi, Sean." She opened up the folding chair she'd brought in with her and sat down. "Al tells me the two of you had a talk yesterday."

Sean nodded. "The admiral? Yeah. He's a good guy."

He was trying to be nonchalant, but Verbena could hear a certain deference in his voice. When she'd gotten back from her date and Al had told her about his visit with Sean, she'd been delighted. She'd bored Eddie to tears, as her mind wandered back to the subject of how to get through to Sean O'Connor no matter what he had on his mind. Al's news had been a ray of sunshine. She hadn't been able to get to Sean at all; maybe Al could. Maybe a male role model who didn't know the first thing about counselors' tricks was just what the doctor ordered. And Al himself seemed to be happy with the assignment. "We like him," she said.

"He brought me a bunch of stuff," Sean said, leaning over and picking up a pile of books. He tossed *Salem's Lot* to Verbena. (She wasn't altogether sure about Al's choice of reading material, but Sean didn't seem too disturbed, so she didn't say anything about it.) "I finished this one already. It's hard to sleep here."

"Would you be more comfortable if the room was cooler or warmer?"

"No, it's not that. I got a lot of little electric shocks. Just, like, little ones, nothing big, but I think it's from the thing that got me here. Leaping. It's electrical, isn't it?"

"I can't even tell you if you're warm or cold."

"I guess not." He pulled himself up onto the table, *The Shining* clasped in one hand. "I started this one this morning. It's really good. Have you read it?"

"A long time ago."

"Do the kid's parents get divorced?"

"Not exactly," Verbena said, noting Sean's first concern with no great surprise. She decided that she'd *really* need to talk to Al about the reading material; *The Shining* was not a book for a kid from a troubled home. It was likely to scare the hell out of him.

"Good. I hate divorces."

"There *are* things worse than divorce."

Sean shrugged. "I guess. But divorce is pretty low."

Verbena sighed. There was some evidence that the damage done to children of divorce often occurred *before* the divorce, from a negative home environment, but that was hard to explain to a kid who missed his father so much that he'd latched on to the first male authority figure to enter his world here. *Oh, well*, she thought. *He could do a lot worse than Al Calavicci.* "Well, aside from the little electric shocks, how are you feeling?"

Sean thought about it. "A little groovy, as my mom would say."

"What do you mean?"

"Well, like I said, I couldn't sleep. But I'm not, like, tired,

99

either. I feel really wide awake and a little jumpy, like I'm on speed or something.''

Verbena felt her eyes narrow. "Have you taken speed, Sean?''

"Speed? No.''

It was hardly a comforting answer. "How about other drugs?''

"I've messed around a little. Everyone does.''

"Not everyone. What have you taken?''

"I smoked pot in fifth grade, and a guy who used to go to Penworth had some acid once.'' He shrugged again. "I wasn't impressed, so you don't have to worry about it.''

Verbena considered telling him what she knew about his future, then decided not to. Nothing in the transcripts had indicated that Sean's "imported merchandise'' meant anything but money to him; in fact, there'd been some implication that his success in the business was related to the fact that he didn't dip into the supplies.

She heard the door slide up behind her, and she didn't have to turn around to know it was Al; Sean's face was sufficient notice. He came around from her right side, carrying a flat pizza box.

"Hey, Beeks,'' he said. "How're you doing?''

"Okay.''

"Hi, Admiral,'' Sean said. "The vampire book was good.''

"You're already finished?''

"Yeah.''

"Our Visitor seems to have a problem sleeping,'' Verbena explained.

"Oh.''

"It's the electricity,'' Sean offered helpfully. "From the Leaping.''

"What electricity?'' Al asked blankly, without missing a beat.

100

Sean grinned, delighted with the game of secrecy. Al mirrored it.

Sean's grin broke into a full smile. "Glad you came back," he said.

Al shrugged. "It's my job." He jerked a thumb at Verbena. "Dr. Beeks here wants me to be a role model for you."

Sean gave him a briefly suspicious look. "You're not going to shrink out on me or anything, are you?"

Al crossed his heart and rolled his eyes.

Sean laughed. "Awesome. If you're going to be my role model, can I have a funky tie like that?" He pointed to the neon modern around Al's neck.

Al pulled it off. "You can have this one, if you want."

"Really?"

"What the hell? You can't take it with you."

"Oh, well." Sean took it, and started fixing it around the stand-up collar of Sam Beckett's Fermi-Suit.

Verbena smiled to herself, watching their interplay. She was beginning to suspect that Al Calavicci needed it, in some deep way, as much as Sean O'Connor did, maybe even more. They were a tonic for each other—a childless man, a fatherless child, each needing what the other could offer. It was like watching benign magic unfolding before her eyes.

Al and Sean seemed to have forgotten that she was there.

"I just got back from visiting Sam in Penworth," Al said, pulling the cot over to sit on.

"Yeah?"

"Yeah. I like your friends."

"So do I. What's going on there?"

"They're at the school doing O.M."

Sean nodded. "Painting the flats. Coach Stover set that up two weeks ago. How do they look?"

"The flats or your friends?"

"The flats. I know what my friends look like."

Al thought about it. "Well, they're mostly gray. Big blocks of dark gray."

"It's supposed to be a cave."

"It'll pass." He opened the pizza box and looked at Verbena. "You want to join us for lunch?"

She looked down at the concoction curiously; Al had a habit of ordering somewhat *exotic* pizza dressings. He said it was a great way to judge how adventurous a person was. He knew, by now, that Verbena Beeks's culinary adventures rarely got above level one.

Today's selection seemed to be double onions with some kind of mystery meat buried under it—not too threatening, but enough to tell her that he wanted her to decline.

She shook her head, with a reluctance that was only half feigned. "No, I think I'll leave this to you guys."

"You sure?" Sean asked.

"Positive." She stood. "I've got some work to do on my records, anyway."

Al smiled an acknowledgment, and pulled a piece of pizza from the box.

Verbena shook her head and left the Waiting Room, satisfied that Sean was in good hands.

They were halfway through the pizza the admiral had brought from someplace "in town," he'd said, wherever that was (Sean got the impression that the admiral didn't think much of "town," although he couldn't pinpoint why he thought this).

The admiral wiped a line of pizza grease off his chin. "So anyway, we're flying reconnaissance over Cuba, and we thought for sure World War III was about to start. I don't think anyone back home had a *clue* how close we got. And my buddy, Chip, says, 'Hey, Bingo—' "

"*Bingo*?"

102

"Don't ask. Anyway, Chip says, 'If the world's going to end anyway, I say we drop down and grab some Havana cigars to give it a send-off.' "

"Did you?"

"No, of course not." The admiral pushed the last of his pizza into his mouth, and crumpled up the cloth napkin he'd been using (they didn't use paper napkins here, he said, because of the trees; Sean resolved to keep this in mind the next time he went shopping with his mom—or *for* his mom, as the case usually was lately) and pushed it into his pants pocket. "The Navy wouldn't have been real appreciative."

Sean laughed. "Your friend Chip sounds like a good guy."

"Oh, yeah. Chip was the best."

"What happened to him?"

"He's dead. Vietnam."

"Oh. I'm sorry."

"Me, too."

Sean, who always felt vaguely uncomfortable talking about dead people (he believed in ghosts, and he wasn't altogether sure they were friendly, although he'd never tell the admiral anything like that), searched for something to change the subject. What he found was, "What did *you* do in Vietnam?"

The admiral looked up sharply, and Sean was afraid for a minute that he'd just pick up his pizza and his books and leave because the question had been out of line. Instead, he just shrugged and answered it. "I was a pilot. I flew some bombing missions, and I did some intelligence work."

"Like, spying?"

"Not really. Just taking pictures from the air."

"Oh." Sean thought that sounded a lot like spying, but he didn't say so. "How long were you there?"

"Longer than I planned to be," the admiral said dryly. "My plane was shot down," he explained when Sean didn't say anything. "I was a prisoner of war for a while."

"Wow," Sean said, unable to think of anything else for the moment. "Jeez, that must've been bad."

"Well, it wasn't Club Med."

Sean barely heard him. His mind kept flashing on all the stories he'd heard about Vietnam, some from TV, others from the endless stream of refugees that had come and gone through the different churches in Penworth (none of them had been made to feel especially welcome to stay) when Sean was little. He had a vague memory of playing checkers with a little boy who didn't know any English and whose left arm had been blown off; he'd screamed every time he heard a loud noise. He's been about four at the time, and his father had explained what horrible things could happen in a war. A couple of years later, he'd had a refugee baby-sitter who'd told him about the V.C., and how they'd killed her cousin and made her aunt and uncle watch while they did it, then blinded them both. The image of the spikes being driven into their unknown eyes had haunted his dreams for weeks (the baby-sitter had not been invited back). He'd lost some memories coming here—he couldn't, for some reason, remember the name of the town his father lived in, or his mother's maiden name, which wasn't too bad, considering his brain had been pretty much rebuilt from molecules up when he came here—but he couldn't put that image out of his head.

"Wow," he said again. He looked across at the admiral, and saw that the older man looked uncomfortable, so he changed the subject again. "Do you like being in the Navy?"

The admiral relaxed. "Yeah. I do. The Navy's done a hell of a lot for me over the years."

Sean smiled. He liked the admiral a great deal; the guy was funny and pretty carefree, but he'd stayed loyal and done his duty, too. (Sean thought that his father—and, even more, Chrissi's no-account dad—could learn something from him.) And a prisoner of war . . . that was way above and beyond, but he still was nice about the people who sent him there. "Aren't you ever mad at them for sending you to Vietnam?"

The admiral wiped a hand across his face. "They only sent me the first time. I volunteered for the second."

"Volunteered?" It seemed inconceivable; all Sean had ever heard about soldiers in Vietnam was about people trying *not* to go.

"I believed in what we were trying to do," he said simply. "I know there are a lot of people who didn't believe, and that's okay; this is a free country, right?" Sean nodded. "But don't listen to people who tell you we went over for bad reasons. I was there. We wanted to help. Maybe we did a lousy job of it, but that's why we went. And that's why I went back."

"I don't think you did a lousy job," Sean said automatically. The feeling inside him was larger though. It was almost awe. This man, who stood for everything Sean's father despised, had stayed true to his beliefs and his country and fought for what was right at a great price, while Dad hadn't even stayed true to his own family or fought for his own son in court. "And I'm really sorry about the way they treated you guys when you came home," he added, a little abashed at never knowing any side of the story except his father's.

The admiral looked at him, surprised. "You're sorry? Jesus Christ, Sean—you were three years old when the war ended. What are you apologizing for?"

Sean looked away, feeling like he'd done something wrong. "I don't know. Everything, I guess."

There was no answer for a long time, and when Sean looked back to the admiral, the older man's face had changed somehow. "You don't owe any of us any apologies, Sean," he said. "Not for anything. And I stayed in the service, so I didn't get too much of the blowout. But thank you."

Sean thought about saying, "You're welcome," but it

didn't seem right. He tried a smile instead.

The admiral returned it, and the tense moment ended.

"Admiral?" a woman's voice said over an intercom.

"Yeah?"

"I've accessed some additional information."

"Okay, Ziggy. I'll be right out."

Sean raised an eyebrow. "You've got someone who works here named 'Ziggy'?"

"You could say that," the voice said.

"And we *will* say that," the admiral cut her off. He stood up and turned to Sean. "You suppose you can entertain yourself while I go take care of business?"

Sean nodded. In the time since his parents' split, he'd become an expert at keeping himself entertained.

"I'll be back, though," the admiral promised. "So don't get into any funny business."

"Okay."

The admiral left.

Sean watched the door close behind him, then dug into the pile of projects he'd left.

The books were good, but Sean didn't feel much like reading. His eyes were already a little strained from last night's vampire marathon. He'd been reading a lot this year, ever since the program started, and he'd found that every now and then, no matter how good the story, he had to close the book or go crazy from eye strain and wasted physical energy.

Beside the books was a Merlin game, which the admiral had said had some kind of problem in its works. Sean wasn't exactly Mr. Fix-It, but he did like to take things apart and see how they worked, which, on occasion, had led to figuring out why they *weren't* working and how to fix them. It wasn't his natural gift, which had always been for working with people, finding *their* natural gifts and putting them to use (even as far back as the Vietnamese boy with no arm, Sean could remember using this gift; his father—like *he* should talk!—had cautioned him over and over about using it selfishly). Fixing things was Chrissi's gift, or one of them, and Sean would've normally just taken it to her and watched over her shoulder while she performed whatever surgery was necessary, but this was hardly a normal situation, and his mind was begging for a challenge, now that even the competition had been yanked away from him.

And besides, the admiral wanted him to do this.

He smiled to himself, and picked up the game.

Al didn't know how much of a role model he was being, but he knew that he liked the job anyway. There was something about being looked up to, about trying to help a kid grow up, that felt good and right. That part of his time with Nate had been long buried under the darker things that had come later, but now it was back, and he was glad of it. Maybe this would be a chance to redeem himself, just a little bit, for everything he'd done wrong before.

But it wasn't just the chance to vicariously repay old debts that brought him here. Sean himself was a good enough reason for that. He was a good kid, with an inquisitive mind and crystal-clear perceptions of the world around him.

"Well?"

Verbena Beeks was standing at the mouth of the corridor that led to the Control Room, her eyebrows raised expectantly.

"Well what?"

"How's it going? With Sean?"

Al debated telling her all the details of his conversation with Sean, decided that it would be betraying a trust, and shrugged. "So far, so good."

She smiled. There was something about that smile, the way it seemed to carry all the good things in the world with it, that had virtually placed her on a pedestal for most of the men at

107

the Project (Sam Beckett not excluded, if Al recalled correctly). Al was sure that he would've placed her there himself, if that interior pedestal had not been filled long, long ago, by someone he had no wish to dethrone. "I'm so glad he tried to get out last night," she said. "I think it is the best thing that could happen for him. And you."

Al knew that she expected him to offer a protest, for form's sake, but he couldn't think of one. Instead, he acknowledged her comment with a smile and started down the corridor. "What do we have on his family, anyway?" he asked. "Aside from the fact that his folks are divorced."

Verbena turned and walked with him. "Not much. They seem to have been a pretty typical small-town couple." She thought about it and amended. "Well, they were bright, of course. His mother was valedictorian of her high school class. His father started his own consulting firm right out of college, and did fairly well with it."

"What happened?"

"The divorce?"

Al nodded.

"You'd have to ask Sean if you want to know. It's filed as a no-fault, without any other information. There wasn't even a custody battle."

"Well, that's good, anyway."

Verbena didn't look very certain of that. "Normally, I'd say it was. But this time . . ." She shook her head. "I think Sean may have interpreted it as proof that his father didn't particularly care about him." She sighed. "And I'm almost inclined to think he was right about that."

"Why?"

"I don't think Stephen O'Connor's been back to visit his family since he moved to Idaho. Sean didn't fly out to see him for any holidays. And all the phone calls were from New

108

York to Idaho, not vice versa. It doesn't prove anything, but it's suggestive."

Al wanted to deny that such a thing was possible. It *should* have been impossible; in a sane world it *would* have been. In a sane world, all parents would fight their way through hell for more time with their kids. But Al had seen enough of the *in*sane side of the world to know that this wasn't always true. This particular insanity had been taught to him very early on. "Poor kid," he said.

"Yeah."

"Admiral?" another voice said, and both of them stopped walking.

Al blinked and turned to the speaker that ran along the top of the hallway. "What is it, Ziggy?"

"As I believe I mentioned before, I have some new information regarding Dr. Beckett's Leap."

Al waited, then prompted, "Yes?"

"I was finally able to access the minutes of the Penworth school board meeting of January 24, 1983. I'm not sure it was worth the trouble of getting into that primitive, parochial archive system. Not very interesting reading."

"Just give me the highlights, Ziggy."

" 'Minutes of the meeting of the Penworth Central School Board, January 24, 1983,' " she read. " 'Six of seven board members present. Herbert Tellanski absent due to cattle emergency'—how quaint—'Mr. Tellanski's votes on tonight's agenda registered with Regina Fairgate, president of the board. Also in attendance were—' "

"The *highlights*, Ziggy," Al interrupted.

"I don't think there *are* any highlights, Admiral."

"Does it say how she gets the program axed?"

"It's a little mundane, I'm afraid. They ran out of money."

"What the hell am I supposed to do with that?"

109

"That's *your* job," Ziggy said cheerfully, cutting off the conversation effectively.

"Calm down, Al," Verbena said. "Why don't you just go back to Sam, tell him what we know. Maybe he'll be able to sort it out."

"Yeah. Maybe." Al started walking again. "Why don't you and Gushie and Sammie Jo start running scenarios while I'm in there. And those techs . . . what are their names?"

"Geary, McNamera, and Corcoran."

"Yeah, them. Don't let them in."

Verbena laughed, and went off to open a conference room. Al went on to work.

CHAPTER
NINE

Sarah left them at the corner of Watkins Avenue, mumbling a good-bye and scurrying off into the cold. Sam watched her go, thinking how alone she looked, then turned left onto Watkins (a residential street that like most streets in Penworth curved down into a gentle bowl shape) with the others. It was the way he'd come home yesterday, and he didn't want to chance getting lost trying a new route in this weather.

Johnny was meeting his brother at work, and the brother was driving him home, and Pigeon, if it was okay, so they had joined Sam and Chrissi going this direction.

"Too bad Sarah couldn't come with us," he commented.

"She, like, lives two miles in the other direction," Chrissi pointed out.

"Oh."

"She's so, like, *weird*."

Pigeon blew on his hands through his thinning mittens. "You can't really blame her," he said. "Have you ever met her parents? Talk about hippie-freaks. My folks used to hang out with them before the accident. All they do all day is sit around talking about the marches and rallies and sit-ins and whatever. It's like everything they ever did or said is totally meaningful. And since we don't do the same things . . ." He shrugged. "I guess they won't be happy with us until we go back to Vietnam, so we can protest it, too."

Sam recoiled, thinking of the stories he'd heard, from Tom and from Al and from countless other men who'd been there. It hadn't been an opportunity for hippies to have love-ins. "That's sick," he said.

Johnny shook his head in disgust. "Why didn't they grow up and become yuppie-freaks like the rest of the Woodstocky people?"

"Probably 'cause they can't afford all the toys for it," Pigeon offered. "They're really broke, all the time. One time I heard my dad say that it wasn't because they couldn't earn the money; it was just because they don't know how to hold on to it."

"Maybe they think it's too *bourgeois* or something," Chrissi said (pronouncing the "r" with the harsh, flat tone of a Western New Yorker, making it sound like "berr-jhwa"), then giggled. "I always wanted to say that."

"Congratulations on achieving a life's goal," Johnny said. "And she's only eleven, folks!" He turned to Chrissi and feigned shoving a microphone in front of her. "Now that you've done this great thing, Miss Martinez, what's left to aim toward for the rest of your life?"

"Well, gee," Chrissi said, raising her voice even higher than normal, and twirling the end of one braid around her gloved finger. "I don't know . . ." She creased her brow and returned to her normal voice. "Jeez. I really *don't* know."

"At eleven, you don't have to," Sam said.

"But when you get to be twelve, like us," Johnny cut in, "you better have it all laid out." He threw an arm across Pigeon's shoulders. "Take Pidge, here. He's got his act together. He studies. Someday, he's going to be a manager at McDonald's over in Oslo. Mark my words, this boy's going

112

places! And me?'' He put his fingertips on his chest. ''I'm going to be a trucker. Get a potbelly and eat greasy food and pick up hitchhikers. What a life!''

Chrissi laughed. ''If you're so smart, what's Sean going to be?''

Johnny raised his eyebrows wisely. ''Sean's a genius. Someday, Sean's going to invent a time machine, so he can come back here and spy on you without you knowing.'' Sam felt his heart skip a beat—it was kind of a shock to the system to hear a true prophecy spoken in jest—but he didn't let it show. Johnny leaned toward Chrissi conspiratorially. ''For all you know, he's spying on all of us right now.''

Sam caught himself instinctively looking for Al, as if the Observer would be summoned by mere mention of his duties, and laughed at himself. Johnny really had a way of catching people up in his schemes; Sam had to grant him that.

''That's stupid,'' Pigeon said. Sam expected him to say that time travel was impossible—that always seemed to be the follow-up to such openings—but Pigeon apparently didn't take impossibility into consideration; Sam liked that in a person. ''Why would he be spying on us from the future when he's here right now?'' the boy asked reasonably. ''I mean, unless he can tell himself things, but that would mean that he can see himself, and if he can see himself, why can't *we* see him?''

''Telepathy,'' Chrissi said, self-evidently. ''He can read his own mind.''

''But can he *tell* stuff to his mind?'' Pigeon persisted.

Johnny dropped back beside Sam. '' 'Fess up,'' he stage-whispered. ''You're talking to yourself right now, aren't you?''

Sam decided to give them something to chew on. ''Maybe I hired somebody *else* to spy on us from the future. Maybe he's only tuned into *my* brain waves, so I'm the only one who

113

can hear him, and maybe he can walk through walls and listen in on everything you say behind my back.''

There were a few seconds of impressed silence, then Chrissi said, ''Awesome!'' (Sam would never know it, but he had started a running thread in their lives—''Sean's spy'' would be a constant presence for years to come, as both a companion and a threat.)

Pigeon laughed. ''Don't tell it to Sarah. She'll make us put it in the script.''

They all laughed at that for a minute, even Sam, who felt uncomfortable making jokes about Sarah behind her back.

Pigeon stopped laughing first. ''I guess we're too hard on her,'' he said. ''I mean, she's pretty regular, when you know her.''

Sam tried to hear a crush or some kind of deep feeling in Pigeon's voice, but it wasn't there. He seemed to just feel bad about teasing her. Too bad. Sarah badly needed to be special to someone.

''And how well do *you* know her?'' Johnny asked, an insinuating tone in his voice.

Pigeon blushed. ''Our parents were friends, that's all. We used to get baby-sat together. We played Superfriends together when we were six. She used to hit me with her doll when she got mad at me.'' He rubbed his head in remembrance. ''I'm glad she doesn't carry that thing to rehearsals.''

''It's weird to think of her *having* a doll,'' Chrissi said. ''I just can't see her playing Mommy.''

''She didn't,'' Pigeon told her. ''She used to make up stories for her dolls, like they were puppets or something.''

''Figures,'' Johnny said.

Sam smiled to himself. He'd known such people before, people who had been focused all their lives on one thing, often without even realizing it. If he could save Sarah, he had a feeling that she would leave her mark on the world.

114

They had reached the bottom of the meandering slope of Watkins Avenue, and Chrissi pulled away from the group, into a salted-over driveway beside a clapboard house. She grabbed Sam's arm to pull him after her. Pigeon and Johnny stood awkwardly by. Sam wasn't sure what to do; Chrissi had been acting cheerful and normal since she'd returned from the ladies' room, and he'd thought her concerns were over for the day. Looking at her face now, though, he thought maybe he'd been wrong.

Chrissi widened her eyes to shoot a look at Johnny and Pigeon. "Get lost, guys," she said. "He'll catch up. Maybe."

Johnny and Pigeon exchanged a knowing look, and Johnny dropped a solemn wink in Sam's direction, then they headed on up the street.

With some trepidation, Sam let Chrissi lead him onto her enclosed front porch.

Chrissi dropped her bag onto a wicker chair that had been gathering dust since summer, a relic of a time of lemonade and swimsuits that seemed impossible to Sam in this time of biting wind and frozen earth.

She looked at him expectantly; he looked back dully, not knowing what she needed to hear.

She let a frustrated sigh escape. "What's the matter?"

"What do you mean?"

Chrissi shook her head, a disbelieving expression on her face. "Are you mad at me or something?"

"No, I'm not mad at you." Sam dreaded the next few minutes; he knew he could make a lot of mistakes here that while probably not fatal could really end up hurting Chrissi, and Sean, too, if he really liked her. What would Sean say to her? Sam realized he didn't even know what he *himself* would've said at twelve, let alone what another twelve-year-old would say. At twelve, girls had been playmates and occasional parts of daydreams about being a teenager like Tom,

115

not the other half of a precariously balanced relationship, with hearts that could be broken by a single word. He decided that feigning complete ignorance would be best; he'd been disappointed to learn, when he'd started dating, that girls *expected* ignorance, almost as a matter of course, and usually brushed it off after a few terse words.

It didn't seem to ease Chrissi's mind. "Is it that you don't like me anymore?" She bit her lip, almost afraid of his answer.

"Is what?"

Chrissi's jaw dropped, and she blinked her eyes rapidly. "You've been avoiding me all day," she said.

So much for ignorance; he could hardly claim it after a succinct explanation. The next step would have to be denial. "I've been five feet away from you all day," he said.

"And every time I tried to get closer than five feet, you moved away." She waved her arm at the door. "Did you suddenly decide that Johnny and Pigeon are cuter than I am?"

"No," Sam said quickly. Where in the hell was an eleven-year-old getting *that* idea? he wondered, but he didn't waste much time on it. Getting out of the current predicament without damaging Sean and Chrissi's friendship-and-whatever-else-it-was was more important than lamenting the lack of innocence in Chrissi's childhood. He'd always hated making excuses (Al had chastised him for this "failing" more than once), but he thought that now might be time for one. "No, I just have other things on my mind, is all. The program, the competition. You know."

It worked. Sam saw Chrissi consider it, turn it over in her mind, almost reject it, then accept it grudgingly, like a broken toy or a wilted bouquet that had been offered with good intentions. She sighed. "Yeah, I guess so." She sighed and fished a key on a string out from under her coat and dress. (*Latchkey kid*, Sam thought, realizing the odd pathos of the phrase for the first time.) "Why don't you come inside? I think

116

Mama's got some hot chocolate mix.''

Sam didn't have the heart to say no. She opened the door and he followed her in.

The porch door led into a blue and white hallway. Carpeted stairs climbed upward on the left, and a closet yawned open to the right. Chrissi quickly led him through this hall and through an almost empty room, then into the kitchen, where she dropped her coat over a chair and busied herself looking through cupboards. Sam pulled his coat off thoughtfully and draped it over his crossed arms, then looked back at the empty room. ''What, uh . . .''

''Happened to the living room?'' Chrissi finished. ''Mama's buying new furniture.'' She groped toward the back of a cabinet under the sink. ''She didn't want Daddy's around anymore.'' She pulled out a can of cleanser, and looked at it, frustrated. ''That's not it. Jeez, she moves the stuff in here around, like, every day. I *never* know where she's keeping *anything* when she's not home.''

Sam thought that Verbena Beeks could probably write volumes on that alone, but he couldn't think of anything to say about it. ''So,'' he said, ''when's the new furniture coming?''

Chrissi shrugged and stood on a chair to look in a cupboard above the refrigerator. ''Who knows? It probably won't be here for long. She's using her credit card; she says Daddy can pay for it with alimony. But Daddy doesn't have that much money, either. I bet they come in, take the furniture, and break our kneecaps or something in a couple of months.''

''They're not going to break your kneecaps,'' Sam assured her.

''They might,'' she said in a quarrelsome tone, then she smiled triumphantly. *''Ha!''* she exclaimed. ''I *knew* it was around here someplace.'' She stood on her tiptoes to reach back into the cupboard, and Sam saw what was coming next without needing an Observer to give him the odds.

117

The chair tipped onto its back legs under her weight, and when she shifted her feet to get hold of the canister of cocoa, it overbalanced to one side, spilling two boxes of rice, the canister, and Chrissi toward the tile floor. She let out a startled scream, and Sam ran for her instinctively. He didn't catch her, but he managed to break her fall, although he landed pretty hard himself.

Chrissi stood up on shaky legs and turned to him. "Are you, like, okay, babe?"

Sam nodded, barely noticing the pet name. "Yeah. Are you?"

"Guess so." She moved her arms around stiffly to check, seemed satisfied, and bent to pick up the cocoa. She pulled the lid off and stared inside with no real surprise. "It's empty," she said. "We just practically got killed, and it's empty."

"We didn't practically get killed."

"Why would she put away an empty thing?"

Sam was trying to think of some kind of Sean-like crack to make when he noticed that Chrissi was not even remotely amused. She looked upset, almost on the verge of tears. "Chrissi?" he said.

She threw the empty canister across the room, and it thudded into a corner underneath the toaster. "Why would she put away an empty thing?" she asked again.

"I—"

"I'm sorry, everything's going wrong, I should've worn my hair down and put on some makeup—"

"What?"

"—there's no cocoa, no chairs to sit down and drink it on, no nothing."

"Hey, Chrissi . . ." Sam put a tentative hand on her shoulder, and she put her arms around him tightly, more like a frightened child than a would-be girlfriend. Sam returned this

118

embrace without hesitation. "It's okay, Chrissi," he said.

"It's not okay. My father's marrying my baby-sitter and my mother's turning into a nutcase. Who's going to take care of me now?"

"Shh . . ." Sam tried to make his voice as soothing as possible. "All this over an empty can of cocoa and a little redecorating?"

"I guess it doesn't sound like much to you," she said, and Sam had time to reflect on the thudding footsteps he'd heard in the dark late last night, "but I'm scared, Sean. I'm really scared."

Sam stroked her hair gently. "I know you are. But you've got me, and the rest of the team, and Coach Stover . . ." He saw her starting to perk up. "And your folks'll get their act together about this pretty soon."

"Like yours did?"

"Don't look at my folks," he said. "They're not how it usually works." He didn't know this for sure—the social sciences had never been his forte—but it was probably true, and it was definitely useful.

Chrissi pulled away from him; he was surprised to see that she hadn't been crying. "I guess I know that," she said. "But everything's so *weird* right now." She smiled hopefully. "Maybe it'll get better after tomorrow, when Daddy's really married and things are set."

Sam doubted that, quite sincerely, but decided that discretion was probably the better part of valor here. He changed the subject. "Was I supposed to go to your father's wedding with you?"

Chrissi's response was immediate and vitriolic. "No way."

"Why not?"

"Because it's, like, totally *gross*." She shuddered.

"What do you mean?"

"I keep thinking about Woodstock."

119

"Woodstock?"

"Yeah. My father didn't go because he thought he was too old for that kind of nonsense. She didn't go because she was in the second grade."

"So?"

"*So*?" Chrissi repeated, eyes wide. "So what can they possibly have in common except sex?" Sam shook his head slightly, as if trying to clear it; he didn't think he was ever going to get used to this kind of candor from children. Chrissi went on. "It's really embarrassing that my father is marrying someone for that. And can you imagine what he'd say if I were dating someone as much older than me as he is than Susie Cupcake? He freaked when I told him I was going out with a twelve-year-old. I mean, what a hypocrite." She smirked. "I ought to do it. Just to piss him off."

And you have no idea how close you are to doing just that, Sam thought, and said, "That's brilliant, Chrissi. Any guy that much older than you who's interested in an eleven-year-old girl has psychiatric problems."

"Ha!" Chrissi said, delighted. "I knew you'd be jealous."

"I'm not jealous."

"Yes, you are, you're jealous."

Sam had meant to warn her about the serious dangers of her suggestion, just to make sure she didn't mean it, but he saw on her face that Sean's "jealousy" on the subject would be a much better tonic. He smiled. "Alright, yeah. I'm jealous. Sure."

She gave him a toothy smile. "I knew it." She squatted to pick up the rice boxes.

Sam watched her for a minute, and decided he'd gotten them both past the moment. She seemed to be fine now. And he thought it better if he left before The Girlfriend decided to come back in full force. "I'm going to go catch up with the guys, if that's all you wanted."

"It was."

Sam pulled on his jacket and turned to go. Chrissi's voice stopped him at the kitchen door.

"Aren't you going to kiss me good-bye?"

Sam sighed. There was no getting around it. "Sure," he said. He went back to her and kissed her chastely on the forehead.

She laughed. "Get out of here, O'Connor."

"You got it."

Feeling better, he went out into the cold.

"This sucks," Johnny said thoughtfully, after nearly a minute of unusual silence.

Pigeon, who knew Johnny Metz better than anyone, said nothing, and waited for him to fill out the thought. They were walking south on Central Street, across from a cement wall on which someone had long ago spray-painted, in capital letters three feet tall, "IT'S ONLY TEENAGE WASTELAND." Beside this, in smaller, fresher letters, was the terse reply, "FUCK THE KIDS." Pigeon always allowed himself a moment to contemplate this when he passed the wall, but he'd never come up with a satisfactory explanation for it.

Johnny kicked a piece of ice off the sidewalk and into the road. "I mean, did you ever think about it?" he asked. "If we lived in Russia or someplace like that, there wouldn't be any arguments. They really *teach* their talented kids. I mean, look at their Olympic athletes."

Pigeon's head jerked around almost involuntarily, but Johnny wasn't paying much attention. Russia? Jeez, Pigeon had third cousins in Poland, and that was the same kind of deal with the government and everything. They sent cards and things sometimes, and Polish cookies. Their letters came with black marks through them, when they came at all. "Sure," he said sarcastically. "Russia'd be great. They'd take us away

121

from our families and make us study calculus or something all day. Also, we wouldn't be able to go to the library and pick up any book we want."

Johnny shrugged. "I guess so. But don't you think there's, like, a happy medium someplace?"

"If there is, it's not in Penworth."

"I hear that parochial school down in Oslo is pretty good. Don't your neighbors go there?"

"Yeah," Pigeon answered carefully.

"Do they like it?"

"I guess so."

Johnny sighed. "My parents asked me if I wanted to go there. Last month, you know, right before Christmas vacation, when the board was going to drop the program because of that zero-charisma guy from the college telling them that it was elitist and everything."

Pigeon stopped walking, alarmed. Johnny was a complete spaz most of the time, but he'd *always* gone to Penworth, and it wouldn't be right without him. "What did you tell them?"

"Not much. I mean, I don't want to bail out on you guys or anything. But this is school stuff, you know? If I don't get it right, it could really screw things up for me."

"Your brother's okay," Pigeon offered hopefully.

"My brother's a great guy," Johnny said. "But my parents have been teaching him outside school since he was four. Me, too, of course, but that's not their job. I mean, they should help and all that, but it's not their job to make up the school-work, and Mike and I don't get any credit for it for, like, college applications and stuff. Penworth Central's got a really bad rating for that. That's why they want to send me to Oslo."

"Great. Then the school test scores will go down, so the rating will drop even further for the rest of us."

"I can't do anything about that!"

Pigeon tried to be nonchalant. "Do what you gotta do."

"I'm only going if they cut the program."

Pigeon turned and started walking again. Johnny was right. It was his education, after all; the rest of his *life* depended on getting it right. It wasn't like Penworth was leaving him much choice.

"Maybe we could all go," Johnny said.

"Who's going to pay the tuition? My grandmother? Sean's mom? And Sarah's folks wouldn't let her go to a religious school even if they *did* have the money, which they don't. They're really psycho about that."

"They're just plain psycho, if you ask me."

"I didn't."

They turned left onto a little street that was known generally as Gasoline Alley, since the only businesses on it were gas stations. The street sign had fallen over or been stolen or something a long time ago, and Pigeon wasn't sure what the real name was. It was the street that Johnny's brother Mike worked on, and Mike was going to drive them both home when his shift was over in . . . Pigeon looked at his watch.

"Oops," he said.

"What?"

"I think we're late for your brother."

Johnny screwed his face up. "He'll live."

There was a loud horn blast, and they turned to see Mike's Pinto sitting at the side of the road. The driver's side window came down, and Mike leaned out, his mop of dark hair flopping to one side. "You guys better be ready!"

Johnny rolled his eyes, led them over to the car, and opened the passenger door. Pigeon caught his sleeve. "What about Sean? He was going to catch up to us, remember?"

Johnny looked at him wisely. "If you were going out with Chrissi Martinez, would *you* catch up with us?"

Pigeon didn't need much time to contemplate this.

123

CHAPTER
TEN

Sean's watch insisted that only fifteen minutes had passed, but Sam was convinced that he'd been walking against the wind for at least an hour. It bit into his lungs like shards of glass; his face felt raw and exposed.

Either his happy childhood memories of winter in Indiana were wrong, or winter in Penworth was really brutal.

Then again, he thought, considering the way Sean's jacket seemed to pull at his shoulders and the way the filling seemed clumped in several places, maybe no one had bothered updating Sean's winter wardrobe for a couple of years, and it just wasn't up to the task anymore.

He'd missed Johnny and Pigeon somewhere; maybe they'd met Johnny's brother already and left for home. He hadn't minded much at first—had, in fact, been rather relieved. When he was alone, he could just be Sam Beckett, and not worry about getting some little detail wrong. A nice, long walk home by himself had a certain appeal in this way. Now, however, thinking of a quick ride in a heated car, the appeal had faded.

He turned the corner from Central Street onto Main Street, and heard the Imaging Chamber Door screech open behind him. Al came through it and fell into step beside him. "Hi,

Sam," he said. "How's it going?"

"You tell me. Have I changed anything?"

"Not yet."

"Figures." Sam's foot slipped on a patch of ice; he tried to catch himself unobtrusively. "How are things going with Sean in the Waiting Room?"

Al's eyes lit up. "Great." He laughed. "The kid's a trip. He's trying his damnedest to get us to tell him all about Leaping."

"You're not telling him, are you?"

"Of course not." The Observer smiled fondly. "He listened to old Navy stories for two hours. I think he liked them. He's pretty impressed with the fact that I'm in the service."

"Probably fills an authority void," Sam suggested.

Al looked annoyed. "Maybe the kid just respects what we do. Not everything has to have some deep, dark Freudian secret behind it."

Sam didn't bother with this. "Do you have anything new on the Leap?" he asked.

Al nodded, and put the handlink in his pocket absently. "Ziggy got a hold of Penworth's school board minutes."

"And?"

"They ran out of money." Al shook his head. "They lost the program because they ran out of money."

"How am I supposed to fix that?"

"I don't know. I came here to ask *you* the same question."

Sam didn't have an answer for it, and Al didn't wait for one.

"You know, it really ticks me off," the Observer said, "the school board had enough state funding at the beginning of the year to run all of its programs without cuts. It's only January and they've already run out. Lousy management. And the gifted kids pay for it, because they have no one to stick up for them. I sat on one of the gifted education commissions a few years ago. It boggles the mind. The smartest people in the world are in the gifted lobbies, but they spend so much time philosophizing and theorizing and arguing semantics that they never get anything *done*."

Sam didn't remember Al sitting on such a committee, but he wasn't surprised. Al, an impulsive if not *com*pulsive joiner, tended to sit on a lot of committees, for just about everything that landed on his desk, it seemed. There was a space committee and an environmental committee (those two were often at odds, causing Al to go into paroxysms of frustrated rhetoric; he was convinced that if they'd stop wasting their energy yelling at each other and start using it to accomplish their respective goals, they'd find themselves on the same side of the line). There was an urban committee of some kind, a research committee, and Sam had no idea how many military committees. He had heard the run-off from many of them over the years, and it had often been heated, but he didn't ever remember seeing this look on Al's face . . . not about something as distant as a cause, anyway. This was the kind of look he got on his face when he was talking about Trudy, or about his mother. "You're taking this kind of personally," he said, trying to draw the Observer out.

Al shook his head. "It just burns me, the same way it burns me to see ships dumping their garbage in the ocean. People don't think about what they're doing. And when it goes toxic, they have the nerve to wonder why."

Sam nodded; it was an apt description. "Well, let's see if we can keep this from going toxic."

"Yeah. Sure." Al nodded. He thought for a minute, and an idea seemed to dawn on him. "Oh, hey . . . how about their parents? Maybe you're here to call in the cavalry."

Sam shook his head immediately. "I've been here a day, and I haven't even *talked* to Sean's mother. She showed up at three-thirty this morning, and she was still passed out when

126

I left at nine. I don't even know if there *is* a father."

"Didn't I tell you? They're divorced. The father lives in Idaho. Sends them money to live on, but never comes around."

It figured. "Great," Sam said, frustrated. "Chrissi's parents are divorced, too, and her father is about to go on his honeymoon with a girl who's young enough to be his daughter. Sarah's parents are apparently stuck back in time worse than I am, and Pigeon lives with his eighty-year-old grandmother. There's not much of a cavalry to call in."

"I'm glad you didn't make that kind of a judgment on me."

"I never needed you to be my father."

The Observer fell silent, and Sam felt immediately sorry. He had obviously hit some vein that he hadn't been aiming for, and hurt Al—again. "I'm sorry. I didn't mean that. I just . . . it's going to be hard."

"I never said it would be easy."

"Easy? Al, it's impossible." Sam quickened his pace. "I mean, I've only got . . . What? Two days?" Al nodded; Sam mirrored it. "Two days! Do you know how much inertia there is around here?"

Al shrugged. "Next time, Leap in earlier. Like around 1970."

"That's helpful."

"Well, you've got what you've got. Work with it."

"Great."

"You've got a better idea?"

Sam sighed. He knew Al was right; he was certainly in no position to sway the school board alone. "I guess maybe it's worth a try," he said. "Their parents, I mean. I'll talk to Sean's mother when I get home."

They reached the top of South Main Street and Sam turned onto Sean's street. Al blinked out and let him walk the rest of the way alone. He was waiting in the entrance hall of the house when Sam let himself in, a look of dismay on his face.

Sean's mother had turned the living room into a sort of cave by closing all the curtains and pulling all the shades. She was curled up in a broken-down easy chair, dressed in her underwear and a bathrobe and nursing a bottle of cheap wine. Sam didn't need to look too closely to see that she had a monster of a hangover.

Al shook his head and looked briefly at the information on the handlink's viewscreen. "Her name's Kathleen Riordan O'Connor. Sean doesn't talk about her much. I guess I can see why."

Sam stood in the archway that led into the living room. He cleared his throat. "Uh, Mom?"

The woman looked up slowly, as if she were swimming to the surface of some murky pond. When she spoke, her voice was thick and slurred—drunkspeak. She slowly raised a sardonic eyebrow. "Oh, Sean," she said expansively. "My favorite son, home from a long, exhausting Saturday at school. What devotion."

Sam cringed mentally. "We were painting the scenery for O.M. Am I late?"

"Since your note didn't say when you'd be home, I couldn't tell you." She stood up (for a minute, Sam wasn't sure she was going to make it, but she did) and started for the kitchen. "So tell me," she said over her shoulder, "are you and your friends going to win?"

"I think so."

"Good." She took another slug from the bottle and went to the sink to splash some water on her face. "Winning's important."

"This was a bad idea," Al said. He was watching Kathleen stagger around with a mixture of pity and revulsion.

Sam shook his head faintly. He had an idea, or the beginning of one, about the deeper reasons he might be here. Oh, the program was important; he wasn't denying that, nor would he. But seeing Kathleen like this, and thinking about Chrissi's mom with her empty cocoa can, and envisioning Sarah's parents with their love beads, and remembering his own horrid loneliness of the previous night . . . all those things were starting to come together, and he was beginning to see a shape.

Maybe it *was* the cavalry.

Or maybe it needed to be.

"Mom," he said, "can I talk to you about something?"

Kathleen sighed. "Well, you're still too young to tell me you got your girlfriend knocked up, so I guess it's okay."

"Nice attitude," Al commented.

Sam privately agreed, but said nothing. "I was in the office yesterday—"

Kathleen's eyes narrowed. "What were you doing there?"

"I was late for a class," Sam explained quickly. He was glad to see that she had some concern over the matter, but he wanted to get to the point. "Anyway, while I was there, Mrs. Fairgate from the school board was talking to Dr. Keller-man—"

"*Regina* Fairgate?"

"Yeah, the school board lady."

Kathleen blew air through her teeth in an extended "Sheesh."

"You know her?"

"Everyone knows Gina. She's been glad-handing since kindergarten."

The shape was getting a little more focused. "You don't like her much?"

"What's not to like?" Kathleen asked in a tone that left no doubt of her feelings on the subject.

Sam smiled. "Look, she was talking to Dr. Kellerman yesterday. About the gifted program." Sam took a few steps into the kitchen. Al recentered near the stove. "They're short on

129

cash or something. They're going to cancel it."

Kathleen turned, anger darkening her already reddened cheeks. *"What?"*

"She's going to ax us."

For a moment Kathleen said nothing, but Sam could see her fingers flexing on the bottle; her body seemed to be trembling with the slow burn.

Then, she exploded. The bottle flew across the room (through Al, although she couldn't have known that), shattering into dozens of shards against the wall and cutting the wallpaper and the floor with deep red gashes. "That goddam *bitch*!"

"Jesus!" Al exclaimed. "If she'd thrown a little bit wrong that would've hit you! And she thinks you're her kid!"

Sam said nothing. He had been trying to provoke a response, some kind of emotional rallying point, but this . . . he knew she hadn't been aiming for him, but drunk as she was, she could've easily misfired. This was too much; it was dangerous.

Kathleen must have seen some of this in his face. She closed her eyes and breathed deeply. "I'm sorry, honey," she said. "I didn't mean to scare you. But I'm sick of that nickel-plated . . ." She stopped herself. "I'm sick of her screwing around with my kid's life. I'm going to get dressed and go over and have a word with her."

Al spoke up quickly. "Not when she's this drunk, Sam. It won't help anyone."

It wasn't a point Sam had especially needed his advice on. "Mom, no. Not now."

"I'm not doing this to embarrass you," Kathleen said patiently. "But someone has to take her on. An adult."

Sam caught her shoulder as she tried to go through the kitchen door and toward the stairs. "Yes. Preferably a sober one."

130

• • •

"Will you slow down, Spaz?" Mike yelled.

Johnny reluctantly let up on the gas pedal, and his heart slowed along with the car. In the back seat, he heard Pigeon let out a relieved sigh. "Wimp," he said into the rearview mirror.

"Pull over," Mike said.

"How come?"

"Because I said so, that's how come."

Wrinkling his nose, Johnny edged onto the shoulder. "Is there a cop or something?"

"No. You were just driving like a complete maniac, and I don't want you wrecking my car. Also, Pigeon's life is valuable."

Mike opened the door to get out and switch places, and Johnny unfastened his seat belt. He was starting to crawl over the emergency brake when Mike poked his head back in. "There's a car just over the hill. Looks like they've got a flat. I'm going to grab the jack out of the trunk and help them out. Do you guys want to come with me or freeze in the car? 'Cause I'm not going to leave it idling."

Johnny looked at Pigeon, and Pigeon shrugged. They got out of the car and helped Mike lug the jack over the hill, to where a small red car was sitting on the shoulder with its emergency lights blinking. The driver's side door opened, and a woman stepped out.

Pigeon leaned over and whispered, "Isn't that Mrs. Fairgate?"

"Yeah, that's her. Mercedes-Benz and all."

Mike stopped for a minute when he saw who he was going to help, then sighed and went on. It was freezing cold out, and both Metz boys had been taught that you didn't hold a grudge when it was dangerous to someone.

"Michael," Mrs. Fairgate said through her best political

131

smile. "I've never been so glad to see anyone in my life. I was about to hike up to the Livingston Inn to call Triple A. I knew I should've learned to change a tire, but I never did."

"No problem," Mike said, and set about changing the tire.

Mrs. Fairgate's daughter, Sharon, climbed out of the passenger side and came over to where Pigeon and Johnny were standing. Johnny liked her okay, and figured she must take after her father. "Hi, Sharon," he said. "Where were you guys off to?"

She smiled shyly. "I have a gymnastics class at Livingston College."

"I thought you took gymnastics in Penworth."

"I used to. But I passed the top level there, so now I've got to go all the way out here."

"Wow," Pigeon said. "Are you going to go to the Olympics?"

Sharon laughed. "I don't think so. Mom and Dad don't really like me to compete so much. They're afraid I'll get stressed out."

"Stress is your friend," Johnny said.

"Also, I think it's really expensive," she added. "I mean, they don't say anything, but I know *they're* stressing about the money. So I probably won't go much further."

Johnny looked at the car, and at the fancy clothes they were both wearing. The Metz family wasn't poor, but next to the Fairgates, they looked destitute. It *must* be expensive, if they were stressing.

"It's too bad," Pigeon said. "It would be cool if you went."

Sharon just shrugged. "Maybe they'll find a way."

Johnny felt an idea try to make a connection in his mind and miss. He shook it off. "Maybe they will," he said.

"Why didn't you tell me that your mother drinks?"

Sean looked at his feet. The admiral was asking a fair

132

enough question, he supposed; unfortunately, there was no good answer. He simply hadn't thought about it since he'd arrived. It had been a welcome respite.

"You know we're trying to help you, don't you?"

Sean nodded.

"And you know Sam's got to live in the middle of your life?"

"I *know*."

"We need to know what's going on." The admiral sat down in the folding chair, leaning forward with his elbows on his knees. "Now, do you want to tell me why you didn't say anything?"

Sean toyed with different answers. *I was ashamed* was not only pat psychobabble, it was false. His mother's drinking was a source of annoyance most of the time, occasionally becoming full-fledged pain, but he wasn't ashamed of it. It was nothing compared to his father's midlife-crisis/run-away-from-the-family-to-go-find-himself routine. If Sean were going to feel shame over either of their actions, it would be Dad's. *I didn't think it was important* was closer to the truth, but not quite there. Thinking about it now, he realized that it could've been dangerous for this Sam not to know. He couldn't even honestly blame it on the little bits of memory loss, because he hadn't not known it. He just hadn't told.

But the truth, *I didn't tell you because it never crossed my mind to mention it*, sounded heartless and not very bright, and Sean didn't want the admiral to believe either of those things about him.

So he said nothing.

The admiral sighed. "Okay. I guess that's your business. But is there anything *else* you haven't mentioned?"

Sean felt his mind reeling full-tilt through images of his life. There were a lot of things he hadn't told the admiral, but most of them were just stupid little things, things that couldn't make any difference at all. Did they want to know about the fort he and Johnny Metz had built in Johnny's backyard when they were eight? Or about the time Chrissi broke her ankle on the pond in the park when she'd gone skating with him? Did they really need to know that he'd seen Chrissi with her shirt off?

No, he decided. They didn't need to know that.

The admiral was still watching him intently, and for the first time Sean felt vaguely uncomfortable with him. It had come down to a choice: to trust this man or not to trust him, and Sean didn't trust anybody very easily, despite the fact that he got along with nearly everybody.

Oh, come on, he chided himself. *The admiral's one of the Good Guys, remember? Big sacrifices for Mom, the flag, and apple pie?*

"Sean?"

Going through his laundry list of peccadilloes, he decided that the information he had to offer wasn't worth the time he'd spent thinking about whether or not to offer it. He thought of a quick, simple answer and decided that it was enough. "I can't think of anything," he said finally, deciding to leave the issue of trust in abeyance for a while.

That's a lie, the voice chided him. *You thought of a lot of things, and you didn't tell because you don't trust him.*

No, it wasn't true. He just hadn't decided yet was all.

"Are you sure?"

"If I said it, I meant it."

"Okay, I'm sorry."

Sean nodded. There was a nervous, fluttery feeling in his stomach, like he was standing on the edge of the gorge over in Aldridge State Park, looking down, and he realized that his quick, simple answer was no answer at all. He had to make a decision, one way or the other—he could back away and say nothing more, go back where he came from with nothing to show for it; or he could step forward and take the risk that

134

there was no hand to catch him.

The admiral got up to leave.

"Admiral?" Sean said when he opened the door.

"Yeah?"

He swallowed hard and spoke quickly. "I thought of other things. But they aren't important. They're, like, personal. I think this guy"—he pointed to the mirror—"can live without them for a few days. Is that okay?"

The admiral thought about it for a moment, then nodded. "It's okay. I'll see you tomorrow."

Sean watched the door close, then took a deep breath.

And stepped over the precipice to see if he'd be caught.

PART THREE

Sunday

CHAPTER
ELEVEN

Sean woke up with a startled scream, his eyes darting around the Waiting Room in the momentary terror of disrecognition. His forehead was beaded with sweat, and his hands were clenched into tight fists. The scream subsided into quick gulps of air that were almost, but not quite, hyperventilating.

Al set down the canvas bag he'd brought in with him without saying anything; many of the Visitors had nightmares here, and most just needed a few minutes to remember where they were without a stranger butting in. It was understandable, Al thought. Leaping wasn't exactly part of their normal mind-set.

After a while, Sean's eyes landed on him. At first, there was no recognition; then, slowly, the panic drained away and the breathing slowed somewhat. He offered a shaky smile. "Hi, Admiral."

"Good morning," Al said. "You okay?"

Sean considered this carefully, turning his arms and legs this way and that, pinching his leg . . . and blatantly avoiding any kind of reflective surface. "I guess so. Just a nightmare."

"You want to tell me about it?"

Sean's eyes narrowed. "Why?"

"I just thought you might like to get it off your chest or something."

"It was probably just one of those electric-shock things going off in my brain." He shrugged. "I dreamed it was competition day, and no one showed up except me. I went out onstage and just stood there with that dumb lightning bolt. There wasn't anybody in the audience either. Just the judges. And they were all Cyclopes." He offered a self-deprecatory smile. "Pretty dumb, huh?" Al said nothing; Sean went on. "Anyway, one of them said that he already ate Johnny and Pigeon and Sarah and Coach Stover, and that he was going to eat Chrissi next, and then me."

"Unless you made him laugh or remembered the whole *Odyssey* in Greek or something like that?" Al guessed.

"No. He was just going to do it, anyway, no matter what I did. I tried to talk him out of it, but it wasn't working. He grabbed Chrissi and broke her neck, and that's when I woke up."

Al was sure that Sean was expecting him to offer some kind of analysis, but he thought that Sean's first guess, about the "electric-shock thing" in his brain, was probably the closest to the mark they could get. So instead of trying to make a philosophical or psychological point, he just said, "Sounds like a pretty lousy dream."

Sean smiled. "Well, it's not my all-time favorite."

"You want some breakfast?" Al poked into the canvas bag and brought out a loaf of bread and some butter. There had been something odd in Sean's smile, something a little distant, but Al didn't want to analyze it too deeply. The nightmare had gotten the better of him for the moment. It was nothing to be ashamed of, but there was no need to harp on it, either. "It's not much, but nothing around here is edible this early in the morning."

"Okay."

Nightmare or no nightmare, Sean didn't seem to have lost

140

much of his appetite. He tore into the bread and butter as if he hadn't been fed for a week.

"Sam's going to try and get your mom dried out," Al said.

Sean looked up, his eyes wide and surprised over a mouthful of bread. He swallowed in a gulp. "He's not staying long enough to do *that*, is he?"

"He's going to get it started today, get her sobered up. It's going to be rough for a while when you get back, though. I just thought I should tell you."

"Yeah, thanks," Sean said absently.

"Do you know all the places she keeps her booze?"

"I think it's all in the cupboard and the fridge. It's not like it's a secret or anything."

Al noticed another odd glance, a strange twist of the head. "Look, Sean, is something wrong?"

"Huh?" Sean jumped a little in his seat. "No, nothing. Just, you know, the nightmare, I guess."

There was something he was holding back, but Al wasn't sure what it was. "I'm going to get back to Sam now, make sure everything's alright."

"Okay, good. I'll find something to do here."

Al left him to whatever was speaking in his mind.

It was technically possible for the senior staff of Project Quantum Leap to conduct meetings without ever seeing each other face-to-face, but it had never become a regular procedure, despite Ziggy's exasperation at having to wait for everyone to arrive. Even the younger members of the staff—Tina, Sammie Jo, a few others—who were fully at ease in cyberspace (Al, for one, still felt vaguely like he was playing a part in a science fiction movie most of the time) preferred the actual, physical presence of their teammates to the distance inherent in remote meetings.

Gushie, Verbena, and Sammie Jo were in the Control

141

Room when Al got there. Gushie looked at his watch ostentatiously. "You're late."

"I was checking in on Sean."

Sammie Jo looked up. "How's he doing?"

"He had a nightmare last night, about a Cyclops judge trying to kill him. But he seems okay now."

"Anxiety dream," Verbena said, brushing it off. "I wouldn't worry."

"So how are *we* doing?"

Al hadn't directed the question to anyone in particular; Sammie Jo picked it up. She waved a hand at Ziggy. "Ziggy and I were working on it last night," she said (it never ceased to disturb Al how easily Sammie Jo spoke of working "with" Ziggy—the computer was, effectively, the woman's best friend, which was not, in Al's opinion, healthy or natural). "We're doing something right, I think, with the mother. The chances of saving the program went up eight-point-six percent when we factored her in. And Sean's chances of making it through even without the program went up to almost eleven percent."

"Ten-point-eight-three-four, to be precise," Ziggy clarified.

"Well, it's a start."

"Pardon me for being a skeptic," Verbena said, "but I've known a lot of alcoholics in my time. What are Sam's chances of getting her dry?"

"Point-oh-two-three," Ziggy answered promptly.

Sammie Jo shot an annoyed look at the closest viewing lens. "Ziggy's a pessimist."

"I simply have no emotional investment."

"What Ziggy meant to say"—Sammie Jo waited for an argument, and continued cautiously when one wasn't mounted—"is that there's only a small chance of getting her to stay dry. The numbers on just getting her sober in time to help are pretty good."

142

"What Dr. Fuller meant to say," Ziggy qualified dryly, "is that, as usual, Dr. Beckett can effect a short-term solution very easily. Unfortunately, human beings rarely thrive on a single short-term solution."

Al nodded and looked at the others. "Any ideas?"

"Well, it's not fair to Sean to dump it all on him," Gushie started.

"I agree." Al looked at Verbena. "How about you, Beeks?"

"It's worse than unfair. It wouldn't work."

"Are we sure she's an alcoholic?" Gushie asked. "I mean, she drinks more than she should, but . . ."

"That's a good point," Beeks said. "Unfortunately, it's not something we can really test for. If Sam can get her sober and she can stay that way on her own, she's not. But we don't have the luxury of waiting around to see, so we're going to have to assume she is."

"Hope for the best and expect the worst?" Sammie Jo said. Beeks nodded.

"In the meantime," Al said, "we have to get back to the basics. Sam's there to save a program that has no money, and we need to work on scenarios to get that done."

The others, who seemed to prefer playing God to playing politics, gave a halfhearted assent.

Al sighed. "Alright, then. Assignment. I want Sammie Jo and Verbena to get outside for a while and get your brains clear. Unfortunately, Gushie has to stay here to hook me up with Sam."

"Woe is me," Gushie commented.

Al ignored him. "Then I want you to think of every scenario you can for the long-term problem. Then we'll brainstorm."

"But I was going to—"

"Sammie Jo, *out*. Now."

143

She gave a sarcastic pout and left. Verbena started to go after her, but Al touched her sleeve. "Are you sure that . . . 'anxiety dream' is nothing to worry about? It had him pretty shook up."

"All kids have anxiety dreams. They don't mean anything. It's probably better to *not* make a big deal out of it. We don't need the kid assigning meanings to it."

"You're sure?"

"It goes against everything Freud taught to leave a dream alone. In other words, yes, I'm very sure."

Al laughed and let her go on her way.

You're going to trust him, remember?

Yeah, okay. Trust. How hard can it be? Even babies do it. *So what are you so scared of? Why didn't you tell him the whole dream?*

Just a dream. No biggie.

If it's no biggie, then what's the problem?

That, of course, was the question.

Because the one image of the dream that Sean could not shake out of his head, the last grotesquerie, was this: As Chrissi's neck had broken, Sean had looked up helplessly at his Cyclopean judges.

Around their huge, solitary eyes, each one of them wore the admiral's face.

Sam had also dreamed of Chrissi, but it had been a formless, aimless dream, just images over images, trying to make a picture, to connect the dots in this particular puzzle.

He shook it off easily when he woke up; he had more important things to attend to.

He went to the kitchen first and, despairing of finding anything healthy to eat, dropped two cherry Pop-Tarts into the toaster. They might be empty calories as far as the higher nutrients were concerned, but they were quick energy; Sam figured, if he was going to get Kathleen O'Connor's cupboards dried out before she woke up, he would need at least that.

Sobering up addicts was never an easy job, and the short time Leaping afforded for it didn't leave much room for mistakes. Sam had a vague, disconnected memory of a beautiful woman named Eve . . . no, not Eve, but something like it . . . fighting him with maddening strength to get at her hidden stash of pills. Wherever and whenever she had been, she'd been out of place somehow, lost . . .

Edie. Not Eve. Edie . . . something. She was a model in—

But the rest didn't come. It could've been New York or Paris or London or Elk Ridge, Indiana; no place seemed to offer itself into his memory.

The Pop-Tarts came up with a sound like a gunshot in the morning-still house. Sam jumped.

"Nervous?"

He spun to find Al standing in the bright frame of the Imaging Chamber Door. It must have come up with the Pop-Tarts. "Don't sneak up on me like that."

"Sorry." Al touched the keypad on the handlink and the Door disappeared behind him.

Sam turned back to his breakfast and plucked the first pastry from the toaster. It burned his fingers, and he dropped it on the floor.

"Try picking it up with a couple of napkins," Al suggested. "That usually takes the sting out of it."

"You eat these things?"

"Now and then. Tina practically lives on them."

"Great."

"Oh, come on. They've got lots of good stuff in them."

"Like what?"

"Well . . . they've got *fruit*, right?"

Sam rolled his eyes and broke the Pop-Tart in half, stretch-

145

ing its thin lining of cherry jam until it broke. He stuffed half of it into his mouth, chewed it ravenously—he hadn't realized how hungry he actually was—and swallowed. "Did you come here to argue about breakfast?"

"No. I just figured you'd probably be starting some kind of scavenger hunt for Kathleen's booze. Sean doesn't think she hides any of it."

"It wouldn't be hidden if he knew where."

"I think he meant that she doesn't bother keeping much of a cover on her drinking. Judging by yesterday afternoon, my guess is, he's right."

Sam considered this carefully. Al and Sean were probably right, but he didn't want to take chances. "I'm going to look around anyway, okay?" He inhaled the other half of the first Pop-Tart and broke the second.

"Probably a good idea." Al went on without being asked, giving Sam a chance to eat. "He says you'll find pretty much everything in the kitchen cupboards and the refrigerator. Do you want me to hang around here for the day?"

"No." Sam swallowed a mouthful of cherry jam and heavily preserved glaze. "You should probably spend some time with Sean. How's it going with him, anyway?"

"I can't tell. I thought it was going great, but he had some kind of nightmare last night. Verbena said it's an anxiety dream."

"Well, he's in a strange place."

"Yeah, I guess so." Al smiled. "His theory is that Leaping gives him 'electric-shock-things' in his brain."

"Residual energy shocks?" Sam finished his breakfast, and pulled open the cupboard over the stove, where a platoon of half-empty bottles stood wearily, waiting for the finishing blow. He took them to the sink, two at a time, and poured their contents into the stained porcelain as he spoke.

"I guess so."

146

"Interesting."

"You think there's something to it?"

"There could be. If there's leftover energy, it's possible that it stimulates the neurons and causes nightmares, if it doesn't keep him awake altogether."

"Actually, he wasn't sleeping very well," Al said, turning the idea over. He shook his head. "But most of the others go out like lights."

Sam reached the back of the cupboard and pulled a kitchen chair over to get high enough up to look for stragglers that may have slipped to one side or the other. There were none. He climbed down and started on the refrigerator. "I wouldn't know. You have better medical data on the Visitors back at the Project than I do here." He opened the crisper drawer and was surprised to find a half carton of eggs sitting behind the lettuce and tomatoes. He took it out, figuring he could make breakfast for himself and Kathleen later.

"We never looked for it. Have you had a lot of nightmares since you started Leaping?"

"No," Sam answered immediately, "I haven't." But hadn't there been a time, at least one time, when the dreams became too much, when they'd kept him up, walking ghostlike through his host's home? Hadn't they driven him nearly to the brink of madness?

". . . last night?" Al was saying. Sam had completely missed it.

"What?"

"Did you dream about anything last night?"

"Oh, well . . . nothing much. I dreamed about Chrissi."

Sam caught his mistake on Al's face even before the Observer cocked a wry eyebrow and said, "You know, kid, I'm really starting to worry about you."

"This is getting really old, Al."

"Oh, yeah. I'd say it's real *old*."

"I mean, it's sick."

"That's what I keep trying to tell you."

Sam breathed out sharply. He had brought this on himself, he supposed, by years of taking little stabs at Al's obsession with women, especially those of the younger variety. "It wasn't that kind of dream," he explained reasonably. "I was just trying to remember where I know her from, I guess. Have you come up with anything yet?"

"Nada. Do you want me to put it on a higher priority?"

Sam shook his head. "No. I don't think it's important." He pulled the last can of beer off the refrigerator door—the tab was pulled off, and Sam could tell by listening to it that it had been flat for quite a while—and dumped it down the sink. "I'd appreciate it if you laid off on the Chrissi jokes, though. I have enough to worry about here."

"You're no fun."

"Yeah, I'm a drag." Sam bent down to start looking in the cupboards below the sink. "I'm not looking forward to this," he said.

Somewhere upstairs, a door thumped open.

"You're on, kid," Al said.

Chrissi had dawdled as long as she could on her regular morning routine.

She spent fifteen minutes in the shower, and towel-dried her hair long enough that she could only stretch blow-drying for five minutes or so without needing to worry about damage. She scrubbed her face with Noxzema, then used toner. She brushed her teeth one at a time (or tried to; toothbrushes weren't really shaped right for it), and flossed them within an inch of their lives. When she was done in the bathroom, she went back to her bedroom and pulled on her underclothes, then brushed her hair for two hundred strokes before pushing it up into a soft bun.

148

But she couldn't dawdle forever.

Sooner or later, she would have to put it on.

It was laid out carefully over her desk chair, yards of pale blue satin, with a swirled design of tiny faux pearls over the chest. The skirt was full, falling from a princess waistline to its hem, which angled down from just below her left knee to just above her right ankle. The sleeves were only wisps of see-through material that hung lightly down to her elbows. She was supposed to wear pale blue heels and a wreath of forget-me-nots in her hair. The flowers matched the bridesmaid's dress perfectly.

Chrissi loved it.

That was the problem.

She didn't want to like anything that had to do with Daddy's wedding, certainly not a dress that the bride herself had designed.

But the first time she had tried it on, she had fallen in love with it—the way the angled skirt showed a glimpse of her stockinged leg, the way the filmy sleeves made her arms look dainty and ladylike, the way the pale blue set off her tan skin and made her hair seem a deep, lustrous red rather than the "bloody-carrot shade" (as Sarah had named it at the drugstore one day while they were shopping for work-weekend junk food) it usually was. It made her really, truly beautiful, not like a pretty girl, but like a Woman.

She took a deep breath and slipped it over her head.

It felt like a cloud sliding down her body, wrapping her inside itself. She closed her eyes as she walked over to her mirror, then slowly opened them.

She curtsied to her reflection and smiled widely at herself. *Queen of the court*, she thought.

Well, no, not today. Today, Jenny was queen, and however she'd gotten the job, Chrissi was going to let her keep the throne, if only because she hoped that someday, she herself

149

would have a day like this, when she *could* be at the center, and she didn't want to jinx it by ruining someone else's.

But my *dress won't be white*, she thought, looking at herself. *It will be blue, like this one, just pale blue with little pearls, and flowers in my hair. If the fogies don't like it, that's their problem.*

She giggled, and imagined Sean standing beside her in the front of the church down on Water Street. He would be wearing a midnight-blue tux, or maybe something a little more outrageous, although she couldn't think what . . . No, she could. *He'll be dressed up old-fashioned, with a dark blue long tailcoat and those pants like they wear at the Victorian museum, the ones that button on the sides. He'll have a top hat on, and one of those big scarves—a cravat—that matches my dress.*

She backed up a moment in her fantasy—mentally, in future time, and literally, in physical space. She bent down and picked up something colorful on the floor (a bunch of clean socks that she hadn't sorted yet) to be a bouquet, holding it in front of her as

she will march down the aisle to him, Daddy holding her arm lightly and crying a little bit. Mama will be in the first pew, dabbing her eyes with a handkerchief. Pigeon and Johnny and Sarah will all be sitting in the pew behind her. Katie Milligan, Chrissi's best friend from Jamestown, will be her maid of honor, walking right ahead of her. She will sweep into the line, leaving just enough space for Chrissi to stand beside Sean.

Then the priest will come out, and she and Sean will kneel at the altar, and the priest will declare them man and wife. Sean will lean down to her and kiss her gently and say that he will love her forever and ever and she will say it back to him. Later on, they will dance together for hours and hours, neither one of them getting tired, while the band plays "Up

150

Where We Belong'' all night. *When it is all over, she will stand in the middle of a circle of her friends, the girls who haven't found their fairy tales yet, and she will close her eyes, and toss the bouquet over her shoulder* . . .

Chrissi felt the cloth leave her hand and laughed at the depth of her fantasy. *Jeez, even* I'd *get sick of "Up Where We Belong" if they played it* all *night.* She turned to pick up her sock-bouquet.

Mama was standing in the doorway wearing a frumpy bathrobe, holding the loose collection of socks in one hand and looking at it blankly.

Chrissi felt herself come down from wherever she'd been with a psychic thump.

She'd been pretending it was *her* wedding, of course, but it wasn't. It was *Daddy's* wedding she was dressed for, and Mama was not a part of it.

Mama, in fact, was going crazy about it.

And I'm dancing in my room and daydreaming. Some daughter.

For a long moment Mama didn't say anything.

Then she began to cry.

CHAPTER
TWELVE

Breakfast, it turned out, had not been a good starting point.

Sam had spent most of the previous night making preemptive strikes—aspirin, vitamins, caffeine—against the monster hangover he had predicted for Kathleen, but none of them seemed to have had any effect. Before she'd been able to finish thumping her way down the stairs, she'd had to sit down three times to regain her balance.

"This is not good, Sam," Al had said helpfully.

Sam had brushed it off, figuring it couldn't be as bad as it sounded. By the time she'd made her way all the way into the kitchen, he knew he was right: it was worse. Kathleen O'Connor looked like she was only a step out of her grave.

"I dumped your supplies," Sam said as soon as she looked conscious enough to register it. "If you're going to be mad, you may as well start."

She looked at him dully. "I guess that counts out 'hair-of-the-dog,' huh?"

"Yeah."

She nodded slowly and put her fingers to her temple. "You're going to push me over the edge, aren't you?"

"Guess so."

"It's not the first time he's done it," Al told her, although she couldn't hear him. "Trust me, it's better on the other side."

Sam didn't answer this, of course, but he wanted to; he remembered very little of his meeting with Al Calavicci, but he didn't think Al had needed to be pushed, just given a reason to step over by himself. All Sam could remember doing was offering him a reason, in the form of an impossible project involving time travel—Al couldn't resist the impossible any more than Sam himself could—and letting him run with it. But Al had always seemed to feel that Sam had single-handedly cured him, and would not listen to any argument to the contrary.

Kathleen snorted and pushed her matted hair back from her forehead. "Well, if I survive this morning, I guess I'll thank you."

Sam went over to the counter, where four of the six eggs were sitting in a bowl. "I'm going to make you some breakfast," he said.

Kathleen groaned. "I wouldn't."

"You need to get something nutritious into your system."

"It's not going to stay there."

"You know, Sam," Al said, "I think she's right."

Sam agreed, but went on breaking the eggs and starting to scramble them nonetheless. It might prove pointless as far as nutrition was concerned, but the machinations of cooking and serving a meal would take up time, and the long, empty hours ahead, while her head pounded, would be the hardest to fill with any voice other than that of her addiction. Even if she spent some of those hours throwing up, it would be better than lying in bed (or on the kitchen table, as it seemed to be at the moment) thinking about how much longer she could possibly go without a drink.

And anyway, Sam had once known someone (he could no

153

longer remember who) who'd sworn that the best cure for nausea was greasy, garlicky pizza, piled with sausage and pepperoni, so there was no telling what the body would do in a given circumstance.

"Do you know where AA meets?" he asked.

"The Methodist Church, Thursday nights," she said immediately, if somewhat wearily. "I went twice last year."

"Why'd you stop?"

"They were . . ." She searched for a word, a befuddled expression on her face. "They were too damned *weird*. Too *nice*."

"Too *nice*?"

"They were just floating around. No one had any opinions, no one ever argued, even about things they should've argued about. One of them was talking about that movie *E.T.* and how much she loved it, and I said it made me sick, so schmaltzy . . ." Kathleen sighed. "It didn't really, but . . . Well, this AA person, she just said, 'Oh, well, I won't judge your opinion if you won't judge mine!' And she gave me this big crocodile smile and went away."

"What's wrong with that?"

"No backbone. I mean, if you've got an opinion, you should stand up for it, right?"

"She's got a point, Sam," Al said.

Sam shot him a look. "But they can help you."

"Help me do what? Become a mindless zombie who can't make a judgment about anything? I think I'd rather be a drunk."

"One bad meeting when you weren't ready to quit is hardly a good measure."

"What do you know about it?"

"I know that you scare me when you're drunk. I know that you can't quit by yourself. And I know I can't help you all day every day."

154

"Now *you've* got a point," Al said.

Sam looked at him over Kathleen's head and mouthed, *You are not helping*.

"Alright, alright. I'll get back to Sean."

Sam tapped his head. *Good thinking*.

The Imaging Chamber Door opened up, and a moment later Al was gone.

Sam finished scrambling the eggs—they'd started to reseparate during his conversation with Kathleen—and poured them into a frying pan on the stove.

Kathleen covered her nose and mouth when they began to cook. "Sean, I really don't think—" She suddenly bolted from the room and up the stairs. Sam heard the toilet flush above him a few minutes later.

He sighed, and put the eggs on to two plates anyway.

When Kathleen came back down, she looked husked out. He led her to her chair, and she looked down at the eggs, turning vaguely green. "I can't, Sean. I just can't."

"Sure you can," he prodded gently. She certainly had nothing left in her stomach now, and that in itself would make her sicker.

"No, really."

"If it comes up, it comes up. Give it a try."

Kathleen picked up her fork and looked at it doubtfully. She lowered it into the eggs, and brought it back up to her mouth, where it hovered beside her lips for a long time. Finally, she put a forkful of eggs into her mouth, chewed it, and fought to swallow.

Sam wasn't sure she was going to do it, and was casting around the kitchen desperately for a basin for her to throw up in when he finally heard the gulping sound of her Adam's apple moving with difficulty. A moment later she breathed in deeply. There was a hitch from her stomach, but the food stayed down.

155

Sam let himself breathe as well. "See?" he said. "I told you you could do it."

Kathleen took some time to read the signs from her body. "It *does* feel a little better." She tried another bite.

Sam looked at the clock.

Forty-three minutes down.

The rest of a lifetime to go.

The minutes marched by at a slow exhibition pace.

Sam had been watching Kathleen try to force down the last few bites of her breakfast for at least twenty minutes, and he was ready to acknowledge that it probably wasn't going to happen.

She noticed him looking at her, and gave him a wan smile, lifting her fork in a salute. Sam thought she was about to put it in her mouth, but instead she turned it over and let the pale yellow chunks of egg bounce onto her plate. She shrugged.

Sam picked up a damp rag from the sink and started to clean the counter. The day seemed to stretch out in front of him into infinity.

He would have to think of something to talk to her about, but he didn't have any ideas. However close circumstances had brought him to her, she was still a stranger, and Sam wasn't even sure yet whether or not he liked her, let alone what kind of conversation he could carry on with her for the unending hours ahead. There were things he wanted to know—chiefly about Sean's family history—but Sean would already know them, so he couldn't ask. He didn't know what else to do. He had never been very good at small talk, even with people he knew and loved; long debates and intricate arguments about science or ethics or music were more his style.

Maybe he should've asked Al to stay, to feed him questions and answers, but he couldn't shake the feeling that Al's job at the Project was more important than helping him beat boredom here.

He supposed he could talk about movies, but he wasn't sure which ones were out. The fables and foibles of contemporary entertainment had only held a marginal interest for him, and it wouldn't be good to bring up a movie that had yet to be released. He had the same problem with television, or music, or even those perennial favorites, the weather and everyone's health. He didn't know if the weather was behaving oddly, because he didn't know the area, and Kathleen's health—or lack thereof—was plain to see. He didn't even know how Sean was doing in school.

He finished cleaning the counter and draped the cloth over the partition in the sink to dry. The kitchen floor was dirty, but sweeping and mopping it would require moving Kathleen, and since Sam didn't want it to get any dirtier, he thought it would be wise to put it off for a while.

He turned to find something else, and found Kathleen staring at him, her eyes glassy and distant. He had a panicked second when he thought she might drift into shock, but then she blinked slowly and sighed. It didn't exactly make her look healthy, but she was, at the very least, *present*. She picked up her fork and started pushing her eggs around again.

He went to her side. "Mom?"

She looked up at him with a ghostly smile and patted his cheek with the back of her fingers. Sam could smell the sickness on her, the sour stench of the human body trying to come to terms with itself. He knew the smell from night after night spent in the emergency room, during his residency, and he'd learned to deal with it, after a fashion, but he hated it. Kathleen took a deep, shaky breath (he did his best not to back away from the exhalation), and said, "What is it?"

"Are you okay?"

She smiled. "I will be." She held out her hand, and he took

157

it and sat down in the chair across from her. "Especially if my handsome son tells me what's going on in his life."

Great, Sam thought. *Maybe I should've risked the movies after all.* But it was too late now. Kathleen had actually asked, so he would have to come up with something that he knew about Sean's life. He just hoped that she didn't ask for too many specifics. "You know about the program . . ."

"Oh, not school. I see your report card. You're doing better. I think that guidance counselor of yours is on to something. What else is there? Do you still have a girlfriend?"

"Yeah. Chrissi Martinez."

"Well, I didn't figure you'd traded up."

"So why'd you ask?"

"It's just that the two of you are so young to be going steady. I was wondering if you'd changed your minds."

Sam shook his head. "No."

"That's nice. She's a nice girl, Sean."

"Yeah, she is."

"I don't want to see either one of you get hurt."

He laughed uncomfortably. "Well, neither do we." He looked down at her plate. "Is that all you can do?"

Kathleen inspected the bits of cold egg, seemed to consult her body, and nodded. Despite her sudden burst of sociability, Sam didn't think she was feeling better at all. As a matter of fact, she looked downright green. But she was trying, and that counted for a lot.

Sam cleared her plate and scraped its contents into the wastebasket beside the sink. He turned on the taps to wash it off.

"Who *are* you?" Kathleen said behind him.

He dropped the plate into the sink, and it clattered noisily. If it had been china, it would no doubt have shattered. "What do you mean, Mom?"

158

She put her hands on her head and groaned. "That was painful."

Sam picked up the plate and started rinsing it. "Sorry."

She nodded, very slightly. "I was just looking at you there, and I almost didn't recognize you. You're acting so grown-up. So different from how you usually act." She winced. "Not that there's anything wrong with that, but I wonder where the old Sean went. Or where the new one came from."

Well, Sam thought, *the "new Sean" had this theory about quantum filaments . . .*

"I'm just worried about you," he said.

"I'm sorry about that."

Sam finished the plate and went back over to her. "Do you want to move into the living room?"

"Sure." She started to stand up, then tipped alarmingly to one side.

Sam caught her and held her up for a moment while she seemed to fade out. He draped her arm around his shoulder and supported her with his own arm around her waist. She came to. "You back?"

"Yeah."

"Ready to go?"

She smiled weakly. "I feel like I'm ninety and in a nursing home."

"You're just sick, Mom."

"Hung over."

Sam didn't argue. He led her into the living room, where the curtains were still drawn, figuring it would be easier on her head than the bright kitchen. He set her down on the couch and took her wrist.

"What are you doing, honey?"

Sam groaned to himself. He hated the excuses that went along with Leaping. "I, uh . . . I learned it in health class. I just wanted to see if your pulse was steady."

159

"My son, the doctor."

"Do we have a sphygmomanometer?"

"A what?"

"A blood pressure cuff."

"No, we don't. I'm okay, Sean. It's a bad hangover, but it's just a hangover."

"I just don't want to see you go into withdrawal. If you start to, I'm going to call an ambulance. I mean it."

"You don't have to worry about that."

Sam didn't know whether or not he had to worry. It all depended on how long she'd been drinking, and how severe the addiction was. "Better safe than sorry," he said.

She started to protest, but decided against it. "I promise to tell you if anything changes, okay?"

He was suspicious of such a tenuous arrangement, but he agreed to it.

The phone rang, and Kathleen winced. "Who's that?"

Sam shrugged. "Let it ring. I don't want you to be alone in here."

"No, please. *Don't* let it ring."

It rang again, and Kathleen covered her ears with the thick folds of her bathrobe's collar. Sam looked at the phone— which might be bringing him a message about the program— and back at Kathleen, who just couldn't stand the sound of it.

"It's okay," she said, patting his arm. "I think I can survive a couple of minutes while you're on the phone."

Another ring.

"Will you get that before I go nuts listening to it?"

With one last suspicious glance at her, Sam got up and went to the phone.

It was Johnny.

His voice was slightly warped by its tour through the phone lines, but Sam didn't need it to recognize him. The theatrical energy behind it was enough.

"O'Connor?" he said.

"Yeah, Johnny, it's me." Sam kept his voice as low as possible, trying not to disturb Kathleen, who he could see out of the corner of one eye. Her back was to him, and he turned to watch her more fully.

"Chrissi's dad's getting married today."

"Yeah, I know."

"And she's going to be in the wedding and everything, and Pigeon and I—Pidge stayed over here last night—thought she might like it if we all, like, dropped in or something."

"No. She said yesterday that she didn't want anyone there. She's really embarrassed about the whole thing." Sam repeated this fact mechanically. In the other room, Kathleen was shivering. She pulled a blanket down around her shoulders.

"Of *course* she said that," Johnny said. "But she didn't *mean* it. She just wants to see if we can figure that out."

"No means yes and yes means no?" Sam repeated. "Do yourself a favor, Johnny, and stop thinking like that."

"Get real, O'Connor. This is *Chrissi* we're talking about. She *hates* being by herself."

"Johnny, I don't think you understand how ashamed she is about all this." Sam narrowed his eyes and looked more closely at Kathleen. She was growing paler, and she looked like she was going to be sick to her stomach again, but the chills seemed to have passed, and she wasn't on the verge of losing consciousness.

"I *do* know that," Johnny insisted. "But I also know the only person anywhere close to her age that's going to be there is the bride. If we don't go, all she's going to do all day is sit alone and brood about it."

"But she asked us not to . . ."

"She asked you not to show up at the court on the day of her custody hearing, too, but you still did. And she said she was glad of it."

161

Kathleen tried to lean back, but sat up suddenly with her hands over her abdomen. Sam could see her chest hitching as she fought with her gorge. The battle was won this time, but Sam didn't think she'd keep ahead of it for long.

"O'Connor?"

"Yeah, I'm still here. Look, my mom's sick."

Kathleen held up one hand to let him know it was alright for him to keep talking.

"What's wrong with her?" Johnny asked.

Sam debated telling him, but he wasn't sure how much Johnny knew about the drinking. "Just a flu or something. But I don't want to leave her by herself."

"But Chrissi—"

"—has got you and Pigeon and Sarah."

"You're the one she's totally nuts about. If we show up and you don't . . ."

Sam didn't need him to finish. He'd lived inside of a number of different people, and he'd learned how the mind worked very well. Chrissi would not see that her friends had come to support her; she'd see that they cared about her more than her boyfriend did, and she'd be hurt.

He had to risk it, though. He didn't need Ziggy to tell him that Chrissi had a better chance of getting through the day without him than Kathleen did. "I know," he said. "But I can't leave, Johnny."

There was a pause. Johnny spoke carefully. "Your mom's really bad this morning, huh?"

"Yeah."

"Okay, then. You stay home. We'll look after Chrissi."

Sam was relieved on two counts—that he'd be able to spend the day keeping an eye on Kathleen and that he wouldn't have to find ways around Chrissi's affections—but it was an empty relief, because he knew that he was letting Chrissi down. Maybe she'd understand—*probably* she would—but deep

162

down, it was a cheat, and Sam knew it. First, her father had cheated her out of her home, and now Kathleen O'Connor's sickness was cheating her out of the support of a boy she thought she loved.

Gives you that warm, fuzzy feeling of familiarity, she'd said of the threats to the program.

Well, here's another square for that warm, fuzzy quilt.

"Look," he said, "tell her what's going on, okay? And that I'd be there if I could, but I can't."

"Sure thing," Johnny promised. "I'll tell her you'll send your invisible spy back from the future."

Sam smiled; he'd nearly forgotten about Johnny's game yesterday. "You do that," he said, and resolved to tell Al to drop by the reception if he came back before it was over.

"I'd better get going then. I've still got to call Sarah."

"Okay."

"Hope your mom's okay."

"Me, too. Bye."

"Bye."

Sam hung up the phone, leaned on it for a minute, then went back to the living room, where Kathleen was sitting very still on the edge of the couch.

"Mom?"

"I'm okay," she said, not expending much breath on the words. "Who was that?"

"It was Johnny Metz. He's crashing Mr. Martinez's wedding. He wanted me to come."

"You could've." There was an ominous rumbling from Kathleen's stomach. "You don't have to stay here and watch me puke my guts out all day, you know."

"If you go into acute withdrawal, I want to be here to call an ambulance."

" 'Acute withdrawal'?" she repeated. "What, have you been watching *Emergency* reruns?"

163

"Uh, yeah."

She nodded, and Sam saw her face go green. She held herself very still, and he thought she was going to win the battle again when she reached out suddenly and grabbed his arm. "Help me upstairs," she said quickly, and clamped her mouth shut. Sam didn't need to ask *where* upstairs she meant.

They barely made it into the bathroom. Kathleen practically dove across the hexagonal tile floor and leaned over the toilet just as the first flood hit. Sam turned away and looked out into the hall, trying not to hear the retching sounds.

After a while they stopped, and Kathleen spoke in a gruff, strained voice. "Honey?"

Sam turned back just as she reached up and flushed the mess down. "What is it?"

"I have some Maalox in the refrigerator downstairs."

Sam had seen it there earlier, and been curious. "Why's it in the refrigerator?"

"That stuff is nasty-tasting enough without drinking it lukewarm."

"Okay . . ."

"It's behind the orange juice, I think. I could really use a shot of it."

Sam was down the stairs before she could finish. He went back into the refrigerator, and rummaged around for the Maalox, which was not behind the orange juice but lying on its side in the door shelves, underneath the butter box. He grabbed it.

By the time he got back to Kathleen, she had lost the rest of her breakfast.

He watched her rinse her mouth out and helped her to her room.

It was going to be a very long day.

CHAPTER
THIRTEEN

"Is everything in place?" Jenny asked, turning slowly in her gown so that the bridesmaids could inspect her.

Chrissi bent dutifully and searched for tiny flaws—a loose button, a snag in the lace, an uneven hem—but there weren't any. Jenny looked like she was in a magazine picture, like in *Modern Bride* or something. Chrissi stood up and shrugged. "Looks okay to me."

The other two bridesmaids (one was Jenny's sister, Laurie, and the other was a friend from high school; Jenny had taken Chrissi to this friend's house once to go swimming—that had been when Jenny was a baby-sitter instead of a stepmother-to-be—but Chrissi couldn't remember her name) took a few more minutes. Laurie gave her okay after a while. Miss Swimming-Pool tilted the angle on Jenny's veil minutely and did the same.

Jenny stepped away from them and looked back, beaming. "So, how do I look?"

"You look beautiful," Laurie said.

Chrissi agreed grudgingly. She'd been listening to this prattle for two hours now, and it was wearing thin. She liked pretty clothes, but this was getting, like, ridiculous. She had expected to feel many things today, but she had never expected what she was *actually* feeling: she was bored out of her skull, and she wished she had never forbidden Sean to come. She wished, as a matter of fact, that she'd dragged him here by his toenails if necessary, so that she'd at least have someone she could actually talk to when this nightmare was over.

It's one day. Can't you handle yourself like a grown-up for one day?

"Chrissi?" Jenny said.

"What?"

"Are you okay?"

She shrugged.

You can do better than that. It's her wedding day; try to be nice. It's just a Little Thing, after all, and Jenny is *keeping the only promise she ever made to you.*

It was true. Jenny had been baby-sitting and her boyfriend had come over. After he'd left, Jenny'd been all excited and started talking about someday getting married. Chrissi, who had liked Jenny a great deal at the time, had begged to be allowed in the wedding party. Jenny had sworn that she could be a bridesmaid.

Chrissi supposed she should've been a little more specific.

This isn't about you. Grow up.

Jenny looked at the other two. "Look, guys, can I talk to Chrissi?"

They nodded knowingly and left the room.

"I know this is hard for you," Jenny said when they were gone.

"Is this supposed to turn into, like, a heart-to-heart or something?"

"No. I know you don't understand this."

"Sure I do. You're pretty. Mama's getting old. Daddy's, like, trading up."

166

"I don't know whether to thank you for the compliment or not."

"I don't care."

Oh, stop it, will you? Why are you being so mean?

Jenny took a moment to think out what she was saying. Chrissi could tell by the small, intense look on her face. "It's just that I want you to try and understand that there's nothing wrong with your father, or your mother, or you. Or *me*. Sometimes things just happen, you know?"

Chrissi nodded, slightly touched despite herself.

You see, there it is. She didn't say anything mean about Mama, and she's, like, taking time right before her wedding to sort it out with you. This is Jenny, *remember? Jenny who taught you how to walk in high heels and put mousse in your hair and talk on the phone with a boy.*

Was that before or after she started "Doing It" with Daddy?

The thought shut the window that was starting to open. Jenny had said she was her friend, but it was only form. In the end she'd taken everything that mattered to Chrissi away, and that wasn't the sort of thing that friends did to each other.

You're acting like a little kid. Stop being selfish.

Okay, yeah. But it *hurt*.

So you think life's supposed to feel good all the time?

Laurie poked her head back in. "Everything's ready," she whispered. "Do you want the organist to start?"

Jenny looked Chrissi in the eye. "You go in first. Are you set?"

Go on. Say yes. It's a Little Thing, right? Just a few steps across the hall and down the aisle.

Last year in January, Mama and Daddy had taken a trip to Hawaii. Chrissi had stayed with her grandmother in Jamestown while they were gone, and when they'd called at night everything had been warm where they were and—

It's not last year and it's not going to be last year. You've

167

got to get that straight or you're going to go crazy. Start thinking forward.

Forward, sure. After going down the aisle, the wedding. After the wedding, the limo ride—that would be kind of awesome. After the limo, the pictures. After the pictures, the reception.

How long would *that* be, all alone?

Skip it. After the reception, sleep. And after sleep, back to school, back to *Sean*, and everything would be normal.

"Are you alright?"

Chrissi looked at Jenny and nodded, realizing in a dim way that she'd been staring off into space for almost a minute. She turned to Laurie, who'd started to come into the room. "Tell the organist to go ahead. If Jenny's ready, I am."

Jenny nodded.

Chrissi went out into the hallway outside the sanctuary. Miss Swimming-Pool (whoever she was) scurried into line behind her. Jenny stood in the door of the bride's room and waited for Laurie to take her place as maid of honor.

There. That was easy.

The first few notes of Wagner's march blared off the organ.

Out of the blue, Chrissi remembered a day on their front porch in the old Jamestown house when Katie Milligan had taught her what she actually thought were the words to the song: "*Here comes the bride, all dressed in white. Where is the groom? He's in the dressing room. Why is he there? He lost his underwear . . .*" An image of Daddy, wearing only his shirt and his long tuxedo coat, tearing through the dressing room in search of his underwear, popped into her head. When he finally found it, it was those dumb boxer shorts with the teddy bears that Jenny'd given him and he always wore around the house on the weekends.

Chrissi laughed.

She felt Miss Swimming-Pool's hand coming before it actually slapped her beneath the nape of her neck, and her breath before she leaned over and whispered, ''Grow up, will you?''

Chrissi did her best to stifle the laughter. It was stupid, she knew, and she knew that there was no one here she could explain it to.

In the other room the organist was playing a protracted note, waiting for the processional to get moving.

Chrissi bit her lower lip painfully, looked down at the bouquet, and trudged dutifully into the sanctuary.

''Psst,'' she heard from her right as she passed the third pew.

She glanced over, trying not to stop and trying not to laugh with relief when she saw Johnny, Pigeon, and Sarah sitting there.

She settled for a sigh and a smile, and went on down the aisle.

Throughout the silly, plain little wedding—they didn't even have communion, for crying out loud—Chrissi tried to sneak as many glances as she could back toward her friends, hoping that Sean would join them at some point.

You told him to stay away, remember?

Well, yeah, sure, but . . .

But nothing. If he doesn't come, he's just respecting your wishes, so don't get uptight. Next time, tell the truth.

Sean never came, but Chrissi's covert glances were not entirely unrewarded. Pigeon, who was also a Catholic, sat through the whole ceremony with a puzzled, quizzical look on his face. Every time Johnny caught her eye, he'd make a face at her, and she'd have to fight to keep from laughing again.

It was over before she even knew it.

And it didn't hurt a bit, did it?

Well, she wasn't quite ready to say *that*.

After all the guests went outside—or out into the foyer, actually, since it was too cold outside—the photographer made

169

the wedding party stop for pictures in the sanctuary. Chrissi did her best to hurry this up, since she was afraid that the others would leave, but it still took almost twenty minutes. When they finally went out into the foyer, Chrissi was sure that her friends would've left, so she was surprised again when Johnny came weaving through the crowd, with Pigeon and Sarah in his wake.

"That's one," he said seriously when he got to her.

"One what?"

"One time as a bridesmaid. Sadie here"—he jerked a thumb backward toward Sarah—"says that if you're a bridesmaid three times—"

"You'll never be a bride," Chrissi finished. "Everybody knows that."

"Do you think that's true?" Pigeon asked.

"I don't know. Ask me two weddings from now." Chrissi looked over Pigeon's shoulder at Sarah, who was wearing a plain gray dress and flat shoes, and who looked like she was trying to hide. "Aren't you going to get in trouble for being here?"

"Huh?"

"I thought your folks didn't like you being in churches."

She shrugged nervously. "What they don't know won't kill them, right?"

Chrissi smiled. Sarah was a space-case, but she'd risked getting in dutch at home to come. It was probably because Johnny had asked her, but still, it was nice. "I'm really glad you guys came," she said. She looked at them carefully, trying to find a way to ask what was on her mind without making them feel like they weren't sufficient for her. Finally, she just blurted it out: "Is Sean coming?"

"No," Johnny said. "I called him, but his mom's really sick."

Drunk, Chrissi corrected in her mind, but even though

170

everyone knew it, no one said it. She looked at the others. "Can you guys come to the reception? Please."

"If it's okay with your dad," Pigeon said. "We all cleared the rest of the day."

"Wait here." Chrissi ducked back into the sanctuary, where the photographer was taking pictures of the happy couple by themselves.

"Daddy?"

He turned his head slightly. "What is it, hon?"

The photographer gave him an annoyed look. "You're out of the light, sir."

Daddy turned away again, and rested his head on Jenny's shoulder.

"My friends came for the wedding," Chrissi said. "Can they come to the reception?"

"I guess so." This time he didn't bother turning. "If it's okay with my blushing bride here." He kissed Jenny's cheek.

Jenny had no objections.

Chrissi went back outside. "No prob-leh-mo, seh-nor-itta," she said when she got back to the others, not noticing that she'd imitated what she wished he'd said instead of what he'd actually said, or having any inkling that this was a habit that would stay with her for a lifetime.

"Awesome," Johnny said. "Where is it?"

"Do you know the Firemen's Hall in the back of the park?"

"That's right around where the carnival is, right?"

"Yeah, that's it. Daddy rented it for the day, and there's going to be a DJ and a lot of food and stuff. He promised there'd be wings."

"Buffalo wings?" Pigeon said in his silly summer-person voice.

"Buffaloes don't have wings," the others said together, and laughed. No self-respecting Western New Yorker referred to the region's most famous snack as anything but wings; if they

171

weren't fried with hot sauce, they were done wrong, period.

"Do you suppose Sean's mom might be feeling better?" Chrissi asked when they stopped laughing. "I mean, maybe he could come."

Johnny shook his head. "I wouldn't count on it, Chrissi," he said. "But he did promise to send his spy."

"Spy?" Sarah repeated.

"From the future," Chrissi explained. "We were joking around about it on the way home yesterday."

"Okay," Sarah said. "If you say so."

"See, Sadie, you live on the wrong side of town."

"Oh, I wind up on the wrong side of just about everything. It's a hobby of mine."

"Oh, my God. Was that a joke? Chrissi, your father's got to get married more often. Sadie made a joke." Johnny goggled in mock amazement.

Sarah glared at him.

Chrissi let it alone. "Just come to the hall about a half hour after we leave here; the reception should be going by then."

"Sure thing."

There, see. Even the reception is going to be fun.

Chrissi had opened her mouth to say something else—she was never sure later what it was going to be—when the tears came, surprising her as much as anyone else. Her throat simply locked up as she looked at her friends' earnest faces, and her eyes grew hot as fire. The foyer blurred, and then her cheeks were soaked.

"Hey," Pigeon said awkwardly, putting a hand on her shoulder. "Hey."

She leaned into their circle, and Johnny caught her and put his arms around her. Pigeon held her from the other side. She felt Sarah's hand tentatively pat her arm, then start to pull away, and reached instinctively for her wrist. She felt all three of them around her, keeping her safe, and after a while the

172

wave passed. She stood shakily and pulled away. "Thanks, I
. . . I'm sorry I did that."

"Don't worry about it," Pigeon said. "You should've seen
me after my folks' accident. I cried about everything."

"That's different." Chrissi didn't look him in the eye. Talking about his dead parents made her feel very small.

He shrugged. "What's different? You want to cry, you cry.
No biggie."

"My father has a right to be happy."

"And you have a right to your feelings about it." He
squeezed her shoulder. "Trust me on this one, okay?"

Chrissi still felt sort of petty, but she nodded.

The door to the sanctuary opened, and suddenly the foyer
was filled with cheers and flying confetti (it was too cold to
go outside, and the church didn't allow rice inside). There was
a rough hand on Chrissi's shoulder, and she turned to find
Miss Swimming-Pool standing behind her. "You're supposed
to be with us."

"I know, I—"

"We'll meet you at the reception," Sarah said.

"Yeah . . ."

"Come on, we're going *now*. The photographer wants to
stop at the lake and get pictures down at the winter park."

Chrissi nodded as she was pulled away. "Meet you there!"
she called over her shoulder. Then the crowd moved in, and
her friends disappeared behind them. Daddy and Jenny were
waiting in the front limo, looking deliriously happy.

You have a right to your feelings, Pigeon had said.

Chrissi looked at her father, at the smile on his face, wider
than she had ever seen it.

Maybe, she thought. *But Daddy doesn't need to know about
them today.*

She followed the rest of the wedding party into the other
limo.

173

• • •

The Penworth Firemen's Hall stood on a patch of gravel in the back of the generous public park. It was a plain cinder-block building, but the heat was steady and the space more than sufficient for large gatherings, so it was in fairly constant use. Receptions and parties were the major functions, but it also served as home to the local theater group (creatively named the Penworth Players), and all of their props and scenery from shows past were stored in the attic, outside the light room.

It was here, in the midst of the moldy, ramshackle sets, that they had decided to retreat after the reception downstairs had become too crowded, too noisy, and too hokey to endure. They could still hear the music from downstairs (right now, the DJ was playing "Eye in the Sky"), but it was part of another world.

Chrissi looked around the space, delighted.

Johnny nodded approvingly. "Yup. This is definitely an O.M. hangout."

"Are we going to get in trouble?" Sarah asked.

Pigeon shrugged. "If we do, we'll just say we didn't know we weren't supposed to come up here."

It was enough for Sarah, who looked like she was totally nuts about the place anyway. She started walking back and forth among the flats, examining them closely.

"Hey!" Pigeon said, going over to a set with marble pillars painted against a blue sky. "Look at this."

"What about it?" Johnny asked.

"Well, it looks Greek. Maybe we could use it. For the skit."

"Pigeon," Sarah said patiently, "everything happens in a cave. What do we need with pillars?"

"I just thought that—"

"—the judges might like it," the others finished for him.

"Well, you never *know*."

174

"Whatever you say, Pidge," Johnny said. He was rummaging around in a costume box, and he came up wearing a Roman helmet made of tin foil and cardboard and carrying a sword made of more of the same. "Too bad we can't have classy costumes like this. That'd knock 'em dead, wouldn't it, Sadie-lady?"

"Why do you keep calling me that?" Sarah asked suspiciously.

"I don't know. I think it fits. What do you guys think?"

Chrissi shook her head. She didn't think that Sarah was really the nickname type; she was too serious and everything.

Not to mention that no one's ever given you a nickname. Could that have something to do with it?

Pigeon shrugged. "If it's okay with Sarah," he said. "Is it?"

Sarah looked dumbly at Pigeon, then shot a quick glance at Johnny, who'd lost interest in the subject already and was rummaging in another trunk. Sarah smiled. "No biggie," she said.

Chrissi wandered over to the dirty, four-pane window set into the wall. It wasn't set very tightly, and there was a draft. She wished that Sean were here to keep her warm.

Great. His mom's so sick that he could barely stay on the phone with Johnny, and you're bummed out because he can't hold your hand while you freeze your silly self at a loose window. That's real grown-up.

Downstairs, "Eye in the Sky" ended, and the DJ put on "Stand By Me," which was one of Daddy's favorite songs from the sixties. Chrissi loved it, too, but it had always seemed to be more than a love song to her, and she'd never really associated it with weddings.

"So what should we do about the program?" Sarah asked somewhere behind her.

"Send it to Mars," Johnny offered. It was his standard re-

175

sponse to any question that they got in the spontaneous competition in O.M., when the judge asked a question and the team had to come up with as many answers as possible. Chrissi hadn't even *thought* about that in two weeks. They hadn't been practicing because there was too much to do on the skit, and Sean could anchor them to pretty good scores in spontaneous every time. He'd come up with an answer, and everyone else would come up with variations on it until all the variations were used up.

"Send it to Pluto," Pigeon followed.

Sarah joined in. "Send it to the moon."

"To the moon, Alice!" Johnny crowed.

"Hey, Martinez, your turn."

Chrissi pointed out the window, which looked out on a scanty woods where the stables for an erstwhile racetrack had once stood. The stables had burned around the turn of the century, killing sixteen horses and the orphan boy who tended them. Some of the horses' names had been preserved in the paper; the boy's had not. "Send the school board out in the woods," she suggested. "They say that horse-kid haunts it."

"He does," Pigeon assured them. "My friend Jason Spiegal saw him once."

"You are so full of it," Sarah said.

"It's true!" Pigeon's voice cracked. "He said that he and this other guy from the religious school were out here last summer, playing forts or something down by that stable door, you know the one that's just lying out there?"

They all knew it. It had stood upright and unscathed until the Blizzard of '77 (or so they'd heard), when the snow had finally tipped it over. Chrissi herself had always liked to pretend that she could swing it up on its hinges and disappear into an enchanted world, like those pools in one of the Narnia stories.

"Well, anyway," Pigeon went on, "they were out there,

and this other kid comes over and asks if he can play with them. He's dressed all weird, but they figured maybe his parents were in some weird religion or something, right? So they say 'Sure' and they all play together 'til dinnertime. This other kid—not the horse-kid, the one Jason was playing with—he invited everyone over to his house for dinner, 'cause he lived right around the corner. Jason says yes right away, 'cause his mom's picking him up there anyway, you know? But the horse-kid says he can't go anywhere. Jason and his friend start to go, but Jason decides to ask again, so he, like, turns around—*and the other kid is, like, totally gone.*" Pigeon looked at them significantly.

"So he hid behind a tree or something," Sarah said, shifting uncomfortably.

Chrissi gestured at the window. "*Those* trees? They're too skimpy."

"Yeah," Pigeon said, "and he can't have walked very far away. You can walk for ten minutes back there and still see everything."

"Well, maybe he hid under those fern things that grow there in the summer," Sarah suggested.

"Why would he do that?"

"I don't know. But I don't believe in ghosts."

Johnny smirked. "For something you don't believe in, you're pretty scared of them."

"I am not."

Chrissi turned back to the window and looked out over the woods, imagining the lonely little boy wandering around out there in the cold. She could see the ghosts of her friends in the glass. "There's nothing to be scared of, Sarah. He just wants someone to play with."

"I'm not scared of something that doesn't exist."

"Hey, I've got an idea!" Johnny came over to the window. "Maybe if we all go outside and play with him, he'd agree

177

to, like, Scrooge out Fairgate for us.''

"Sounds like a plan to me," Pigeon said.

Sarah nodded sarcastically. "Sure. Maybe we can send along Sean's spy from the future, just to make sure."

"Why not? Sean promised to send him tonight, to check on Chrissi."

Chrissi giggled. "Hey, spy! Are you here?"

"Now how's he supposed to answer that?" Pigeon pointed out. "Sean's the only one who can see and hear him."

"How do you know?"

"That's what Sean said yesterday, remember?"

"Oh, yeah." Chrissi was still smiling; she spoke to the air. "If you *are* here, tell Sean that I'm going to run off to Vegas with Johnny here if he doesn't start paying some attention to me."

"If he's from the future," Sarah said, "he already knows whether you ran off with Johnny or not."

"You guys are no fun."

Johnny leaned forward over her shoulder, dancing around behind her. "I'm fun, baby. Do you like blackjack or roulette?"

Chrissi giggled and elbowed him away. She could see Sarah behind him in the window, watching the whole game with a hurt look on her face. "We better not joke around like that, Johnny. I *am* going out with Sean and everything." She thought about his spy and giggled again. "And he *is* watching."

Johnny put a hand over his heart. "You're killin' me, doll." He went to Sarah and draped a casual arm over her shoulders. "Sadie's going to have to comfort me now."

Sarah blushed deeply and pulled away from him. Chrissi couldn't figure her out; she obviously liked Johnny in a big way, and this should've been the perfect time to play it up. Instead, she sat on top of an old trunk, sending up a cloud of

178

dust, and stepped back into safer territory. "If Sean's spy *is* here, he knows if we win tomorrow. And if we keep the program."

"*I* know both those things, too," Johnny said. "Yes to the first, no to the second. You don't have to be psychic."

"Do you think there *is* anything we can do about it?"

"Hey, Sean shot down *my* best idea yesterday."

"If that was your best idea," Pigeon said, "then you're in the wrong program."

"Prude."

Chrissi tuned out as the conversation steered onto the familiar path. She could hear them, and answer if she felt like it, but she didn't want to think about Sean's spy being there for anyone but her. She was secretly delighted by the thought of an invisible companion, one that represented Sean, and she didn't want to share him, so she put herself on autopilot while the conversation dragged on, imagining what the spy might answer to everything that was said instead of answering it herself. *Me and my shadow*, she thought to herself with a secret smile. *Awesome*.

CHAPTER
FOURTEEN

There had not, in fact, been a spy from the future at the Penworth Firemen's Hall in January of 1983. The man who normally would have filled such a position—if anything about the situation could be called "normal"—had spent the day in the Project Quantum Leap Waiting Room with Sean O'Connor, eating pizza and playing old Atari games (Tanks and Space Invaders, mostly; he'd won the latter several times).

Verbena Beeks, meanwhile, had been doing some observing of her own, from the small post just above the Waiting Room.

At first, Verbena hadn't been thrilled with the concept of what was essentially a spy room, but it had proved itself useful from time to time. A camera was mounted in a light in the corner of the Waiting Room, and three microphones were placed strategically near the furniture groupings. Verbena was settled in behind a small desk, wearing the headphones that were hooked up to the mikes, watching the old black and white monitor perched on the far wall with growing concern.

This morning she had dismissed Sean's anxiety dream without a second thought. Many of the Visitors slept restlessly; a few had even complained about bad dreams. Sean's dream of the Cyclops judges was clearly rooted in concrete aspects of his life. It had looked like a simple release of tension.

It was only later, when she'd gone to the observation deck to watch him with Al, that the alarm bells had started going off. They were distant at first, muffled by the pleasantness of watching the way Al was relating to Sean (he was so relaxed and open that he'd even mentioned Beth once—in *passing*, no less, which had shocked the hell out of Verbena, although she doubted he realized that he'd done it) and by her own mellow mood after a long walk in the desert, but she couldn't ignore them, and they were growing louder. Sean was doing all the right things and saying all the right things, but Verbena noticed a certain hyperalertness in his eyes. He looked like a rabbit in a snare, waiting for the hunter to find him.

Al either didn't notice it (Sean *did* seem to be going out of his way to mask it when the admiral was looking at him) or was choosing to let it be. Verbena rather suspected the latter; the admiral's philosophy on mood swings seemed to be "just ride it out and it will go away." So far, his instincts had proved better for Sean than her own had, so she forced herself to sit on her hands and watch things unfold. Maybe it would even be for the best if something exploded, anyway.

There was an electronic popping sound, and Sean laughed and said "Shit!" as the low-resolution tank spun on the screen in a jerky circle.

Al laced his fingers behind his head and leaned back with a self-satisfied grin on his face. "Gotcha," he said.

"Let's try another game. Do you play Demons and Dragons?"

Al wrinkled his nose. "I hate that game."

"How can you hate D&D?"

"Kids get too into it. A couple even end up killing themselves over it."

Sean shrugged and said cautiously, "Kids kill themselves

181

over a lot of things. I seriously doubt D&D is top of the list.''

Verbena had to agree, although she hated the game herself. It was a fixation that kids got, but like most fixations, it was usually covering something a little deeper. The kids who'd killed themselves undoubtedly would've found a different, probably more mundane reason to do it if Demons and Dragons had never been invented, but they still would have done it.

Al was disconnecting the Atari and winding the cords around the joysticks, and Verbena glanced over at Sean. That furtive, trapped-in-a-snare look was back. The waiting-for-the-other-shoe-to-drop expression. What was he expecting? What had Al done? Or what had Sean dreamed he'd done? Then Al turned around and Sean covered it up. He reached behind himself and pulled out some kind of plastic electronics game. ''I've been working on this thing.''

''Yeah?''

''Yeah.'' He pulled off the back cover (there was a vague, squeaky protest from the plastic) and held it out to Al. ''You see,'' he said, ''a couple of these things are warped.'' He pointed to two or three circuits. ''I had one of these things, and I left it in a window during the summer. It got dew on it or something. It never worked right again.''

''So you think it's a lost cause?''

''It *might* be. But maybe we can do something with it. Maybe there's some way to, like, clean the wires or something.''

''I don't know if you can do that with stuff this small.'' Al took the machine and looked inside it, squinting to get his eyes to focus. He had a pair of glasses for close work, but he never carried them with him; he seemed to prefer to pretend that they didn't exist. ''If it was just the battery wires, it would be different. We could strip them and reconnect them further up.''

182

Sean nodded wisely. "I noticed you already tried that."

"Yeah. A long time ago."

"What happened?"

"It worked for a few minutes, then quit."

"Figures. It looks like it's mostly in the circuits where the problem is."

Verbena smiled to herself, despite the weird vibes she was getting. Al's knowledge of computers was surprisingly limited for the job he held; Tina took care of most of the technical aspects. The likelihood that he knew about the circuitry of an extinct game was about as high as the likelihood that she herself could repair a fighter plane, and she had serious doubts that Sean knew much more about the subject. Yet, here they were, quite seriously discussing the subject, as if they were both experts called in for consultation in this grave matter. *Men and their toys*, she thought, and loved them both achingly for a moment.

Sean smirked. "Too bad my girlfriend's not here. She can fix these things in nothing flat. Probably with a bobby pin or something."

Al laughed. "Mine, too. I swear, Tina can fix *anything* with nothing. We've got a computer here that goes down all the time, and—Sean?"

Verbena stood suddenly, her good feelings fleeing as suddenly as they had appeared. She banged her knee on the sound console, causing a wave of static to pass through the earphones. Too late, she realized what shoe Sean was waiting for. His face had passed through several emotions, from vague puzzlement to dawning realization to cold withdrawal.

"What is it?" Al said.

"You have a girlfriend?" Sean asked carefully.

"Yeah. Tina."

Even more carefully. "You're not married then?"

"Not anymore."

Almost excruciating. "Your wife's, like, dead?"

"No . . ." Al answered dubiously, trying to understand the sudden change in the conversation. "I'm—" Then he understood, too late.

"Divorced," Sean finished coldly.

Al nodded slowly and carefully. "I have five ex-wives."

Sean breathed in sharply, pulling out the knot of the tie Al had given him. "So how many kids did you leave behind?" he asked coolly.

Verbena didn't expect Al to answer, least of all civilly, but he said, "I don't have any children."

"If you did, would you have five ex-wives?"

"I wish I could just say no—"

"But you can't. I should've figured." Sean turned away from him.

Al tried to explain. "Look, Sean, there are other things involved. Things you don't understand yet—"

Sean turned back, with a sarcastic expression on his face. "Oh, let me guess. It just wasn't fulfilling anymore. You found someone you care more about. You needed to go find yourself. You felt stifled—"

"Stop it, right now," Al cut in. "Who the hell gave you the right to pass judgment on me?"

Sean's jaw dropped. "You walk in here and tell me you're supposed to be my fucking role model, and you can't even get your own life together! I think I've got a right to be a little bit pissed off."

"What you've got is a lot of growing up to do."

"I'm *twelve*!" Sean cried. "When are you assholes going to get that through your heads? I'm a kid. *You're* supposed to be the adults. Why don't *you* all grow up, instead of telling *us* to all the time?"

Al stopped and breathed in sharply. He held the breath, as Verbena herself had taught him, and then let it out slowly.

184

"I'm going to leave now," he said at last. "Before this goes much further."

Sean said nothing; Al left. Verbena ran out of the spy room, and caught him outside the Waiting Room door. For a moment he just looked at her with dull anger, then he rubbed his temples and sighed. "I guess you were watching?"

"Yeah."

"I handled that one like a pro, don't you think?"

"I should've gone in," she said.

Al shook his head. "No. It's bad enough *I* blew it. He doesn't need to know that you were spying on him, too." He started down the corridor; she followed.

"It's not your fault," she insisted. "I should've seen it coming sooner, warned you . . ."

"And had me do *what*? Do you think he wouldn't have caught a lie? It was bound to come out sooner or later."

"Still . . ."

"Look, Verbena, it's done. We're just going to have to find some other way to get through to him. Right now, I don't care much."

"I don't believe that."

"You were listening in there. You know what he said."

"And I have a pretty good idea how it made you feel." She touched his hand. "Look, Al, I think the kid wasn't ready to trust you. I think he was looking for an excuse to stop."

"Is that so?"

"Yeah, it is. Everything was fine yesterday, then he has a normal anxiety dream and then he snaps at you on almost no provocation. It's pretty cut and dry."

Al nodded tightly. "Tell you what, Beeks. Why don't you go back in your observation booth and watch your cut and dried little scenario play out. As far as I'm concerned, he can go to hell."

Verbena watched him until he disappeared around a bend in the corridor.

Al went to his quarters and locked the door. He leaned back on his desk chair until he was almost seeing upside down, took a deep breath, and sat up straight again. "Ziggy?" he said.

"Yes?"

"How bad did I just screw that up?"

"I have no new projections on the subject."

"Then he'll forget about it?"

"Admiral, Sean O'Connor is likely to forget *all* the specifics of what happened here. The best we could have hoped for from your relationship with him was a residual memory, anyway."

"A residual memory," he repeated. "What are the odds of him going into the drug trade?"

"Eighty-seven-point-four-two."

"Were they lower before?"

"No, Admiral. As I said, there was no change."

Al nodded, but didn't carry the conversation any further. Maybe he'd talk about it with Verbena later, but probably he wouldn't. He felt like he'd been stung in some deep place, a deeper place than his few days acquaintance with Sean O'Connor should've allowed, and he needed some time to tend the wound privately. He also felt like any concern he was giving Sean was perfunctory, because right now, at this minute, he hated the kid.

He didn't need Verbena to tell him what the problem was, of course. It was simple: the adult in him, who had gone through five marriages and knew that things weren't always black and white, had wanted to take Sean and shake him for being insensitive and self-centered, not to mention rude and way out of line. But there was a five-year-old boy inside of

186

Al Calavicci who was always lying in a dark room, wrapped in tattered old blankets and clutching a mildewy toy (a stuffed rabbit named Fuzzy, even though the boy had never known it before it was bald), listening to his papa's smoke-damaged, heavily accented voice saying, "I think your mama's not coming back this time, and you're going to need to be a big boy and be strong for your sister," and that little boy had known what Sean O'Connor was saying, and agreed with every word of it. The child, of course, would no more have said those things to his papa—they would have been *unthinkable*, this was *Papa*, after all—than Sean would say them to his own father, but he had heard and he had responded.

Al breathed deeply and counted to ten. He had long since learned to silence that cheated voice—much, he thought, to his credit. He found self-pity boring.

And if Sean O'Connor couldn't learn to keep his own locked up, Al Calavicci decided, he was done with him.

End of story.

Al went to his bed and lay down on top of the covers, one arm resting over his eyes.

I never needed you to be my father, Sam had said yesterday.

Well, dammit, why should he be anyone's father? Sam had his own father, and so did Sean. Even Nate had had his own father, if Ruthie had ever bothered to figure out who the man was.

They weren't Al's responsibility.

Except that all of them had trusted him, and that *was* his responsibility. And he'd let all of them down when they needed him.

"Admiral?" Ziggy said tentatively.

"Leave me alone," he said. "And turn off the damned lights."

There was no answering dimming of the inset bulbs in the ceiling.

"Ziggy, the lights."

"Admiral—"

"What?"

"There is one more small problem."

Sean let out his breath in a shaky sigh.

Everything seemed to be shaky right now. His hands were quivering at his sides, his jaw was trembling, his heart was racing, rabbitlike, in his chest. Even the bright lights set into the ceiling seemed to have a tremulous shimmer.

Sean knew the feeling well enough; it had been almost constant in the weeks following his father's disappearing act. It came in the aftermath of what his mother called a "hissy-fit" and his father called a "temper tantrum." He guessed it was partly physical, with hormones or something from the fit, but mostly it was in his head. He hated himself when he lost control.

He felt a dull ache on his right hand, and looked down to see the admiral's tie woven tightly through his fingers, turning the tips blue. He unwound it slowly and set it on the table beside him.

When the admiral had started talking about his girlfriend, Sean had felt himself—the higher part of his mind, the part he liked to *think* of as himself—pushed aside by some huge, bloated hand inside of him. It was made of childish things, things like anger and selfishness and self-pity, but it was strong, and it felt betrayed.

But you had no business feeling betrayed. The admiral didn't lie, and he didn't hurt you.

The higher voice didn't seem to have much power in the matter. Sean had dared to trust the admiral, and trust hadn't come easily to him for a long time. But the guy had *five* exwives. Even Sean's father only had one.

He'd stood back and watched the horrible things come out

188

of his mouth, things that the Admiral would probably never forgive him for, things

(*why don't* you *grow up?*)

that should never be said, not even to bad people, and the admiral wasn't bad, just divorced.

Sean felt the trembling begin to quicken; he thought he might pass out.

Divorced.

Judy Blume could write *It's Not the End of the World* as many times as she wanted to, but Sean knew it was a lie. It *was* the end, maybe not of *the* world, but definitely of *some* world, some inside world where grown-ups were forever and kids didn't

(*look, sean, there are other things involved. things you don't understand yet—*)

need to know anything else.

"Sean?"

Dr. Beeks was standing behind him; he hadn't even heard the door open.

"Are you okay?" she asked.

Sean meant to say, "Yeah, I'm fine," and ask her to let him be alone for a while, but he found he couldn't speak. He shook his head dumbly from side to side.

She came across the room and put her arms around him, saying nothing at all, and Sean was glad. If she'd spoken, if she'd started to counsel him or analyze him, it would have been wrong. He just needed to be held tight, and that was all she did.

After a long while, he pulled away a little bit. He still felt shaky. "Thanks," he said, hearing the tremor in his voice.

"You're welcome," she said simply.

"Are you mad at me?"

"No."

"Is *he*?" Sean didn't think he needed to clarify who was

189

meant. He suspected that Dr. Beeks had probably been watching through a mirror or a camera or something anyway.

"Al's heard worse from time to time."

Sean tried a smile. "With five ex-wives, I don't doubt it." But the joke tasted sour in his mouth, and the smile, which had not been on firm footing to begin with, twisted into something that felt almost lunatic to its wearer.

"Sean?"

He took two quick gulps of air. "I didn't mean it," he said.

"What didn't you mean?"

"I was just so mad."

"Because Al's divorced?"

Sean shook his head. He didn't know *why* exactly he was mad. "It's not that, it's . . ." He shrugged helplessly.

"*What* is it, Sean?" she asked. "I can't help you until you tell me."

"You can't help, anyway."

"I wouldn't be so sure of that."

Sean wanted to tell her that he didn't mean it personally, that it wasn't about counseling or understanding or any of the other things she thought. He wanted to tell her that she was trying to fix something that just couldn't be fixed, like the admiral's old computer game with its warped circuits. But he didn't know where to start. "It's not just me," he said after a while. "Or my folks or the divorce or anything. It's, like, *everything. Everything's* divorced."

"I don't understand."

"I wish I didn't." He pulled himself onto the table, and she sat down beside him and took his hand.

"Tell me," she said.

Sean struggled to turn the nasty snarl of feelings inside him into words; he wasn't sure there *were* words for some of them, and, hug or no hug, he wasn't sure he wanted to find them for a shrink. If he finished some long speech and wrenched

190

all of it out of his head, then she raised an eyebrow and said "I see," he thought he might scream.

But if he *didn't* say it, if he kept it inside much longer, it would explode, like it had with the admiral. He could already feel it growing again, big and poison, ready to push the higher Sean out of the way with a flick of its wrist.

"Are you alright, Sean?"

He looked up, startled at the sound of her voice.

"You look a little pale. Do you need to lie down?"

"No." he said. "I . . ." But there weren't any more words behind it.

"What did you mean about everything being divorced?" she asked, letting his judgment on his health stand.

"I meant . . ." Sean looked into the far corner of the room, as if trying to read the words from an invisible cue card. *I meant that everything in the world feels about as secure as my folks' marriage*, he wanted to say. *I meant that nobody's making any commitments to anything. Nothing means anything. There's nothing worth fighting for.* What he said was, "I just meant that nobody gives a shit about anything anymore. That's all."

"That's not true, Sean."

"It *feels* true." He turned back to her. "My mom drinks a lot now," he said. "Maybe she did before and I just didn't know it, 'cause Dad took care of her. Now *I* take care of her when she's really bad off. At least when she's home. She's not home much."

Dr. Beeks didn't say anything.

"And Chrissi's folks . . . God, they used to be, like, great. They loved each other and all, you know? But then they got divorced. Chrissi's mom keeps throwing out his stuff now and not talking to him or anything. Sooner or later, she's just going to pack Chrissi and their furniture into a U-Haul and leave town so she doesn't have to see him on the street."

191

"Is that what Chrissi says?"

"No. But it happened to a couple other kids from school."

"That doesn't mean it's going to happen to Chrissi."

"But I think it is. It's like, I know what Mrs. Martinez is thinking. I know how bad it hurts her to see him with Jenny, just like I know how bad it hurts my mom to know my dad wasn't happy with us. I know how my dad had to go, too, 'cause he felt like someone was strangling him."

"That's a lot of people to understand."

Sean nodded. "I don't *want* to understand any of it," he said. "I don't even want to *know* about it. I want to worry about winning the O.M. competition, not about if my mom's going to drink herself to death. I want to worry about catching a couple minutes with my girlfriend, not whether or not having a girlfriend is even worth it when it's all going to come down around us anyway."

"But you *do* understand, don't you?" Dr. Beeks said. "You understand all of it, and you worry about all of it."

Sean tried to say yes, but couldn't. The word stuck in his throat, held there by the giant hand that was swelling inside of him again, making it hard to breathe. He *didn't* want to understand; understanding meant too many horrible things.

But he *did* understand. To the core of his being, he understood.

And he wept.

His tears weren't just for himself, or for Chrissi, or for their parents, or for the admiral.

In four months, he would come across a horror novel called *Lord of the Flies*, in which another boy in another land wept "for the end of innocence, the darkness of man's heart," and he would turn off the lights in his room and cry tears that would feel somehow familiar, although he wouldn't remember why, but right now they were fresh, and they were cleansing, and he let them come.

CHAPTER
FIFTEEN

Kathleen had pulled herself out of bed at around three, and insisted on trying to cook Sunday dinner. Sam had offered to help, but she'd refused, saying that she wanted to keep her hands busy, so he'd merely stayed in the kitchen with her, making small talk and watching her preparations with resignation.

She'd produced a small chicken from the back corner of the freezer, where it had grown icy new feathers across its plastic wrap, and proceeded to pry it from its packaging. She chiseled the bag of innards from the bird's cavity, looked at them blankly for a minute, then threw them into the sink's metal basin, where they landed and bounced with a series of dull thuds. She hadn't touched them since, and Sam was wondering what she planned to do with them. The chicken itself had gone, fully frozen, into a five-hundred-degree oven—''Just to thaw it for a few minutes,'' Kathleen had explained when Sam questioned it. A few minutes became nearly half an hour when a brief question about the school board had turned into an amusing but seemingly endless rant about ''that Fairgate bitch,'' and by the time she remembered the chicken, the outer layers were dry and the inside still frozen solid. She shrugged sheepishly and turned down the heat. Less than twenty minutes before she planned to serve everything, she'd thrown two potatoes in to bake.

So Sam couldn't claim surprise at the meal in front of him, but he couldn't very well refuse it, either. No matter how awful it was—and he thought that if it wasn't the *worst* dinner he'd ever eaten, it was high on the list of them—she had stayed sober and alert (well, sentient anyway) long enough to make it, and that had to count for something. He was sawing at a piece of chicken when Kathleen put her fork down and looked at her watch.

"Five-thirty," she said, with a nervous smile. "Twenty-four hours down."

It took Sam a minute to realize that she was talking about her drinking; it had seemed both longer and shorter than twenty-four hours since he had arrived home and issued the challenge. But she was right. He lifted his glass of milk. "Here's to twenty-four more."

"Cheers." She raised her coffee cup and drank, then looked down at her dinner plate with a rueful smile. "I guess I thought sobriety would miraculously cure my cooking. I don't know why. I could never cook before I started drinking."

Sam considered arguing the point, for form's sake, but didn't see any point to it. "It's a, uh, valiant effort," he said.

"Maybe I'll take that cooking class they have over at Teoka Community College sometime," Kathleen suggested, mostly to herself. "Jesus, it's been a long time since I thought about taking a class."

"And the one you want to take is cooking?"

"Maybe," she answered defensively. When Sam didn't challenge her, she went on. "I did pretty well in most of my classes, but I never paid much attention in Home Ec. At the time I was taking it, I figured I'd be rich enough to hire a maid by the time I was twenty-five." She laughed. "I sure never figured on being where I am."

"Me, neither," Sam said.

"Oh, really? And where *did* you expect to be at the ripe old age of twelve?"

"Well . . ." Sam rolled his eyes, trying to think of some light thing to say to get himself off the hot seat. "I figured I'd be King Tut by now. He was king when he was nine."

"And he was dead when he was nineteen!"

"Well, I admit the idea has drawbacks."

"I'd say so." A wicked smile tried to surface on Kathleen's face. "I'd love to see Gina Fairgate try to push King Tut around, though."

Sam wiggled his eyebrows—*See what I mean?*

"We've got to think of some way to do this." She managed to pry a small bit of chicken from the piece on her plate, and she chewed it thoughtfully for a minute before spitting it into her napkin and shaking her head. "This is a washout."

"The chicken?"

"Yeah." She thought about the double meaning he could've taken. "The thing with Gina . . . I don't know, Sean. The meeting's tomorrow, and whatever they decide is going to stick. I don't know if we have enough time to put a fight together, even if I stay stone-cold sober."

Sam leaned back in his chair, rubbing his chin thoughtfully. "Do you think we have to?" he asked. "I mean, maybe, if everything else is okay, with us and all, we don't need the program at school."

"I'm not a teacher, Sean. Drunk or sober, I don't have the patience for it. I can love you and I can support you, but I can't educate you. I wouldn't know where to start."

Sam considered this. When the idea of sobering Kathleen had first entered his mind, he'd thought he'd grasped the secret of the Leap—not to save the program, which was incidental, but to save the more important inner core of the kids' lives. But what Kathleen was saying made sense; not every parent was cut out to be a teacher, and teaching wasn't a job that could, in good conscience, be left to the inept, no matter how wonderful their intentions might be. There was no guarantee, of course, that the teachers assigned to Penworth's gifted program would be top quality, but they would, at least, have training, and be able to connect with educational resources that an average parent simply wouldn't know to look for.

"Besides," Kathleen said, "you kids need to be together, to learn together. Not just the academic stuff; that you could pretty much learn without school at all, if you put your mind to it."

"What, then?"

She took a deep breath. "I don't know the best way to put it . . . Your father and I were very concerned about you for a long time, Sean. Your grades were good, and you could do everything that people put in front of you. The problem was, you . . . you *knew* it."

"Why was that a problem?"

"You were never with people your own age who could keep up with you." She bit her lip. "You picked friends that you could push around and intimidate. I don't think you did it on purpose, and your father didn't think so, either, but it was a problem. You were starting to talk down to people. We were worried."

Sam looked at his feet. Neither of his parents had ever spoken to him this way, but his brother Tom had, when he was nine. It was easy to fall into the idea that you were better than other kids, somehow, if there was no one to check the image, and Sean, to top it off, seemed to be a natural leader. Sam thought about Sean's future without the program and shuddered. "I guess I can see that."

"But in the last year, in this program, you've changed. Now that you're in a class with people who beat you to an answer sometimes, you've grown a lot. And I'd bet the other kids have, too."

Sam nodded.

Kathleen winced. "I'm sorry, honey. It was mean to say that to you, especially when you've been so good to me all day."

"No, it's true." Kathleen still looked miserable, so he touched her hand gently. "I wanted to thank you for doing this," he said. "It means a lot that you want to fight for us."

She smiled. "Will you think less of me if I tell you my motives aren't that pure?"

"Of course not."

"Good. 'Cause I'll tell you, part of it is just that I've been spoiling for a good fight ever since your father left town. He always gave a good fight."

"Is that good or bad?"

"It was good." She looked away wistfully, and sighed to herself. "I miss him, you know."

"Yeah, I've gotten that impression."

She blinked twice, and came back from wherever her brief reverie had taken her. "I'm sorry, Sean," she said. "All the fighting must have been hard on you. I don't mean to make light of it."

"I'm sure I knew the difference between a good fight and a bad one."

Her eyes rested on him comfortably, and she smiled wearily. "You're a good boy, Sean. You always were. It's Somebody's sick idea of a joke that you got your father and me for parents." She stood up and started to clear the table. "I'm going to do the dishes now. And when I'm done, how about we go out for some ice cream or something?"

"Sure. Maybe we could catch a movie or something."

"Don't you want to watch *Voyagers!* at seven?" she said.

Sam felt the corner of his mouth twitch. He had vague memories of the show from the early eighties, about, of all things, a time traveler who had a mission to fix mistakes in the time stream. Katie's kids had loved it—he thought. It was hard to be sure. It had been a kids' show, anyway, with little attempt at plausible scripts and no attempt at good science fillers. "I'd probably live if I missed it," he said.

Kathleen shook her head. "You have your competition to-morrow. You don't want to go in sleepy, do you? And I don't think the next show even starts 'til nine."

"I guess you're right."

"Of course I'm right. You've gotta shine tomorrow, kiddo. Show that old Pride-in-Penworth spirit." She flashed a devil-may-care smile that managed to be cynical and absurdly hope-ful at the same time. Sam wondered what she really felt about the "old Pride-in-Penworth spirit."

"If we win tomorrow," he tried, "it's for us, not Pen-worth."

She stopped in the archway to the kitchen. "I admit it's not always easy to love this town," she said, "or even to like it, for that matter. But it's yours, so you may as well try."

"Do *you* love it?"

She let out a brief snort that might have been a laugh. "It made me everything I am today." Without explaining this (and Sam didn't think it needed too much explaining), she picked up the pile of dishes and went to the kitchen.

Sam hadn't spent much time in Sean's room, despite having been here for nearly three days. The first night, he'd only come here in the dark, panicked (and surprised) by loneliness, then gotten up in the morning and set off for the school without any time to spare for exploration. Last night, he'd stayed up with Kathleen in the living room, pouring coffee into her and listening to three or four crying jags that he was glad the real Sean O'Connor had been spared. When he'd finally gone to bed, he'd been so tired that he hadn't even bothered to turn on the lights before stripping down and crawling between the covers. This morning, he'd wanted to be out and about soon enough to get rid of the bottles, so he'd gone immediately down to the kitchen.

But now, Kathleen was asleep (she'd dozed off around

198

seven-fifteen, shortly after they'd come home from an uneventful trip to a local ice cream parlor and found out that *Voyagers!* was going to be preempted by a special; Sam had found himself ridiculously disappointed at this), there was no pressing school engagement, Al was nowhere to be found, and Sam decided to take the time to explore Sean's life.

The bedroom was a not-too-unruly mess, much like the rest of the house—a boy's domain. The walls were covered with posters, like walls belonging to most early adolescents. There were some rock groups, including the Stray Cats and the Pretenders, and several fantasy posters that were either connected to Tolkien or one or another of the role-playing games that had been so popular in the eighties. Sam hoped it was the first. There was also a small, autographed picture of Pat Benatar, her eyes hyper-widened and encircled with thick jet-black liner, and her hair teased into a ponytail that stuck straight up. It had been framed and placed on the dresser.

He started with the desk. There was no revelation there, unless it was that twelve-year-old boys should probably not be called on to design filing systems. There were half-done homework assignments from two years ago, a notebook with three or four unfinished letters to Sean's father (none of them had much to say beyond "Hi. I'm fine. How are you?" and the like; one had opened with the almost daring "It was nice to see your checkbook is alive. Maybe next time you'll write more than your name") as well as the same assortment of jumbled notes that Sam had found in his other notebooks, and the usual collection of unused and overused school supplies. The most revealing thing the desk offered was a picture of Sean and Chrissi at a costume party that was taped to the top drawer, and all it revealed was that they were clearly "going out." The dresser had nothing to offer but a few piles of wrinkled clothes and a tattered issue of *Playboy* that had been haphazardly buried in the back of the top drawer. Its discovery

199

was clearly not an imminent threat. Sam put the socks and underwear back over it, shaking his head.

A stack of cassettes lay on the corner of the small table where the stereo was set: Michael Jackson's *Thriller* (of course), *1999* from Prince (or whatever his name was lately), *Built for Speed* from the Stray Cats, *Rio* from Duran Duran, *Get Nervous* from Pat Benatar (this cover was graced with the same photo that was on the dresser) . . . the sound track for an early eighties nightmare, as far as Sam was concerned. There was an empty case for *American Fool* by John Cougar, and Sam deduced that the cassette was in the tape player. He hit PLAY, and John told him that even after the thrill of living is gone, life still goes on.

Charming, he thought. *Just what a twelve-year-old needs to hear.*

But there was something about it, something truthful, that Sam could relate to after only three days in Sean's life. He himself had grown up bright in a small town, and until now had believed that his life was the normal way to live. He'd been happy and well treated, and people went out of their way to help him grow. Leaping into Sean O'Connor's life, he could see that it wasn't always like that. Sean and his friends lived in a world he didn't recognize, a world where a good mind was as much a curse as a blessing, a world where the only constant was a nagging fear that the rug under their feet would be pulled out at any minute. There was a wretched monotony here, a kind of desperate, hopeless boredom that permeated everything and sullied even the good moments with the knowledge and expectation that they wouldn't last.

"Good tune." Al was standing by the window, holding a cigar but not smoking. There was a distanced look on his face that Sam didn't like, but he didn't comment on it. "My fourth . . . no fifth . . . wife said it was great for roller skating. I never did get around to trying it."

200

Sam tried to imagine Al, at sixty, speeding around a roller rink to John Cougar, and found that it was the first image of his friend that he simply couldn't contrive. "What's up?"

"We have a little problem."

"How little?"

Al shrugged apathetically. Sam was again concerned—Al was many things, but he was rarely apathetic—but he knew that Al would tell him what the problem was if he wanted to, or needed to. "Well," he said. "Now Ziggy's saying that there's a seventy-eight percent chance that the kids are going to lose the competition tomorrow."

Sam furrowed his brow. "You said they were going to win, with or without me."

"Well, when I said that, there was an eighty percent chance that it was true. But that's been dropping since you got here."

"You might have mentioned that."

"We hadn't had Ziggy check that scenario for a while. She just came up with it."

"Does it matter?"

"It matters to the kids," Al said. "And losing the competition won't exactly help you save their program, either."

Sam sat down on the edge of Sean's bed. "What happens?"

"Well, you're going to do okay in the skit . . . that's really on autopilot. But now it looks like you're going to blow the spontaneous question, and that's Sean's event."

"The what?"

"The spontaneous question. Haven't they been drilling?"

"I don't even know what you're talking about. All we've done is paint flats and rehearse the skit."

"Oh. Well, the basic idea is that the five of you are going to be asked a question, and you come up with as many answers as you can. It's like a relay race. You'll have one minute to think, three minutes to respond. One point for each answer, three points for creative answers. The team with the most points wins the event. Apparently, Sean's good at starting strings of answers.''

"What kind of question?"

"I'll see if I can access one."

"Why don't you just ask Sean?"

Al gave him an odd look, but didn't answer. He keyed in the request to Ziggy. "Let's see . . . Okay. Try this one. I'll have Ziggy keep score, so I'll have to repeat whatever you say. The United Nations decides unanimously to outlaw the game of Ping-Pong. There are ten billion Ping-Pong balls left in the world. What do you do with them?'' He pulled a stop-watch out of his pocket.

"Why would the U.N. outlaw Ping-Pong?"

"That's not the point."

"What *is* the point?"

"It's a game, Sam. It teaches them to think."

"About ten billion Ping-Pong balls?"

"About alternatives. Kind of like we do back at the Project. You ask me a stupid question like 'What am I doing here?' and we come up with as many stupid answers as we possibly can. The only difference is that these kids run it by a judge and we run it by Ziggy.''

"That, and people's lives are depending on it."

"It's the same principle. Would you rather we stopped do-ing it?"

"I see your point."

"Let's try this again. Since you don't like the Ping-Pong balls, we'll try another one. You're twelve years old and it's up to you to keep your underfunded gifted program on its feet. How are you going to do it? Three minutes to respond; I'll start." He clicked the stopwatch. "Call in their parents."

"Um . . ."

"Come on, Sam. Say anything."

Sam glanced at the stopwatch, tried to think of some reasonable answer, glanced at the stopwatch again, and blurted: "Rob a bank."

Al nodded approvingly and repeated it for Ziggy's benefit. "Good. Have the program go underground."

"Get the town to donate the money?"

"Find volunteer teachers."

"Kidnap the school board for ransom."

"Assassinate the school board."

"Blackmail the school board."

They kept volleying the answers back and forth for the longest three minutes Sam could remember, and then, suddenly, it was over. Al checked his stopwatch and prodded the handlink for a score. "We got forty-three answers. She says seven were creative, so that's . . . fifty-seven points."

"Is that good?"

"No. But we were slower because I had to repeat, and this was a tough question. I think you've got the idea."

"What are the odds on losing now?"

"Down to twenty-one percent."

Sam nodded. "Okay, then."

Al put the watch back in his pocket thoughtfully. "So how'd it go with Kathleen?"

"Okay, so far. I hope Sean can help her when he comes back."

"I wouldn't count on it."

"Al, is something wrong back there?"

"Wrong?" The Observer's hand hovered above the handlink.

"With Sean. With Project Role Model."

"Let's just say we're thinking about other alternatives."

"Why? What's going on?"

"I don't want to talk about it." Al hit a button and disappeared.

Sam stood alone in the cluttered room, and thought about alternatives.

PART FOUR

Monday

CHAPTER
SIXTEEN

For Sam, the last day of the Leap began with another culinary adventure from Kathleen—hard fried eggs, limp bacon, and cold toast. He struggled through it as best he could, kissed Kathleen's cheek, and left for school.

He didn't like leaving Kathleen alone, of course. She'd given her word not to drink, but the word of an addict on such a subject was usually no more than wishful thinking. Unfortunately, there weren't any options here; Sean (and therefore Sam) had to be at the competition today.

The morning was cold, even by the standards of January in the Northeast, but beautiful. When Sam turned right onto Main Street and saw the valley of downtown Penworth jump into view in front of him, he stopped for a moment to catch his breath. It was the kind of clear, photographic image that belonged only to the north country in winter, with each line, each angle etched against the pale sky like a crystal minaret. The quaint, false-fronted buildings looked like children's toys left carelessly on a staircase; Sam felt like he could reach out and touch each one, although the farthest might have been more than a mile away. He could see the edge of the library roof cutting the sky at the far end of town, where it stood beside a ramshackle white house with a sagging cupola. Six church steeples pointed heavenward. The sharp sound of ice cracking under its own weight in the trees was all the sound track the morning needed.

"Looks cold," Al said beside him.

Sam nodded. "Pretty, though."

"Guess so."

Sam felt the moisture in his nose start to freeze, and he pulled his scarf up over his face and started moving, veering left onto Central for most of the trip ahead. Al hovered beside him, maintaining a comfortable walking distance. "Been in to see Sean yet?"

"I'm not going."

"You want to tell me why?"

"I'm not really the role-model type. Why don't you call his father and tell him to get his butt back home where it belongs?"

"I have a funny feeling that wouldn't work." Sam tried to move his fingers and found they were numb inside his gloves. He blew on his hands through his scarf. "You got a number on it?"

"One point three percent."

"Kind of what I thought." He sighed. "Al, I *need* you in there. I don't know what happened yesterday, but—"

"What happened is that I blew it, okay?"

"How did you blow it?"

"I got divorced."

Sam thought about the notebook of unfinished letters, and Sean's empty house. "He found out you're divorced and got mad. What did you do?"

"What else did I need to do?"

"Did you keep your cool?"

"While I was in there, I guess."

208

"I see. So *you* didn't blow it. Sean did, and you're angry at him."

Al started to argue, then changed his mind and nodded.

"Angry enough to let him throw away the rest of his life?"

"He would've before."

"If we start thinking like that, then what are we doing here?"

"I can't." Al stopped following. "I'm afraid that if I go in there, he'll say something else, and I'll really lose it."

Sam turned to him. "That's something you've got to deal with. Because I need you there a lot more than I need you here."

Al looked away sullenly, then punched most of the code for opening the Door into the handlink. "I hate it when you're right," he said, then the Door opened, and he stepped through it.

Sam waited for it to close, then went on down Central. He turned right onto Watkins a block away from the high school.

Chrissi was waiting on her porch steps, and she bounced up and ran to him as he walked by her house. She was surprisingly understanding about his absence at the wedding yesterday, which had been, in her words, "totally lame" and "pretty grody," anyway. He let her take his hand with no protest as they turned the last corner and faced the school.

The next forty-five minutes were a confused jumble of people and action. Johnny and Pigeon had already moved most of the large props out of the storage room and down to a back entranceway, where Sarah was keeping inventory and trying to organize for the best packing on the bus. Chrissi took over the latter job (Sam couldn't tell if Sarah was relieved or chagrined by this), and when the bus arrived (there was a vague idea that it was late), it was she who directed the loading. Sam noticed that he, Johnny, and Pigeon did most of the heavy work. Coach Stover had a bad back, and the girls seemed to take it for granted that lugging the flats and large props around was a boy's job. The boys, for their part, didn't so much as blink at the idea of taking their directions from girls. Sam didn't know whether the scene would be a feminist's dream or nightmare.

The bus ride to nearby Livingston College took twenty-some-odd minutes, but Sam didn't have much of a chance to appreciate the scenery that was flashing by the windows (which was stunning, judging from what little he could see; the entire area was nestled in gently rolling snow-covered hills, with frozen streams glittering like diamonds every mile or two). Sarah insisted on running lines; Johnny accommodated by getting up and running up and down the aisle until the bus driver growled, "Will youse kids settle down? Christ."

Coach Stover, who had been going over papers in his brief-case, looked up. "What are you doing, Johnny?"

Johnny pointed to the grooves in the rubber aisle mat. "I'm running lines," he said. "Sarah told me to."

Stover laughed. "Running lines. You kids."

"You grown-ups," three voices said in unison.

After that, Stover lined them up and drilled them on spontaneous questions ("Name things that are blue," "What would you do with a million boxes of Chex cereal?" other easy ones) until the bus pulled up to the Student Union in Livingston, where the competition was going to be held.

Stover went in to take care of the paperwork, and Sarah ran a quick mission to find out where they were supposed to stow their equipment for the day. She came back a minute later and started leading the team to an empty spot along the ballroom wall, above which a sign read "Penworth Central Junior-Senior High School, Division II." Chrissi orchestrated the move with casual expertise, and when Stover joined them again, the bus was gone and they were settling into the new quarters.

"Okay," the coach said. "You're third on the skit and eighth on spontaneous, so get your costumes on first."

"TO-GA!" Johnny chanted, imitating a fraternity brother after one or two too many.

Sarah opened a suitcase and pulled out the togas, and three triangular patches of fuzzy stuffed animal covering. "I brought beards," she said.

"What do you plan to attach those with?" Sam asked suspiciously.

Sarah produced a jar of rubber cement.

"Oh, no," Johnny said. "No way."

Sarah raised an eyebrow.

"I mean it, Sadie-lady. No way." He looked at Sam. "Come on, O'Connor, back me up here."

"That'll be really hard to take off."

"Rubber cement rolls off skin," Sarah said implacably. "I experimented with it last night."

Sam tried another approach. "What do we need beards for?"

"Makeup points. There's ten points there, and I want to get at least a few of them."

"Chrissi's drawing whiskers on her face," Johnny offered desperately. "And she's always got black stuff on her eyelashes."

"It's not black," Chrissi interjected. "It's burnt sienna."

"Whatever." He turned back to Sarah. "I'm not doing it."

"And here I thought you were going to cut your wrists with a rusty steak knife."

"Not one with rubber cement on it."

The ballroom doors opened, and another team filed in. They were carrying boxes of cardboard scenery, and were already in costume. Each one wore an authentic-looking toga, sewn from a pattern and trimmed with gold ribbon, and laced sandals on the feet. Heads were wreathed with leaves, and two

211

of the five young faces sported beards.

The Penworth team stared at them in a kind of mute shock.

"We're dead," Sarah said.

Johnny sighed, and took the rubber cement from her. "The things I do for art."

He marched off toward the men's room to change, and Sam and Pigeon followed.

Sean was sitting cross-legged on the table, bent around the Merlin with an intense look on his face. He said nothing when the door opened, and nothing when Al came in. It was only when Al had been standing in front of him for nearly a minute that he looked up. He held out the game. "I hoped I could fix it. Symbolic and everything, you know?"

"It's a cheap computer game, Sean. It doesn't make much of a symbol."

"I guess that's good. 'Cause the only thing that's going to fix it is if your pal"—he glanced at the mirror—"goes back and tells whoever owned it not to leave it out in the rain in the first place."

"I doubt it's a top priority in the time stream."

Sean wiped a hand viciously across his face, and Al was surprised to see a damp trail fading away from his eye. "I didn't think you'd come back after yesterday."

"I almost didn't." Al pulled the chair around and sat down. Coming into the Waiting Room this morning had been difficult, but Sam was right. No matter how angry he was, it would be wrong to walk out on the kid completely for one outburst, no matter how obnoxious it had been. There were things Sean O'Connor needed to learn, now and for good, and Al Calavicci had been chosen by Whoever or Whatever, for reasons of Its own, to be his teacher. "You said some pretty lousy things."

"I know. I'm sorry."

Al sighed. "Does 'sorry' fix it?"

Sean stifled a sob and turned away.

Al put a hand on his shoulder. "Look," he said, "I know your folks let you down. I know you hate everything about divorce. I don't know everything that went on between your parents, but I'd bet it happened fast, they didn't try to fix it, and they never asked you what you thought about it."

"You'd win that bet."

"I figured. And for what it's worth, I'm sorry it happened to you."

"It's been two years." Sean laughed weakly, and wiped his nose on his sleeve. "Do you know that's the first time anyone apologized to me? And you weren't even there."

Al smiled. "I was there when it happened to me. No one apologized then, either."

Sean looked at him with guarded curiosity. "What happened with your folks?"

"My mother ran off with a traveling salesman."

"Did you ever see her again?"

"No."

"Did you ever look, even from here?"

Al thought about it. It had never occurred to him to look for his mother through Ziggy's databases, and the idea filled him with revulsion . . . or worse, with no feeling at all. She was likely dead, and he thought he should feel some kind of dread, at least, about knowing for sure, but he just didn't care. And if she wasn't dead, what the hell would he have to say to her after half a century, anyway? *Hi, Mom, what kept you?* "No," he said. "I never looked."

"I'm sorry it happened to you," Sean said.

"Sorry" had never been among Al's favorite words, but for the second time since Sean's arrival, it carried a certain comfort with it. "Thanks," he said.

"Is all that why you keep getting divorced? Because of getting burned like that when you were a kid?"

213

Now, what answer was he supposed to give to that? Beeks, of course, would say "Yes, it was," and little Dr. Ruthie would undoubtedly concur, and there might be some truth to what either one of them was saying, but it wasn't the whole truth, and it definitely wasn't the truth that mattered here and now. "No," he said firmly. "Now I want you to listen to what I'm going to say, and I want you to think hard about remembering it."

"I'm listening."

"I didn't get divorced four—no, five, I'll admit five—times because my mom dumped me at an impressionable age. I don't cheat on my wives or on my girlfriend because I feel abandoned. And I don't drink too much because my father died when I was ten. I do all those things because I made bad choices. Do you understand me?" Sean was looking at him blankly; he could've been speaking a foreign language. In a way, he supposed he was; Sean had been raised in the firm belief that explaining a problem made it go away. "All right," he said, "I'll try again. I'll make it simple. I know your folks walked all over you, but that doesn't give you the right to do it to everyone else. *Now* do you understand? The question isn't 'What happened to you?' It's 'What are you going to do about it?' "

"I don't understand."

"I think you do."

"Am I going to do something bad?" Al didn't need to answer; Sean's eyes widened in horror. "I am, right? That's why they wanted you to come in here and be a role model, 'cause someone else screwed the job up already."

Al held up one hand. "You're doing it again, Sean. Yes, you're going to do something bad. You're going to kill three people because they get in the way of your drug-smuggling business."

"No."

214

"*Yes*." Al grabbed Sean's shoulders and made him look up. "And it *isn't* because someone else screwed up. It's because *you're* going to, just like you did yesterday, only by then you've done it so often that it doesn't bother you anymore."

"It's not true."

"It *is*. It doesn't have to be; you can change it. But right now, it's true." Sean was shaking his head in negation. Al could understand; it couldn't be a great moment to find out you were the scumbag, after all, especially for a twelve-year-old kid who was still basically pretty good-hearted. But if Sean was going to stand a chance of changing his future, he had to understand what he was capable of, how far he had to sink. Al put one hand on either side of the boy's head, and stilled it as gently as he could. He could feel the trembling in Sean's body, but he couldn't tell if it was fear or self-revulsion or both. "It's *true*," he said again.

Sean's chest hitched twice, and Al thought he was going to cry, but he didn't. Instead, he closed his eyes and nodded. The trembling escalated, until it was actually visible in his hands and face.

On an instinct that was as out-of-use and almost as rusty as Nate's defunct Merlin, Al Calavicci put his arms around Sean's shoulders. "You're okay here," he said. He thought he should say something more, something deep and lasting, but there wasn't anything in his head. Instead, he just held Sean tight until the shaking stopped, then let him pull away when he was ready.

"Kill me," Sean said.

"I'm not going to kill you."

"I don't want to be like that. I'd rather be dead."

"You don't have to be dead."

"Then what?"

"You just have to decide who you want to be. Then you

215

have to stop thinking about what other people owe you and pay up what you owe yourself.''

''How?''

Al thought about this carefully. He'd never had to be aware of his own philosophy of life before, and he'd certainly never articulated it. He sighed. ''You have to . . . think of something that you do that pays for itself. Something that you don't expect to be anything more than what it is, and what it is is enough for you.''

''Something I get a charge out of.''

''Not just a charge. Something you love.''

Sean looked into a corner. ''What if I love smuggling drugs and killing people?''

''I don't believe that for a second.''

''I can't think of anything.''

''You have a while.'' Al turned to go.

''Admiral?''

''What?''

''What do *you* love?''

The answer came into Al's mind not as words, but as a memory, a series of images. He saw himself blasting off from Cape Kennedy on a tower of fire, climbing into the cockpit of his A-4, speeding across the desert in his prototype car . . . but under all of them was one simple memory of being seventeen years old, racing along the highway on the used motorcycle he'd bought with his summer stock earnings, with Ruthie riding pillion, her small hands pressed tightly against his chest, screaming ''Faster, Albert, go faster!'' into the wind. It hadn't been Ruthie, though, no matter how good it had been an hour later behind the bandstand, and it hadn't been the bike, or the sunshine, or even the freedom. ''The wind,'' he said at last. ''I always loved the wind.''

Their fears had been baseless.

If the first two skits—one (the one by the ribbon-bedecked

216

team that had first intimidated Sarah) had been a version of the Circe episode that not only added no humor but subtracted what was in the original; the other had been a thoroughly incomprehensible (and inaudible) Cyclops play, in which Polyphemus was somehow metamorphosed into Pac-Man—had not been enough to convince Sam of this simple fact, the response of the audience and judges to the Penworth team's performance surely would have cinched it. Bed-sheet togas, rubber-cement beards, and all, there was no mistaking it: the quality of the skit was on an entirely different level than anything that came before or after it, at least so far.

The competition was on a lunch hour, and Sam had tagged along with Johnny and Pigeon first to the men's room, where he and Johnny removed their beards ("I'm gonna kill her," Johnny had said, as a thin layer of skin peeled away at the base of his chin, "slowly and creatively"), then to the Student Union's video arcade. The arcade was frequented by students, and they took pleasure in pushing the "little dweebs" out of the way. Johnny had finally staked out a claim at the Space Invaders machine, and Sam and Pigeon were standing guard. The girls were still in the ladies' room, doing whatever it was girls did there.

Al had not made an appearance since this morning, and Sam was glad. He hoped the Observer was taking the time to fix things with Sean—for Al's sake, even more than Sean's. A part of him seemed to have been waking up, and Sam would hate to see that undermined.

"AAARGH!" Johnny pounded his fist on the game as it made the weak popping sound that passed for an explosion in old video games.

"Is he done?" Sam asked Pigeon.

"Nah. He's got two lives left."

"Great."

"Why?"

217

"Are we ever going to eat?"

"I thought we were waiting for Chrissi and Sarah."

"Oh." Sam didn't remember anyone mentioning it, but he supposed they shouldn't have had to. They were spending the day as a team, after all. He pointed at Johnny. "What if he's still got two lives when they get here?"

"I'll unplug the thing."

"I heard that," Johnny said.

Pigeon shook his head, and turned away. Sam smiled to himself. His memories of his own friends were scattered and, for the most part, nameless. There was someone named Sibby, he thought, and a girl named Lisa, but he couldn't find the faces the names matched, or the names the faces matched. But he knew *these* kids, and he liked them, and he hoped he would remember them enough to miss them when he left.

He felt Chrissi slide up beside him before he heard her or saw her in the crowded room. Sarah was standing behind her, looking away nervously.

"Hey, guys," Chrissi said, "I need you to look at something for me."

Johnny's attention was diverted for a second, and another popping sound indicated the end of another life. "Look at that, Chrissi. I died for you." He nodded toward Sam with twinkling eyes. "Would he do that?"

"On request," Chrissi answered smoothly.

Johnny laughed, and the third life ended, unnoticed, behind him.

"So what do you need us to see?" Sam asked.

Chrissi tugged at Sarah's sleeve. "Come on," she said. "They can't see your face if you keep looking at the floor."

Sam knew what he was going to see even before Sarah slowly lifted her eyes to them, revealing a lightly and carefully painted face. Her light blue eyes had been ringed with dark lashes, striking against pale skin, and her hair had been parted

218

to one side. One of Chrissi's combs was placed above her left ear, catching a honey-colored wave. She may or may not have been wearing rouge—she was blushing too furiously to tell for sure.

"Well?" Chrissi demanded. "What do you think?"

"I don't think Sarah needed any makeup," Sam said gently.

Johnny shrugged. "I don't know. I like the mascara. I think she needed the eyelashes." He gestured toward her. "Turn around. Let me see your hair."

Sarah turned nervously in a circle. Her hair moved softly across her shoulder blades, and Sam noticed that the new style revealed a wide wave near her neck. It didn't look like something that Chrissi had done with a curling iron, but like something that had just been there, waiting to be unleashed. She faced forward again and bit her lightly reddened lip. "What *do* you guys think?" she asked.

"I think you look great," Pigeon said simply. "I also think that Chrissi better have something to help you get the crap off your face before you go home, because your mother will kill you if she catches you wearing makeup."

Chrissi wrinkled her nose. "Why would she do that?"

"She doesn't believe in makeup," Sarah answered. "She says it's just a way that the men in the world make women hide who they are."

"Do you feel like you're hiding?"

Sarah didn't answer for a long time, and Sam could tell that she was considering the question very carefully, reevaluating some of her most basic assumptions. Sam found himself reconsidering some of his own. He thought he'd been forced to wear makeup once, and found the experience degrading, but he'd never thought about what it might mean to wear it voluntarily. There was an element of cover-up still, but looking at Sarah now it was hard not to see the other side of the story. She seemed to have pulled her natural beauty forward, rather

219

than creating an unnatural, fit-with-the-crowd, magazine-model face.

"No," she said, shaking her head in a slow, surprised way. "When I looked in the mirror in the ladies' room, I thought..." She stopped, a faraway, dreamy expression on her face.

"What did you think?" Sam prodded her.

"I thought it was the first time I ever saw myself." She looked at them quickly, seeming to measure their reactions. "I know it sounds crazy," she said, "but sometimes, almost all the time, really, I look in the mirror, and the person I see there isn't the one I see when I think about myself."

Sam Beckett, who'd had occasion to think more than casually about mirrors over the past five years, said, "I don't think it sounds crazy at all."

"Me, neither," Chrissi said firmly.

Pigeon nodded. "And if you ask me, the only thing you're hiding behind right now is this." He pinched the peace sign hanging around Sarah's neck.

"I want peace," Sarah protested.

"That's not why you wear that."

Sarah sighed and nodded, but didn't remove the pendant.

"Are we done philosophizing?" Johnny asked. "I think Sarah looks great. Can we get some lunch now?"

Sarah laughed. "Good idea. I'm starving." She turned and headed out. "We can drill on spontaneous while we eat," she told them casually.

"Oh, yeah," Johnny said. "That's Sarah."

Sam laughed, put an arm around Chrissi, and went with the others.

CHAPTER
SEVENTEEN

The question was: "The *Odyssey* takes place in Ancient Greece. Name things that are ancient."

One minute to think, three minutes to respond.

Ancient, Sam thought. The Egyptian pyramids were ancient, and the tombs around them, and the hieroglyphs in them, all of which would count as separate answers. The Sphinx. The Phoenician alphabet. The Dead Sea Scrolls.

Ancient, Johnny thought. What did people do then? Chariot racing. The Olympics, the real ones. Riddles; he remembered reading someplace that riddles were the big thing way back when.

Ancient, Sarah thought. There was the black shadow at the heart of her nightmares; that was ancient. And the hands of a priest, resting lightly on her head to drive it away; that was ancient, too.

Ancient, Pigeon thought. He could feel his grandmother's fragile skin under his fingers, see the way the tiny blue lines crawled across her arms.

Ancient, Chrissi thought. But all she could see were eyes, old and tired . . . the eyes of the Mariner.

"Your time begins . . . NOW."

• • •

Johnny let out his breath in an explosive gasp and collapsed onto the table, feigning exhaustion.

Sam could feel his own heart beating loud and fast in his chest, as the adrenaline rushed through his veins, looking for an outlet. His mind was still generating answers, even though time had been called. *Andromeda galaxy, Milky Way galaxy, the constellations, astrology* . . . Some had been used, some wouldn't be, but they all kept beating at his skull like newly caged birds or unbroken horses.

The spontaneous judge smiled. "Good job. Now go relax."

"Yeah, right," Pigeon said, getting up.

Sarah stood. "Now, nobody mention any answers outside. The next team might be there."

Johnny jumped out of his chair and dropped a bow at her. "Yes, ma'am, coach."

They left the room, laughing. As they went out into the lobby, Chrissi wound her fingers through Sam's and tiptoed up to kiss his cheek. "You were totally awesome in there, babe!"

"We were *all* totally awesome in there," Pigeon said. "I think we just kicked some major butt."

"You know, Chrissi, you may very well have a brain under all that hair spray." Sarah pulled at a hank of red hair.

Chrissi offered a wide Cheshire grin. "Who'd've guessed?"

Johnny leaned his head on her shoulder, then changed his mind and fell to his hands and knees, bending over her feet. "I would've," he cried. "But you never notice me, I'm nothing . . ."

Laughing, Chrissi pulled him up and threw an arm around his shoulders.

Pigeon was the first to notice Coach Stover walking toward them, and he waved his arms. The others looked across the lobby and saw him, striding toward them with a pipe in his

222

mouth, looking more serious than he should've.

Sam's chest tightened. He knew what was coming.

Well, you should. What have you done to stop it so far?

But that was unfair to himself, and he knew it. The opportunity to take on the issue directly hadn't come yet. Sometimes, Leaping was just a question of finding new variables to introduce, and that's what he's done with Kathleen yesterday. He'd also stopped the kids from making a foolish mistake by breaking into the school on Saturday, and gotten them thinking about what they might do by giving them an advanced warning of what he'd heard in Kellerman's office Friday afternoon. As Sean O'Connor, that was all he *could* do.

And, of course, there was the matter of the real Sean. Even if Sam failed completely here, it was possible that Al was clearing a path for at least one of them to survive, anyway, and if one did, maybe he could help the others. It wouldn't be perfect, but the time wouldn't be wasted.

He braced himself for the crash of everyone's high spirits.

"You kids look happy with yourselves," Stover said.

Sarah nodded enthusiastically. "I was keeping score," she said, tapping her forehead. "Not counting creatives, even though I think Chrissi came up with a bunch of them"—she nodded at the other girl—"we got a hundred twenty-five points."

Stover nodded. "That's terrific. I've been eavesdropping around, and I don't think anyone else has come close."

"Awesome," Chrissi said.

"And I don't think I even need to tell you that no one's touched you on the skit. I mean, maybe I'm prejudiced, but I don't think there was even competition there."

"There wasn't," Johnny said. "I've got to admit, Sadie was right about running it and running it. And running it. And running it. And . . ."

223

"We get the picture," Sam said.

Johnny shrugged.

Sarah smiled, unembarrassed by the compliment. Sam thought she'd also be quite unperturbed if someone pointed out that what they'd been running over and over was *her* script. As shy as she might be about her looks and her personality, she was coolly confident about her talent. She didn't crave compliments on it, but she accepted them gracefully when they came.

"So we're going to win?" Chrissi asked, breathless.

"Looks like it."

Sarah's smile widened into genuine excitement. "We're going to States!"

Stover shook his head. "No, I'm afraid we aren't."

"What do you mean? You said we won."

"They're cutting the program," Sam said quietly. He looked directly at Stover. "Right?"

"Yeah." Stover sat down on a low bench by a window. Behind him, the frozen campus gleamed in oblivious beauty. "I just called Dr. Kellerman to give him the good news, and he told me. The board took an informal vote this afternoon. It was unanimous. We're being cut. Right away. The meeting tonight is just a formality."

Sam could feel the news falling on the group like a cloud. No one said anything.

"Hey," Stover said, offering a smile, "look at it this way. You got to compete, right? And you won. The team that's building the robot isn't even going to compete." He smiled an apology at Chrissi, who seemed not to hear him.

Sarah wiped a hand viciously across her eye, and the unfamiliar mascara traced a line over her temple. "Oh, yeah," she said. "That makes *everything* all right." She stalked off toward the ballroom.

After a minute, the others followed her.

• • •

They won.

Out of three hundred fifty possible points, they earned three hundred thirty-seven. Seven of the lost points were in makeup, and four were in costume. The remaining two came from a category nebulously labeled "style." The second-place team had a score of three hundred six.

Despite the rout, the mood on the return trip was low.

No, it was beyond low. It was despair.

Chrissi was sitting beside Sam, her arms clasped tightly around his neck, crying against his cheek. Sam kept his arm around her and rocked her quietly. Pigeon was sitting across the aisle, trying valiantly but unsuccessfully to hide his own tears.

Johnny Metz alone was not sinking into a void. He was pacing up and down the center aisle, swaying with each curve, getting angrier with each passing mile. But his anger was constructive, after a fashion; he was trying to think his way out, and Sam Beckett respected that.

"Okay, okay," he said, stopping. "This vote this afternoon was informal, right? Right. It's the one tonight that counts. So what we have to do is, what we have to do is . . . anyone?"

"Go to the meeting," Sam said.

Johnny nodded. "Yeah. Go to the meeting. Raise a little hell."

"Bad idea."

"Yeah, they'll just think we're spoiled." Chrissi pulled away from Sam a little. "Like with the air ducts, right, babe?"

"Right," Sam agreed.

"Right, yeah." Johnny resumed his pacing. "But we can't just sit there either."

Pigeon sniffed and slid toward the aisle in his seat. "We can think of something, maybe."

225

"Sure. Definitely. That's what we do, right? Think, I mean."

"There's got to be something," Chrissi mused.

"For starters," Sam said, "our parents have to come."

"Yeah, right," Chrissi said. "My folks will give us that nice mature look. Should my stepmother come along, too, in case we need a cheerleader?"

"My folks are cool, but they aren't exactly 'in' with the school board. You know, bad blood with my dad and everything." Johnny sat down on the edge of a seat, apparently found it unbearably confining, and bounced up again. "Besides, this is our fight. We ought to do it ourselves."

"Yeah," Pigeon said. "We don't need to bother them with it."

"They are not going to take a bunch of twelve-year-olds seriously!"

"I'm eleven," Chrissi corrected.

"All right, a bunch of twelve-year-olds and an eleven-year-old."

"Maybe if we refuse to take those tests again?" Pigeon suggested.

"The tests are already in for the year," Chrissi said.

"We could purposely start flunking. That would bring the Board of Regents in."

"Oh, that's brilliant, Pigeon."

Johnny nodded. "Sean's right. That's a really bad idea. We'd have to flunk regular classes for a long time before the state noticed, and that would screw up our records for good."

"Where's Sarah?" Sam asked, suddenly realizing that he hadn't seen her since they'd finished packing the bus.

Chrissi shrugged, looking vaguely jealous. "I saw her go to the back. She didn't look too good."

"I'll go get her. We need to do this together."

"She won't come," Pigeon said. "She wants to be by her-

226

self. She used to do this all the time when we were little.''

"Well, neither one of you is little anymore, and maybe it's time for her to get out of that habit.''

"But I need you here,'' Chrissi protested.

"I'll be back.'' She looked at him doubtfully. "I promise.''

He was afraid that Chrissi's objection would get louder—it was, after all, a jealous protest rather than a rational one—but she acquiesced quickly. Johnny had caught her attention; he was, at least, offering something to do other than sulk. She let go of Sam with no more than a token pull, and didn't argue when he got out of the seat and headed for the back of the bus.

The canvas flats had been folded in half and stood on their hinges in the aisle. They leaned over a row of seats, making a line of small cubicles. It was from one of these that Sam heard Sarah crying quietly. He tipped the flats to the other side of the aisle, found her in the second seat, and sat down beside her. "Are you okay, Sarah?''

She turned to him, her face a wreck of mascara and eyeliner, her hair slipping out of Chrissi's comb. "Do I *look* okay?''

"Sorry. Dumb question.''

"What do you want, anyway?'' She wiped her face efficiently with the back of one hand, and tucked her hair behind her ear, trying to look as if she hadn't been disheveled only a second ago.

"I was just concerned about you. I noticed you weren't up front with the rest of us.''

"That's because I didn't want you guys to see me like this,'' she said. "Not today.''

"It's okay, Sarah. Chrissi's up there crying her eyes out. Pigeon is too, almost.''

"I'm not Chrissi or Pigeon.''

"Of course not.''

Sarah shook her head slowly back and forth, staring blankly

227

out the window at the ice-white cornfields. "Just for a few minutes there, I thought everything was going to be okay."

"Everything *can* be."

"No it can't. Not ever." She slammed her fist on the back of the plastic seat. "It's just not fair! They take everything, and it doesn't matter what we do or say. Whether we win or lose, we lose."

Sam thought about saying something comforting, or telling her that there was still a chance at the meeting, but he had a feeling that she needed this less than she needed a simple understanding ear. He put his hand on her shoulder. "I know it's not fair, Sarah."

"I'm sick of all of it."

"I know."

She bit her lip viciously and hugged her knees up to her chest. "Why is it always a fight?" she said. "I'm tired of fighting. I'm tired of bashing my head against a brick wall. I just want to give up."

"What's stopping you?"

She turned toward the window and rested her cheek on her knees. At first, Sam didn't think she was going to answer, then she said, in a soft voice, "Because I don't want to be like them. Small town, small minds. That's what they have in mind for us, you know. Grow up and be just like them. Big fish in a puddle." She turned and offered him a sweet, ghastly smile. "I want . . . more."

"*What* do you want, Sarah?"

"I want . . ." Her mouth twisted anxiously for a few seconds (Sam figured that sooner or later she would become a smoker or a compulsive gum chewer—he hoped for the latter—to soothe her fears), then looked at him helplessly, like she was confessing her darkest secret—which, Sam supposed, she was. "I want the world to know who I am," she said in a quick, staccato voice. "I don't want anyone to ever forget

228

that I was here." She turned on him, suddenly savage. "And if you try to give me some *It's a Wonderful Life* speech about how we all touch each other in some little way, I swear to God I'll break your face in half, because you know exactly what I mean, Sean O'Connor."

Sam nodded. He spent his life fixing little wrongs, helping touch up all the small pictures that made the infamous Big Picture, but he knew what Sarah meant. Nothing in the world could've convinced him to stay in Elk Ridge, not even his father. He had always felt that he had something huge inside of him to give the world, and the passion to give it had often been overpowering. "Yeah," he said. "I guess I do."

Sarah fingered the peace sign around her neck. "So I have to keep defying them," she explained. "In every way I can think of."

"You'll do better if you defy them with the rest of the team."

"They laugh at me."

"Did we laugh at you this afternoon?"

She shook her head.

"So come up and be with us now."

"They don't want me there. If they did, they would've said something."

"Well, they're pretty convinced you don't want them to."

"So why did you come?"

Sam shrugged. "I'm contrary that way."

She laughed, despite herself. "I'm glad."

"Good. Now, come on out of here."

He slid out of the seat, and stood up and held out his hand to her.

She stared at it nervously and tried to pull back into her enclave, shaking her head.

Sam didn't allow it. He reached down to her and pulled her up into the world.

• • •

They hadn't been able to settle on a strategy during the ride home, but Sam had convinced them to make sure their parents appeared at the meeting with them. Pigeon said that his grandmother wasn't feeling well, and probably wouldn't make it, and Sarah had said that she wasn't sure where her parents would stand at all, but they'd both agreed to try. Chrissi had suggested that they call people on the other two O.M. teams (the first, Sam found out, had competed a month ago and placed second in an engineering problem dealing with balsa wood) and get them to come to the meeting with their parents as well. They'd made up a list of names and split it up among them.

The O.M. bus had pulled into the lot just as the late afternoon bus, the one that the country kids who'd had to serve detention used, was arriving. They unloaded the bus quickly and quietly, carting all of the equipment back to the storage room.

"What are we going to do with all of this?" Sarah asked.

"Nothing 'til after tonight. We might still need it at States."

"Yeah, right."

Stover put his hand on Johnny's head. "I don't want you to get your hopes up. They're serious."

"Yeah? Well, so am I. I don't want to go to the religious school, and my parents are going to send me if they cut us. Probably starting tomorrow."

"I think you'll have to wait until fall."

"If it doesn't change tonight, it's not going to change by fall."

"You can't go there," Chrissi protested.

"You say that like I had a choice."

"Have you told your parents how you feel about this?" Sam asked.

230

Johnny shook his head tightly, and went to the other side of the room, where he started clearing a storage space.

"It's not just his parents," Pigeon said.

Stover nodded, then turned to Sam. "Sean, would you mind going back to the bus and making sure we didn't leave anything? Last time we used a bus for a field trip, Pigeon spilled some M&M's, and the bus drivers complained to the school board that the gifted kids weren't learning respect for 'real' jobs like bus driving."

"I'd like to think you're joking," Sam said. "But I have a feeling you're not." He pulled Sean's coat around himself and went back outside.

All he found on the bus was a filthy, unmatched mitten that looked like it had been lying against the wall for two or three seasons. He picked it up and stuffed it in his pocket, checked each seat one more time, and jumped down from the back door of the bus.

Al was standing under a bare tree at the edge of the parking lot, looking rather incongruous standing on the ice in a lightweight green suit. "Congratulations," he said.

"What for?"

"Well, aside from a pretty lopsided win over in Livingston today, you managed to save Sarah's and Pigeon's lives."

"How?"

"Well, with Sarah it's easy. You got her into the group, and she never got in trouble trying to force herself into the counterculture at college. Ziggy hasn't got a clue how that kept Pigeon out of a parking lot brawl."

"Is she sure they're connected?"

"No. But Sarah and Pigeon *do* wind up getting married out of college, so she thinks there's something there. Maybe they were out on a date the day Pigeon would've gotten stabbed."

Sam checked the internal barometer that told him when his work was done far more accurately than Ziggy did. It didn't report any changes. "So, where's the happy couple now?"

"They still live in Penworth," Al said. "Pigeon's the manager of the Factory Outlet on Main Street. Sarah works as a legal aide at the County Court in Oslo."

"Big fish in a puddle," Sam muttered.

"What?"

"That's not good enough, Al."

"Of course it's not."

"You agree?"

"Yeah, I agree. If it was good enough, you'd have Leaped." He took a long pull on his cigar and blew the smoke out. "And if it was good enough, these kids wouldn't be who they are."

"So the program's still the best bet?"

"The next best is to talk all their parents into moving away or getting them all scholarships to private schools."

"That's not going to happen."

"No kidding."

"So we're back to square one."

"Maybe not."

"What do you mean?"

"Well," Al said, "when we were running our practice spontaneous last night, I had Ziggy keeping score."

"I remember."

"I got to thinking it wouldn't hurt to see just how good the answers were."

"And?"

"We came up with a sixty-four percent chance of saving the program on one of them."

"That's great." Sam brought his hands to his mouth and blew on them for warmth—and for cover, since the bus driver had come back to the bus and was looking at him curiously from the back door. "Which one?"

Al winced. "Blackmail."

"Blackmail?" Sam repeated. He started walking toward the school. "Sixty-four percent isn't that good when you're talking about a felony."

Al followed. "Well, I know that. But I talked about it with Sean, and he's the one who thought of the right answer."

"What answer is that?"

"If there's a sixty-four percent chance that blackmailing someone will work, that means they've probably got something unkosher going on to begin with. And if it were to come out . . ."

"Someone on the board might take a dive."

"Exactly."

"So what's going on?"

"We don't know. Do you?"

"How would—" He stopped walking. "You said they had all the money at the beginning of the year?"

"Well, yeah, but . . ." Al realized what he was hitting on. "You think they've been . . . Oh, sure. They grab the money, cut some programs . . ."

"And a bunch of kids crash and burn."

The handlink let out a series of high-pitched beeps. "Bingo," Al said. "We've got 'em."

Sam shook his head. "We've got them seventeen years from now. That's not going to help tonight."

A car pulled around a corner and into the parking lot. Sam didn't take any notice of it until it pulled up beside him. The driver's window rolled down, and Kathleen O'Connor looked out. "Hey, kiddo. Need a lift?"

"Yeah. Just wait a second." He ran inside quickly, left the glove with Johnny ("What do you want me to do with this?" he asked; Chrissi said, "Send it to Mars," and Sarah suggested that he bomb Russia with it), and went back out to the car, where Al had centered himself in the back seat.

Kathleen was sober.

Better than sober, she seemed well groomed and energetic, a different woman entirely than the one Sam and Al had found shut in the living room on Saturday afternoon. Sam commented on it.

She smiled. "Well, I spent the morning cleaning up around the house—mostly *your* things, young man—and then I realized that if I spent another hour sitting in my clean house doing nothing, I'd be out in a bar before you got home from school."

"So you went out and did something fun?"

"No. I went out looking for a job." She steered the car onto Watkins. "No luck today, but there's always tomorrow."

The handlink gave a concurring beep, and Al clarified, "She gets a job at a bank a couple towns over. She ends up a vice president."

"That's great," Sam said.

"I think so," Kathleen agreed.

"Uh, Sam?" Al was gesturing with the handlink. "The program?"

Sam nodded. "Mom?"

"What?"

"I need you to help me do something before the meeting tonight."

CHAPTER
EIGHTEEN

"Can I call a family conference?" Johnny asked when his mother got home. He'd called the three kids on his O.M. list already, and hoped they were trying to call conferences of their own.

"I don't know," Mike said. "Do you think we should let the spaz start thinking he's, like, part of the family or something?"

Mom reprimanded him with a look that was too severe to be real, and unwound the scarf around her neck. A few strands of permed blond hair were dragged with it by static electricity. "Can I peel while we talk?"

"Sure."

Dad came out of the living room, where he'd been trying to start a fire in the fireplace, as he did a few times every winter, usually with spectacularly bad results. "Is this about the board meeting tonight?"

"You know?"

"I keep track of what's on the agenda. It's a hard habit to break."

Mom stopped in the middle of unbuttoning her coat and looked at him with a sort of dull incredulity. "Not again."

Johnny nodded. "Again. And they're going to do it before we can even get to States."

"Did you win Regionals?"

"Yeah," Mike said. "They kicked ass."

"Michael!"

"Well, they did. I think we ought to have a party or something."

"Not on a Monday," Mom said absently, ruffling Johnny's hair. "I'm so proud of you."

Johnny pulled away with the compulsory distaste, even though he didn't really mind. " 'Tweren't nothing, ma'am," he said.

Mom freed herself of her coat and sat down at the kitchen counter. She looked at Dad. "So what's the scoop this time?"

"Money problems."

"How can they have money problems?"

"I don't know. Most of them are incredibly bad businessmen, but Gina Fairgate ought to know what she's doing. Someone screwed up, and I want to know who."

"Then you really believe them? You don't think it's just another pot shot at the kids?"

"You think they'd lie?" Johnny asked.

"Of course they'd lie," Mike said sagely. "They're politicians. Look what they did to Dad last time."

Johnny sighed. He remembered it well enough; Mrs. Fairgate had accused Dad of child abuse. Johnny himself had been held up as the victim, by virtue of an arm that had been broken when Dad tried to catch him from falling down the stairs. His own protestations on the subject had been labeled "denial" and summarily dismissed.

"I believe them," Dad said, ignoring his sons' exchange. "School finances are a matter of public record. They can't very well lie about it."

"Did you check?"

236

"I called Herb Tellanski earlier."

Mom reached down and pulled off the thick socks she wore under her boots, revealing a stockinged foot with four runs around the toes. Johnny couldn't remember ever seeing her wear stockings with a whole foot intact at the end of the day. "Herb Tellanski couldn't add two and two with a calculator," she said.

"Maybe not, but he was always pretty good at greater than and less than. And the total budget is greater than the amount of money we have to pay for it."

"So what do we do?" Johnny interjected, feeling a little left out of his own conference. "Just lay down and die?"

Dad turned to him, a flash of his more usual humor in the green eyes he'd passed on to both of his sons. "If you die as well as you did in that skit, that might get us someplace."

Johnny grabbed his throat and started to go into his death scene, but Mike pulled him up by the collar of his shirt. "Not here, Spazmoid. We've all seen it. About a hundred times."

"I can do it at the meeting," Johnny offered.

Mom laughed. "It would be entertaining, but I don't think it would get us very far."

"But we have to do *something*."

"What for?" Johnny was surprised to see that Mike looked serious, even speculative. "I mean, what's the point, really? We can pack the spaz off to St. Stephen's, if you guys can't teach him yourselves. Although I think you've done a pretty good job with me."

"I think we have, too," Mom said gently.

Johnny kept his mouth shut, because he knew that there was an unspoken truth in the house: Mike was a wonderful brother, a great athlete, and a good student, but he wasn't as smart as Johnny himself was, and they all knew it. This had been a painful thing to acknowledge, because Johnny adored his brother, but it was true. Even with a four-year age difference,

237

Johnny could run mental rings around Mike, and had been doing so since he was eight. He easily aced classes that Mike had found challenging, and was only a year behind him in math—and bucking for an early finish at that.

The last thing he expected was for Mike to speak the unspoken, but that was what happened. "I know Johnny's special," he said. "And I know that the way you've taught me wouldn't be enough for him, at least not the specific stuff. But you're with him, all the time. You know what he needs better than those assholes on the school board."

Johnny squirmed uncomfortably, hoping that one of his parents would say something to change directions. Anything he could say right now would sound like he was agreeing.

Mom sighed. "Michael, if we were going through your school years again right now, I don't think we'd be able to give you all we did."

"Taxes are up," Dad said. "Your mom's had to take a bigger caseload. And we just lost an associate professor in the department, so I'm teaching double as it is."

"What about St. Stephen's?"

"If it comes to that, it comes to that."

"Uh-uh," Johnny said. "I don't want to go there. It wouldn't be fair."

"Fair to whom?"

"The other kids. If the test scores go down, it'll make the school look worse for them."

Dad rubbed his temples and considered this. "I'm glad you're concerned, but I'm not going to let you throw your mind away for your friends."

Johnny looked at his feet.

"I want us to go to the meeting tonight," Dad said. "We'll go as a family, alright?" There was general, if sullen, agreement. "I don't know if there's anything we can do or say that will change things, but we can definitely put on a show."

238

Johnny smiled. No one spoke.

"All right," Mom said after a while. "Now that that's settled, I believe I told your brother to pick up a gift for you."

Mike smiled wickedly and pulled out a looseleaf folder. "Your homework, Spazmoid. I went around to your teachers while you were playing games with your little friends today. You didn't think a little crisis would get you out of geometry, did you?"

Calling the two strangers on the list they'd made on the bus was one of the hardest things Sarah had ever done. The others had been nice enough to give her two kids who were almost as shy and unpopular as she herself was—pimply Simon Ferkler and Neil Kiernan (who had a harelip), both from the balsa wood team—so that she would be less intimidated talking to them, but it didn't really help. She found their numbers in the phone book quickly enough, but actually making the calls was another matter. What if they didn't even know who she was? Or if they did, and hung up laughing?

But she'd promised, and she made the calls. She was perversely pleased to find that they were even less secure than she was on the phone. They both agreed to come to the meeting.

Now, the hard part.

The word "gifted" had never been mentioned in the Easton household, and Sarah wasn't sure what the reaction to it would be.

Oh, her parents had gone along with the others in refusing to let her take the tests last year, but the entire comment on the subject had been, "The tests are unfair and biased, anyway." And they hadn't objected to her being in the program, but they always seemed uncomfortable discussing it with her.

They seemed, in fact, uncomfortable with the entire concept of Sarah's intelligence—or, for that matter, their own.

239

It was understandable, she supposed. All the philosophers they liked were into the strength of the masses against the elite, and the idea of an above-average mind *was* drawing awfully close to elitism, or at least it was easy to see it that way. There'd been enough talk of such a connection that Sarah would've had to be blind and deaf not to know about it.

So it was with some trepidation that she approached her parents about the board meeting.

It couldn't have started on a worse note.

"Is that makeup on your face?" Mom asked, blinking her eyes in the slow, deliberate way she had when she was getting angry.

Sarah was caught entirely off-guard. In the tangle of the afternoon, she'd forgotten all about it. "I . . ." she started. "Well, we did a play today, and I put a beard on my face with rubber cement, and it left a red mark, and Chrissi Martinez said she had some stuff to cover it up, and then—I just wanted to see what it would look like to wear, you know, mascara and stuff."

"And?"

"And what?"

"What did it look like?"

Sarah bit her lip—the waxy taste of lipstick had disappeared hours ago—and considered her options. She wanted to tell the truth, as she had when she'd first put it on, but she wasn't sure that it would be a good idea to cross Mom's ideas on a day she needed help.

"What did what look like?" Fred asked, coming into the kitchen with a tuna sandwich in one hand.

"It seems we've been playing with war paint," Mom said.

"Turn around." Fred put his finger under Sarah's chin and tilted her face up to look. His eyes grew concerned. "I'm not too smart about this stuff," he said, "but I thought the black stuff went on the eyelashes, not the cheeks."

240

"It doesn't go *anywhere*," Mom grumbled.

Sarah answered Fred. "It was on my eyelashes before. It looked pretty good."

"I bet it did. I always said you had pretty eyes."

"Fred, I don't want her getting obsessed with this . . ." Mom struggled for a bad enough word, gave up, and pointed vaguely at Sarah's face.

"I think Sarah's old enough to make up her own mind about that, Rainie," Fred said absently. "I'm wondering how it got from her eyelashes down to her cheeks. Have you asked yet?"

Mom's anger faded abruptly into concern. "No, I haven't. I'm sorry. Here you've been crying, and I'm worried about a little mascara. I'm sorry."

"It's okay. We can talk about that later," Sarah offered. She didn't want to promise never to do it again, although those were the words that came first to her mind. The idea that Fred would be on her side if she decided to defy Mom had not occurred to her, and it deserved some thought. She had no desire to pit them against each other, but at the same time the idea that they *could* disagree about something like that was heartening. Maybe there were other things they would be open to. Maybe she could go back to Pigeon's church someday, and get her throat blessed.

But that was a long way off, if it would ever be, and right now she didn't need to wonder about it.

"Did the game go bad?" Fred asked.

Sarah shook her head. "No, we won."

"So what's with the tears?"

She explained as briefly as she could, willing herself not to cry again. Her parents wouldn't mind (that had never been one of their hang-ups), but she couldn't think of any use that more tears would serve.

She looked back and forth between them when she finished, trying to judge their expressions. They had both listened silently, even stoically, and their faces revealed little of what they might be thinking. Sarah had long ago noticed that in her family the deep Anglo-Saxon-Puritan roots were only visible in anger, when the warm and even hot emotions were submerged beneath a thick layer of ice, but she had never been good at judging where the anger was directed. "Will you come?" she finally asked.

Mom shook her head, surprised. "Of *course* we'll come. Why wouldn't we?"

"I thought you might think it was elitist or something."

"I'll tell you what's elitist," Fred said coolly. "Elitist is letting money make decisions over talent."

"But all the books in the living room, the ones you like—"

"Just because you agree with some basic idea doesn't mean you have to swallow everything that goes with it whole," Mom said.

Sarah felt the same disorienting mental shift that she'd felt that afternoon, when she first looked in the mirror and saw the face she knew belonged to her. She'd invested a lot in a particular viewpoint, even though it had rendered her own feelings invalid on more than one occasion, and it was a dizzy, terrifying feeling to be loosed from it.

Imagine all the people, she thought, and this time the image came without the muumuus and flowers. She saw people in business suits and blue jeans, people in a church and people on a march, people on the stage and people in a boardroom, people toeing both sides of a thousand different lines. None of them carried a chasm within them.

Mom sat down at the table and pulled a spiral notebook out from under the lazy Susan and a pen from behind her ear. "Now, where should we start?"

"Children's rights?" Fred suggested.

"No. Maybe someplace else, but I don't think there's a real

acceptance that children have rights here, so it's not a very good jump-off point.''

"How about the right to the pursuit of happiness?''

"That's not a law. That's the D of I.''

"No kidding. But they're big-time flag wavers.''

"They'll say if the other kids can be happy without programs, we can,'' Sarah tried.

Mom nodded and doodled on the paper.

Fred sat down in one of the other chairs. "Wasn't it Tom Jefferson who said 'There's nothing more unequal than treating unequal people equally'?''

"Yeah, that was him. But I think 'unequal' was a bad word choice. It makes people defensive.''

"You're right. Besides, it's too easy to misuse that.''

"Good point.''

"How about freedom of assembly?'' Sarah suggested. "That's law, isn't it?''

"That's a good try, but I don't think it applies to classes,'' Mom said. "Does it, honey?''

Fred shook his head. "I like the way you're thinking, though. Know your rights.''

"Wait a minute,'' Mom said, her eyes widening. "What about the special ed laws, the ones they were going to invoke last year?''

"Yes!'' Fred exclaimed. "That's it!''

Sarah laughed. "You guys are really into this stuff, aren't you?''

"Honey,'' Fred told her, "you're on our turf, now.''

Pigeon hadn't had any intention of telling his grandmother about the meeting. She'd been sick, and she was old, and her battles should've been long over.

But when he came home after the long, twisting after-afterschool bus ride, the Spiegals were sitting in the living room

243

(Jason and Erin were watching *Quincy*), and his grandmother was dressed in her best "going-out" suit.

"The Spiegals have been nice enough to offer us a ride to the meeting tonight," Gram said. "I thought it would only be fitting to invite them to dinner first. I hope you don't mind."

"We're going to the meeting, too," Mrs. Spiegal said. "I'd like to get the kids back into a public school, and if we can get a commitment out of the board . . ." She shook her head from side to side.

"That's great."

"I think it would be cool not to wear a tie to school," Jason said, putting his hand to his throat as if he were afraid his hated St. Stephen's uniform had reappeared after hours.

"Or a skirt in the winter," Erin added. "My knees are all chapped."

Pigeon's eyes wandered down to Erin's knees, but she was wearing jeans now and he couldn't see the chap marks. He felt himself blush; he hadn't really been looking for marks, just an excuse to look at Erin, who was even prettier than Chrissi, in Pigeon's humble opinion. "What's for dinner?" he asked.

"I'm showing Mrs. Spiegal a proper Polish dinner," Gram said. "We're having *galumskis* and pierogi . . ."

"How about a couple of knishes and gefilte fish?" Jason said under his breath, and Pigeon shot him a warning look. He didn't know what either of those things were, but he had a feeling they were related to things it was better Gram didn't know. There was no need to risk anything tonight. Jason shrugged.

"Could you help me in the kitchen, Peter?" Gram asked.

Pigeon followed her into the tiny room (really just an alcove separated from the rest of the trailer by a counter) and squeezed himself behind the table as she started pulling things

244

out of the oven. "How did you find out about the meeting?" he asked.

Gram poked her finger at the *galumskis*—rolls of stuffed cabbage—to test the temperature. "Mrs. Spiegal was in town, returning a book to the library. She met one of your friends, the Irish boy, I think—"

"Sean?" Pigeon mentally added the names on Sean's phone list to his own. Great. Four calls to make, and there was company.

"I think so. He was with his mother, and they were looking at school records. The mother told Mrs. Spiegal about the meeting, and Mrs. Spiegal told me." She sniffed at the *galumskis* and put them on the table beside Pigeon. "These will do. Put them on a platter, please."

"Sure, Gram."

"You weren't going to tell me about it, were you?"

"No."

"Why not?"

"You haven't been feeling good, Gram. It's cold out, and it's a long trip into town, and the meeting's going to be mean. I don't want you to get sick."

"I'm *your* guardian, Peter. You are not mine."

Pigeon wasn't sure if he was being reprimanded or consoled; Gram tended to do both in the same curt tone.

One dry, twisted hand came to rest on his arm. "I know what you're frightened of, Peter. I know you need me. That's why I don't do things I don't have to. But this is something that has to be done."

Pigeon sniffed the air deeply. "I think the pierogi are done."

"Do you need any more help, Mrs. Janowski?" Mrs. Spiegal asked from the other room. She could no doubt hear everything, but she was politely aloof.

245

"No one else can fit in here," Gram answered, cheerfully enough.

"Thanks anyway," Pigeon said.

"I'll take care of the pierogi," Gram said. "You go set up the card table. Put it at the end of the coffee table. We should be able to seat six."

Pigeon nodded, and retrieved the card table from behind the television. Jason helped him assemble it. There wasn't room at the end of the coffee table, so they put it in the center of the room, deciding in some unspoken way that the adults would sit around the coffee table on the sofa, and the kids would face them from three sides of the card table. Pigeon set out glasses and mugs.

"My mom brought wine," Jason said. When Pigeon only got three wineglasses, Jason looked at him oddly. "What about us?"

"I'm not allowed. Are you guys?"

"Yeah, sure."

"Right," Erin said. "We're allowed to taste, not to have whole glasses. Jay's just a budding alkie."

"You're such a twerp."

"You're the one who's being a twerp," Pigeon said. "You want to come to my school, you better shape up."

"You better shape up whether you go to his school or not," Dr. Spiegal said from the couch.

"Okay, Dad." Jason offered a pout that was about as real as Johnny's usual theatrics.

Pigeon watched the interplay with a stab of jealousy that he hadn't felt in a long time, mixed with a grief that always had a way of surprising him. He imagined himself as Jason, goofing around, with his dad to catch him up if he pushed a joke too far. The others would all be bringing their parents tonight, even the ones who had troubles. Pigeon knew they would all come, except maybe Sean's dad who was far away. They'd overcome whatever difficulties there were and come to the meeting to defend their kids.

His own parents would not.

Oh, Gram would come, and the Spiegals, who were practically family sometimes, would come, but it wasn't the same.

He felt suddenly very alone in the crowded trailer.

"Pidge?" Jason said quietly beside him. The spoiled child he'd been a moment ago seemed to have disappeared; there was a genuine concern in his voice. "Are you okay?"

Pigeon nodded.

"Lie." There was no doubt in the assessment. Jason had known Pigeon longer than anyone else outside his family, and there was no lying to him, at least not without getting caught.

"Okay, yeah. Lie."

"Anything I can do?"

"No."

Erin appeared with the tray of cabbage rolls. "What's going on?"

"Pigeon's got a malaise of the soul."

"Maybe some *ga*—whatever they are—will help," she said, then offered a smile that did more for Pigeon's heart than any food on the planet.

He returned it.

Jason wiggled his eyebrows wisely. "So *she's* the secret?" He shook his head. "Pidge, you don't know what you're wishing for."

Erin giggled and set the platter down.

"What, no heated denial?"

Pigeon shrugged, and started spooning out the *galumskis*.

Mama was not especially sympathetic at first.

She had her first real date since the divorce, with a guy named Marcus O'Something—there were so many O'Somethings in Penworth that Chrissi had a hard time sorting them—

and a school board meeting wasn't exactly the top of the list of romantic places she knew.

"I said I'd go, didn't I?" Mama said, soaking a cotton ball in baby oil to remove her evening-out makeup.

"Yes, but, Mama—"

"Do you want me to be thrilled about it, Chrissi? Is that it?"

"No, but you could at least pretend it's important to you."

Mama took a deep breath and rested the cotton ball on her cheek. "It *is* important to me. Your education is *very* important to me. This meeting just couldn't have come on a worse night."

"I know."

"I needed to do this. I needed to prove to myself that I was still . . . That I still had it, you know?"

Chrissi nodded. It really wasn't fair to Mama, when you thought about it. It wasn't her fault that the school board was mostly made up of jerks, but she was the one who was paying for it with a night that should've been part of her healing after the divorce. "I'm sorry," she said. "I—you don't have to go. Go out with Marcus."

"I'm going to the meeting, Chrissi," she said dully.

"No, really, Mama," Chrissi insisted. "It's just a Little Thing. I shouldn't have bothered you with it."

Mama turned and looked at her oddly. "Telling me about a school problem is not bothering me, and it is *definitely* not a 'Little Thing.' Where did you get that idea?"

"When we were in counseling, they said—"

"I doubt they were talking about school. Are there any other 'Little Things' like this that you haven't been telling me about?"

Chrissi swallowed hard and dared herself to say something. "I wish you hadn't, like, trashed Daddy's chair."

Mistake. Mama's eyes flared. "I meant in school. At home,

248

you have to get used to things."

"What, like you've been doing?" It was out before Chrissi knew she intended to say it. She snapped her mouth shut, but it was too late.

"What do you mean by that?"

"Nothing."

"Wrong." Mama set the cotton ball down on her dressing table. An oily stain spread out on the cloth cover. "If you have a problem with something, tell me."

"I just told you one. You told me I had to get used to it."

"I don't know what to *do* about that. Your father and I *are* divorced. I didn't want it to happen any more than you did, but your father had different ideas. That's not going to change. We have to make a break."

"You don't have to throw out his stuff. That's how I remember him."

"He's not dead, Chrissi." Mama stood up and walked to the window. "He lives across town with whatshername. You can go over there whenever you want to."

"Her name's Jenny, Mama," Chrissi said, bored. "You know that. And it's not the same. I meant, like, remembering him when he was here with us."

Mama came over and put a warm hand on her cheek. "But don't you understand, Chrissi? That's just what we can't do, either of us. We have to accept what *is*, and the more we worry about what used to be, the more it's going to hurt. It's like rubbing salt in a cut."

"Yes, Mama."

"There you go." She brushed a strand of Chrissi's hair off her forehead. "Your face is hot. Why don't you go splash some cold water on it? You'll feel better."

"Okay."

She closed Mama's bedroom door lightly and went down the hall to the bathroom. The cold water *did* feel good on her

249

face, and she took off her shirt to splash it on the rest of her body. She clasped her hands behind her head for a moment to do her nightly check, and decided she wasn't any closer to the low-cut tops than she'd been this morning, or yesterday, or the day before.

Maybe you're going to be eleven forever.

She rejected this consciously, of course; it was crazy talk. The only way to be eleven forever would be to die now.

And yet . . .

There was something inside of Chrissi that knew a little more about the world than she admitted to herself, and it had been that something that had spoken to her. It told her that home would always be as much a time as a place, the time when she invented herself, and it told her that the time was now and the place was here. There was life before now, and there would be life after now, but this was where the dividing line would always stand, and the part of her that she was looking at in the mirror, the pretty girl with big eyes and small breasts, was always going to be the self she carried inside.

Why now?

Because this is the first time you've needed *a self, and if you don't find one, you'll go crazy.*

Mama's door opened down the hall, and Chrissi heard the quick thump of her low-heeled shoes as she went downstairs, then her muffled voice as she spoke to someone on the telephone—probably Marcus, to call the date off.

Chrissi put her shirt back on slowly, relishing the spread of warmth as it covered her skin, and went down to join her.

Mama made hot dogs and macaroni and cheese while Chrissi made her three phone calls to other members of the robot team. All of them promised to try and come. Mitch O'Shandlin suggested that they send the robot after Mrs. Fairgate to suck off all her jewelry. Mama dished the food out onto paper plates.

250

They ate dinner as they watched the news from the living-room floor, and didn't speak until after Mama had finished the dishes.

"Chrissi?" she called from the kitchen.

Chrissi turned away from the television, which was now showing a sitcom that she couldn't seem to focus on. "What, Mama?"

"Could you come in here?"

She got up dreamily, and found Mama at the table, with two mugs of tea sitting out for them. She sat down in the empty chair. "What is it?"

"I'm sorry I threw out your father's chair," Mama said. "It's too late to get it back."

"I know."

Mama stirred her tea intently, watching the spoon circle around the edge of the mug. "Chrissi," she said, "I want you to promise me you'll remember something from now on."

"What?"

"As far as we're concerned, there's no such thing as a Little Thing."

"But you said—"

"I know what I said. I was wrong." She shrugged and shook her head. "You didn't get divorced. I did."

Chrissi looked away. It didn't make everything better. It didn't make anything better, actually. But it was a start.

CHAPTER
NINETEEN

The library had been Kathleen's idea.

During a quick meal at a downtown restaurant (creatively named "Joe's Restaurant"), Sam explained his theory as clearly as he could.

"Do you have any idea how serious an accusation this is?" she asked.

Sam nodded.

"And you're sure this isn't just a last straw you're grasping at to save your class?"

"I'm sure."

"How?"

"You want the figures?" Al had commented, offering the handlink.

"I can't tell you. But I know I'm right."

"Well," she said, "if you're right, there'll be discrepancies in the town records. There's no way in hell we'll be able to prove where the money went tonight, but maybe if we can show that they've been screwing around with the books it'll be enough."

So they left the restaurant and went to the public library, a building with which Sam was utterly delighted. It was small, but well stocked. The bookshelves were wooden, stained to a deep mahogany color to match the chairs and the long tables where people worked quietly. The ceiling lights were bulbs, not fluorescents, which made for a more natural, cozier space. There was a braided rug in the foyer and an old (and unfortunately unused) fireplace in the lounge area. Sam wished he'd come in earlier in the Leap.

He vaguely remembered Kathleen talking to a pretty brunette woman (who he would not recognize at the school board meeting later, although she would be there with Pigeon and his grandmother and her own two children) while the librarian was retrieving the school board finances and he himself was browsing a shelf of new acquisitions. That had been over an hour ago.

Now, they were sitting at a small round table in a corner of the main room, surrounded by unnoticed cookbooks and pattern books, examining row after row of figures from the school budget ledgers.

"There," Al said, pointing at another discrepancy. "Tell her to check the receipt for . . . uh . . ." He squinted at the handlink. "For phys ed supplies."

"Check the phys ed supplies," Sam advised.

"How do you know?"

"I told you—"

"You can't tell me." Kathleen turned her attention to the folder of receipts, and rooted through the papers. "There is no receipt for this. Maybe they lost it."

"Sure," Al said. "Just like they lost the receipts for the new office typewriter and the Xerox machine."

"They didn't lose it," Sam said.

"I just can't believe—"

"That Mrs. Fairgate would steal," Sam finished. "I know."

"That she'd steal?" Kathleen repeated. "No, *that* I believe. I can't believe she'd do it this *stupidly*." She added the phys ed line to the tally sheet she was keeping.

"Maybe she didn't mean to."

"What?" Al and Kathleen said together.

"Well . . . maybe she thought it would just be one time, and she covered it up fast, figuring she'd pay it back. But no one caught it, and she didn't pay it back, and the next time it was easier. Maybe it just sort of happened."

Kathleen looked down at the folder of receipts. "How many times?"

"Ziggy says there are fourteen unaccounted deposits in Regina Fairgate's bank account over the last two years," Al said. "You want to know what the total comes to?" Sam shook his head; Al told him anyway. "Twenty-three thousand dollars. She stole twenty-three thousand dollars from a bunch of kids." Al swore softly in Italian for a minute. "And you want to let her get away with 'But, Your Honor, I didn't mean to do it'?"

Sam didn't answer. Motive was important, of course, but he'd never thought that letting a mistake get out of hand was an excuse for making it in the first place. However the embezzlement had started, it had ended with a serious consequence for students whose only crime was being in a program that Regina Fairgate knew would be an easy target for a cover-up. That was not something to be taken lightly.

"What about this one?" Kathleen was pointing to an expenditure line for a six-hundred-dollar oven repair in the home ec classroom.

Al looked at it. "No, that's legit. Some kid cut the wires that led to the burners. That really takes a genius, huh?"

"No," Sam said. "I remember that. It's real."

"Sam!" Al put his finger on the line under the oven work. "How about the one right under it?"

"You think she bothered to steal fifteen dollars?"

Al shrugged.

254

"Yeah."

"Jesus." Kathleen riffled through the receipts, found nothing, and recorded the line with a disgusted look on her face.

"Sean?" A short, balding man with a pretty blond woman on his arm was standing behind Al, looking at the O'Connors with curiosity. "I saw your car in the church parking lot across the street, and I know you're not Baptist, so I thought you might be over here."

"Small towns," Al said. Sam couldn't tell if his tone was derisory or just disbelieving. "This is Chrissi's father, by the way. Chet Martinez. He's the e-in-c of the local paper."

"Hi, Mr. Martinez," Sam said. "Do you know my mom?"

"Kathleen O'Connor," Kathleen said, extending her hand.

He shook it. "Chet Martinez. And my wife, Jenny." He looked back toward the main desk. "The librarian told me you have the school board records. My ex-wife tells me they've got a surprise vote planned for tonight. I was just going to send one of my reporters, but Ann thinks Chrissi would want me there."

"She's right," Sam said.

"I suppose she is."

"Why'd it have to happen this week?" the woman, Jenny, asked, with a tired smile.

"Florida's been around for a few centuries," Chet said. "I'm sure it'll still be there if we leave next week."

"Florida?" Sam repeated.

"We were supposed to leave for our honeymoon an hour ago."

"I feel like such a bitch being mad about it," Jenny said.

"It's not your fight," Chet said.

"Well, I'm glad you're coming to the meeting," Kathleen said. "We may have a surprise or two of our own for Gina Fairgate."

"Really?"

255

"Mm-hmm. I've been looking at some of our equipment purchases over the last year."

"Stover tried that already, remember? I covered it last year. They'll say that equipment is a one-time expense. The program's ongoing. Believe me, it's been done."

"Have you ever done a story on all the equipment the school's been buying lately?" Sam asked.

"What?"

"Let's just say, that's a story I'd be interested in reading," Kathleen said, pushing the pile of papers across the table to him.

Mr. Martinez pulled his chair up to the table and started reading.

Chrissi and her mother arrived at the Penworth town hall for the school board meeting twenty minutes early, but they weren't the first to get there. Actually, except for Sean, Chrissi thought, they might be the last.

The room was nearly full. Chrissi could count at least eleven families. The Metzes had taken the second pew (well, *row*; Chrissi didn't think the wooden benches were called pews outside of church), and Sarah and her parents were across the aisle from them. Sarah's folks were carrying signs that said, "Education is for everyone" and "A student is only as good as her best teacher." Chrissi noticed that they'd passed one across the aisle to Mrs. Metz, which she couldn't see completely. The quote on it was attributed to Thomas Jefferson. Pigeon was sitting with an old woman who Chrissi guessed was his grandmother, and a family she didn't know at all (the boy was cute, though). The long table where the board would meet was still empty; the only thing on it was the tabletop podium with the president's gavel resting on it. Coach Stover was wandering through the room, his pipe clenched tightly in his teeth. He stopped occasionally to talk to each of the families, and stare at the table with a certain discernible dread.

Chrissi waved to him, but he didn't see her.

Mama leaned over her shoulder. "Do you know these people?" she asked.

Chrissi nodded, and pointed each family out to her.

"Is there somebody we should sit with?"

"I don't know. Maybe the Metzes. Don't you know them?"

"I might have met them once when we first came here. Where are Sean and his mother?"

"Probably just running late or something." Chrissi didn't want to think too much about where Sean was; he'd been acting so weird over the last couple of days that she didn't want to make a guess as to whether he'd show or not. Of course, he'd been really serious about the program and everything, but still . . .

"Chrissi!" Johnny hailed her. "Come on over here."

"Well," Mama said. "There you go."

"Yeah." Chrissi led the way down the aisle, and stopped between the Eastons and the Metzes. Sarah smiled a hello; the makeup was gone, but she'd left the natural part in her hair. Chrissi smiled back. There was still time to get her used to makeup and clothes that weren't, like, totally behind the times. If she could stick with the hair all day, it was a good enough start.

"Where's your boyfriend?" Johnny asked.

"I don't know."

"He'll be here," Sarah said.

Chrissi felt a twinge of jealousy. She didn't know what Sean had spent so much time talking to Sarah about on the bus, and now Sarah was talking like she knew him inside out. "Unless his mother's sick again."

No one said much.

"Aren't we going to invite Pigeon to come up here?" Chrissi asked.

"I already talked to him. They've got to stay back there.

257

That's where the heat is. His gram, you know?''

"Oh, yeah. I forgot.'' The town hall was over a hundred fifty years old, and the heat circulation was nonexistent. Chrissi still had her coat on, and hadn't completely warmed up from being outside, but she could tell how much warmer the back of the room was than the front.

Johnny shook his head dismissively. "Well, anyway—''

"Oh, my God,'' Mama said. She was looking toward the back of the room. "Wonders never cease.''

Chrissi looked up. Daddy and Jenny were standing in the doorway. Daddy's press card was pinned to his coat, and he was carrying a tape recorder and a camera. Jenny was dressed in a business suit that made her look a lot older than she ever had in Chrissi's presence. She looked out of place and a little embarrassed to be there.

They spotted Chrissi, and came forward.

"Hi, Daddy. I . . . I thought you were going on your honeymoon.''

Jenny smiled tightly. "So did I.''

Daddy bent over and kissed Chrissi's cheek. "Your mother called. She told me what was going on here.'' He looked at Mama. "Why are you so surprised, Annie? I told you I'd come.''

"I didn't want to make any promises for you. You seem to have enough trouble keeping the ones you make for yourself.''

Daddy's eyes were cross, then he looked back at Chrissi. "I wish you'd told me yourself. I'd never let my little girl down.''

Chrissi didn't believe him, not really, but she believed that he believed himself, and that was good. "Thanks, Daddy,'' she said. "Maybe it'll scare them a little to have the paper here.''

"You never know.''

Jenny touched his shoulder and he stood up. "I'm going to

258

find a place to sit," she said. He waved her off impatiently, and she headed for the back of the room.

"Aren't you sitting with your wife, Chet?" Mama asked sweetly.

"I'm going to tell you guys a secret," Daddy said, leaning into the group.

"What?"

"There's going to be a story here tonight. A big one, at least for this place."

"How do you know?" Chrissi asked.

"I ran into your boyfriend and his mom at the library," he said cryptically. "I want pictures of this."

"What *is* it, Daddy?"

He shook his head. "No. This one's Kathleen's scoop. I'm just going to back her up. We'll just have to keep the board distracted until she gets here." He spied a place on the balcony that would give a good angle on the podium. "Now, if you folks will excuse me, I'm going to go set up." He hugged Chrissi again, and set off for the stairs.

Jenny stood and craned her neck. She started to say something, then sat down again, frustrated. Mama gave her a vindictive shark's smile that managed to be oddly commiserating at the same time.

Chrissi didn't pay attention to either of them. Mama and Jenny would never be bosom buddies, and that was okay. She watched Daddy come out of the stairwell and set up his tripod on the balcony. Some things would never change, and this was one of them. Whether he was concerned about Chrissi, or sorry to be missing his honeymoon, or mad at Mama, Daddy was a newspaperman, and where there was a story, it came first. Sometimes it was really irritating, but Chrissi loved him for it.

"May I have your attention please?"

Mrs. Fairgate was standing at the podium, holding her hands

259

in the air. A few other board members had taken their seats.

The chatter in the room died down slowly, and Chrissi and her mother slid into the bench behind the Metzes.

"It's always good to see such a good turnout at our open meetings," Mrs. Fairgate said. "But you should all know that nothing on our agenda tonight is subject to change."

"We have a right to be heard," Sarah's mother called out.

"As long as you follow the proper rules of order."

"What, like taking the vote before the meeting?" Mr. Metz said.

Mrs. Fairgate looked at him harshly, then banged the gavel officiously. "Can we come to order, please?"

"You've got to go now, Sam." Al was standing impatiently near the table. "You've got enough to go on, but if you miss the vote, you're dead in the water."

Sam nodded. "Mom, it's getting late."

"I know. I just want to be sure about this."

"You're *not* sure?"

Kathleen looked at the tally sheet. They'd verified nine of Al's fourteen deposits, to the cent, although of course knowing it wasn't enough to convict her. "I don't know, Sean. This is really serious."

"Yeah, it's serious!" Al repeated. "It's Sean's education, for God's sake."

Sam put his hand over Kathleen's. "Mom, look. You know in your heart that we're right, don't you?"

"Yes."

"And we aren't pressing any charges tonight."

"I know."

"Don't you think it's our right to get some questions answered?"

"I know, but—"

"Mom, it's the only shot we have. We've got to take it."

260

"This just feels so low."

"Do you think that would stop Fairgate?" Al asked.

"It *is* low," Sam said. "But it's not as low as what she's been doing."

Kathleen looked up at the clock on the wall, watched the second hand sweeping around it, then looked at Sam again. "Is this enough?" she asked.

"It'll have to be," Sam said. "It's the best we can do."

Al met them outside at the car. He looked distracted. "Sam, this is your show now. And Kathleen's. Ziggy says the chances to succeed are about ninety-eight percent."

Sam nodded.

"You might Leap right out of the meeting."

"It's possible."

"What's possible?" Kathleen asked.

"Uh . . . to win this."

"Who are you trying to convince?"

"Both of us, I guess."

"Sam?" Al said impatiently. "Can you do this without me? I mean, I've told you everything we know." Sam looked at him blankly. "I want to say good-bye to Sean," he explained. "I don't want him to Leap out without saying good-bye, okay?"

Kathleen got in the driver's seat and shut the door. She was looking more alive and involved with her life with every second. Well, she said she'd been spoiling for a fight.

Al was still waiting for a response—a little impatiently, but a far cry from the days when he would leave the Imaging Chamber to take a phone call from Tina.

Sam smiled. "Yeah," he said. "It's okay. Try to come back, if you can."

"I will."

Al opened the Door and disappeared.

"Come on, Sean!" Kathleen urged. "You're going to freeze to death out there if you don't hurry up."

CHAPTER
TWENTY

The meeting was going well, but Chrissi thought that Mrs. Fairgate probably didn't think so. She looked like she was about to cry, to tell the truth.

Daddy had said that Sean's mother had something to say here that would change everything, so everyone was trying to buy her time. Coach Stover was standing now, up front, in the middle of the aisle.

"Do you have any idea how hard these kids have worked to win 'Homer' today?" he asked. "They beat some strong teams. They were *good*. It's not fair to cut them off at the knees like this. It's just not right."

One of the other school board people—Chrissi didn't know this one at all—stood up. "I don't think it's right that they get special treatment anyway."

Mrs. Fairgate was a good enough politician to know that it was a bad idea for him to bring up a fight that he'd already lost at a crisis point, and she waved him down impatiently. "This vote is not a judgment on the children, Mr. Stover," she said. "I know they're all bright, and if I hadn't known it before, they certainly proved it today. They did us proud at the contest."

I wonder if she even knows the name of the contest, Chrissi thought.

"You sure have a funny way of being proud," Sarah's father interrupted. There was a muted cheer from the crowd, as there had been at every successful interruption.

"This is *not* a personal issue."

"Like hell it's not."

"Mr. Easton, this is not a demonstration or a sit-in. This is a meeting of a respectable school board, and I ask you to use appropriate language in the presence of children."

Chrissi bit back a laugh. The language on any school bus trip was worse.

"The woman's concerned about language!" Mr. Easton stood and faced the rest of the room. "They're cutting our kids off at the knees, and the woman's worried about their tender ears."

"Seems to me she ought to be more worried about what's between them," Pigeon's grandmother said from her place in the back row.

This time the cheer was louder. Gram (as Chrissi herself was beginning to think of her) was a corker, and everyone liked it when she talked.

Mrs. Fairgate smiled tightly. "As I was saying, this is not motivated by any personal animus toward your children. The budget will simply not cover the program any longer."

"So we're, like, getting screwed because you guys can't handle your money?" Johnny said.

Mrs. Fairgate answered him by talking to his father. She had, so far, not addressed any child in the room. "Mr. Metz, if you can't control your son, I'm afraid I'll have to ask you to leave."

Mr. Metz nodded, and gave Johnny a sharp look. Johnny lapsed into sullen silence, which Chrissi predicted would last about two minutes.

"May I speak?"

Chrissi turned to see Jenny standing up in the back row, a little way from Pigeon. She looked very young and very alone.

"Certainly," Mrs. Fairgate said. "That's why we have these open meetings."

Jenny swallowed hard. "I . . . I'm just not clear on why it has to be the gifted and talented program that you cut. Couldn't it be something else? Like . . ." A dim light went on in her mind. "Like maybe the football team or something. That costs more."

Oh, well, Chrissi thought. It had been a good try.

Mrs. Fairgate spoke down at her. "The football team is self-supporting, with tickets and sales programs."

Jenny sat down miserably, and Chrissi felt bad for her. This wasn't her fight, and she'd done her best to help out. It hadn't been much of a contribution, but it was a nice gesture. Chrissi stood up on the bench and flashed a thumbs-up at her. Mama pulled her down by her elbow and gave her a stern look.

"Now," Mrs. Fairgate said, "if there are no further questions . . ."

And that was when the door opened, and Mrs. O'Connor and Sean blew in on the winter wind.

"I have a question, Gina," Kathleen said.

Sam closed the door behind them, then stood at her side. If this were a court of law, he wouldn't be very sure of his position, but here, in a public forum, they had enough to get the wheels turning. Now it was just a matter of forcing Mrs. Fairgate's hand.

"Well, good evening, Mrs. O'Connor. I'm glad to see you could make it."

"Yeah, I'm sure you're ecstatic." She looked at Sam. "And my son is not invisible."

Mrs. Fairgate's smile widened. It looked like it was about to shatter. "Hello, Sean."

"Hey, Mrs. Fairgate," Sam said. He toyed with the idea of calling her "Gina"—he was feeling cocky enough to do it—but he decided against it.

She nodded nervously and shuffled some papers on her podium. "We're just about ready to vote."

"Where did the money go?" Kathleen asked pleasantly.

"I beg your pardon?"

"You heard me. There was enough money in the school treasury to pay for all the programs all year. What happened to it?" Kathleen opened the paper portfolio she was carrying, and started pulling out the Xerox copies she'd made at the library.

Regina Fairgate's face went blank. "We didn't budget enough for emergencies," she said, her voice hardly above a whisper.

"*What* emergencies?" Kathleen pulled her gloves off, and handed them to Sam, then unzipped her coat. "Perhaps you'd like to discuss the whereabouts of"—she looked ostentatiously at the papers—"twenty-two thousand six hundred dollars that are missing from the treasury."

"Twenty—?" Mrs. Fairgate started, and Sam could see that she was genuinely surprised at the figure. She straightened her shoulders and spoke calmly. "Everything is accounted for."

"Oh, really?" Sam said. "We couldn't find the receipts, Mrs. Fairgate. Maybe you could show us some of the stuff you bought for the school, like the new ropes for gym class." There was a questioning buzz in the room. "Or maybe the new bookshelves in the library."

"I don't know what you're talking about."

"Or maybe we could just talk to a few of the repairmen you've hired this year," Kathleen finished.

Mrs. Fairgate's jaw tightened. "What are you implying, Kathleen?"

"You tell me."

"Yeah, Gina," Chrissi's father said from his position on the balcony. "I'd really like to hear all about it."

She looked from face to face in the crowd, then turned to the other board members, who shrunk away from her.

It was over.

The admiral was smiling when he came in.

"They're going to win it," he said.

Sean smiled back, a little confused. "I thought we already won."

"No, not the contest."

"The meeting? The board meeting?"

"Yeah. Your mom came through, kid."

"Wow."

The admiral sat down. "You're probably going to go back really soon."

"Probably?"

"It's hard to tell for sure when Sam will Leap out. He may stay another day, for all we know. But chances are, you're going to find yourself at the town hall in about half an hour, maybe less. I just wanted to make sure I came in to say good-bye first."

"Thanks," Sean said absently. It was insufficient, of course. The admiral and the people here had saved the gifted program, helped his friends, helped his mother, and helped him. "Thanks" didn't seem to make much of a dent in the debt. "I owe you guys a lot."

"You don't owe us anything."

"Is this what you and this Sam guy do that pays for itself?"

Al laughed. "I ought to take *that* one to the Committee. They'd laugh for a long time."

266

"I guess that was sort of a dumb question," Sean said, looking at all the fancy equipment he could see even locked up here.

"No question is dumb. And I *would* do this for free, if that's the way it had to be."

They sat quietly across from each other, neither of them knowing exactly what to say next. Finally, Sean asked, "Will I remember you after I go back?"

"I don't know. We can't really get any feedback on that. There's no data. The most I can tell you is that one Visitor told the paper that he was kidnapped by a UFO, and his details were a little fuzzy. Some of the others might have remembered more, but they never told anyone, and it never got back to us."

"You couldn't call or something?"

The Admiral shook his head. "We're classified, Sean. We couldn't explain what we were calling about."

"And nobody's ever tried to get in touch with you?"

"No."

For Sean, who couldn't imagine *not* wanting to come back here, that closed the subject. "So it's all been pretty pointless, hasn't it? I'll probably forget it all, anyway."

"Truth?"

Sean nodded.

"You might. Until you've Leaped back, we're not completely sure about anything."

"I still might kill three people?"

"Probably not. Saving the program will most likely give you something better to do with your brain, no matter what happened here."

"I don't want to forget."

"I know that, Sean." The admiral leaned toward him, his elbows on his knees. "What we think most people remember—we can't be sure, but we *think* this is it—is a sort of dream."

"I almost always forget my dreams." Sean smiled weakly. "Maybe we could tie a ribbon around my finger or something."

"It wouldn't Leap with you. Your body's the only thing you can take back."

"Figures."

The older man sat back. "Do you want me to stay until you Leap?"

Sean shook his head. "If you did that, the other guy'd probably decide to stay a week."

"Good point." He stood. "I'm glad you came here," he said. "It was good talking to you."

"You, too."

"Good-bye."

"Good-bye."

And that was it.

The admiral opened the door and walked out.

Well, what did you expect? That he'd adopt you or something?

No. It was time to go home. Time to forget.

But Sean rebelled against it. He might not be able to remember everything, but he was *not* going to forget it all.

"Your body's the only thing you can take back."

Maybe so, but it was going back *to* something, wasn't it?

Of course. That was it. If he could just think of some way to leave himself a message, some small reminder. Maybe the guy, Sam, could leave something in his room.

Second thoughts killed that idea. First, if Sam was at the meeting now and might Leap anytime, there was no way he could be sure to leave anything in Sean's room. Second, Sean had so much crap in his room that he wouldn't notice if someone parked an alien spaceship on his bed.

268

So maybe there's something at the town hall.

Maybe. It was possible, anyway, that he could find something to leave in a coat pocket. Except that Sean shoved *everything* into his coat pockets. What would that accomplish?

Something unusual then. And something that would be in his hands when he got back.

Yeah, that would work. No one would think twice about him picking something up; he was a pack rat, he did it all the time. And if it was something specific enough, maybe he'd remember why. If he remembered exactly, he'd remember that it was classified, and not tell. If he didn't remember exactly, maybe it would trigger whatever was left, and make him think really hard about what he'd learned here, sort of like those posthypnotic suggestions they liked to show on television, like "Every time you hear the word 'peanuts,' you'll sing the National Anthem" or something.

Okay, then, he told himself. *Every time you see whatever you're holding in your hand when you get back, you'll remember that there's someone out there who cares what you do with your life.*

All well and good, except for two things:

(1) Sean had no idea what was in the town hall that could possibly have such an effect on him, and (2) he didn't know how he would make sure that anything at all was in his hands; the admiral was gone, and he had no idea how to get him back.

But there *was* a system, somehow. The admiral had gotten called out of here once. There had to be a way to call him back. Someone was watching. He'd mentioned a name.

You've got someone who works here named "Ziggy"?
You could say that.

It was worth a try.

"Ziggy?" Sean called into the thin air. There was no answer. "I know you're listening. Or maybe you're someone

269

else. Dr. Beeks? Anyone? I know someone's there."

No answer.

"I have to talk to the admiral," Sean said, praying that his suspicion was right, and he was being watched. "Please. Call him back here, or open the door." Nothing.

Sean bit his lip. Time was short. He could feel it, no matter what the admiral said about Sam staying longer than he thought he would.

Open the door.

He'd promised not to, but he didn't see any option. He ran over to the door across the room and reached for the panel he'd pried open when he first arrived. An electric shock bit his hand and threw him backward.

"Hey!"

No one responded. Sean stood and went toward the door again. He reached for the panel, ready to ignore the shock, but it didn't come. The metal was cool under his skin. He twisted his thumbnail trying to pry the upper left corner. It came off with a force he hadn't anticipated, and he fell again. The wires stared at him blindly, and he couldn't remember which ones he had crossed before. There was no time to experiment. He sat down on the floor and buried his hands in his hair. It was hopeless.

The door opened.

"Sean!" The admiral knelt down in front of him and put his hands on his shoulders. "Are you okay? What is it?"

"You came back."

"Ziggy told me you were going a little crazy in here. What's going on?"

"I need you to do one more thing for me."

Sam was standing on the porch of the town hall, reading the notices on the bulletin board beside the door. It reminded him a great deal of Elk Ridge's perennial announcement board, with birth notices, recruiting posters, sale flyers . . . it wasn't quite like going home, but it was a welcome taste of it.

It was cold out, but Sam had a feeling that Al would be back soon, probably for the last time on this Leap, and he didn't want to have to make excuses to anyone. It would take time, and his time was running out here. After five years on the merry-go-round, he'd learned how to read the signs that said this circle was almost closed.

Kathleen was inside with Chrissi's father, who'd insisted on interviewing her for Thursday's *Crier*, which would carry the meeting as a front-page story (he said it very importantly, but Sam suspected that such things as school board meetings and town council meetings were as much a staple of the *Crier*'s front page as they were of the Elk Ridge *Gazette*'s). Regina Fairgate had left with "no comment," and the other members of the board had suddenly remembered pressing business elsewhere as well.

The Imaging Chamber Door opened.

"I was wondering if you'd get here," Sam said. "We did great in there—"

Al waved it off. "Of course you did. I told you you would. But you have to do something else."

Sam rolled his eyes. "Don't tell me: I was really here to help Chrissi pick out a new shade of lip gloss."

"I'm serious, Sam. Sean wants me to leave him some kind of message, so he doesn't forget the things we talked about."

"Are you crazy, Al? We can't—"

"I'm not talking about leaving him a phone number, Sam. Just something that might make him think. A little bit." He stopped, and pointed at the bulletin board. "That's it."

"What is?" But Sam didn't really need to ask. There was only one thing on the bulletin board that would have called to Al. Sam reached out and pulled down the Navy recruiting poster. "And you really think this will work?"

"Just keep it in your hand."

Sam looked at it skeptically (as Kathleen O'Connor would in twenty minutes, when she would come outside and ask her son if he was planning on joining up; Sean would make a joke, not really knowing why he was holding a Navy poster, but he would not put it back, nor would he throw it out at a later date). "If you say so."

Al was checking the scenarios in the handlink when Sarah came outside.

"I loved the last-minute entrance," she said. Her parents were at the door, talking to Mrs. Martinez. "It was very . . . dramatic. And here I thought Johnny was the ham."

Sam smiled. "I aim to please."

"Did I hear my name?" Johnny demanded, appearing over the brick rail on the stairs. Pigeon was with him. "Are you bad-mouthing me, Sadie-lady?"

Sarah blushed.

"Where's Chrissi?" Pigeon asked.

"She's inside with her father," Sam said. "She said she likes to watch him work."

"Oooo-kay," Johnny said.

"So, what happens now?" Sarah asked. "I mean, they're still out of money. Are we going to get to States?"

"Oh, yeah," Al said. "They don't win, but they go. They come in fifth. The town cuts a deal with Fairgate. She pays back every cent, and they don't prosecute her. Of course, she and her husband have to sell their house and one of their cars, but it's a small price."

"I bet we go," Sam said.

"And where, oh wise one, do you come by your information?" Johnny asked, bending at the waist.

"I told you Saturday," Sam said. "I have a spy from the future."

"Sam!"

"Oh, yeah. I forgot." Johnny stood up again. "Well, if we can't trust your spy, who can we trust?"

"Damn right," Al agreed.

"I don't know about you guys," Sarah said, "but I'm freezing cold. I'm going inside."

"I'll keep you warm, baby," Johnny offered, putting his arms around her and leading her inside.

Pigeon stood on the step beside Sam for a minute more. "Aren't you coming in?"

"No, I think I'll stay out here and wait for my mom."

"You sure?"

"He's sure," Al said.

Sam nodded. Pigeon went inside. "So what else happens?"

"Well, next year, the whole board gets voted out of office. Johnny's father gets reelected, and winds up president."

"And the kids?"

"Well, Johnny never goes to private school. He graduates in 1988, goes on to Yale, then comes back here to teach. He's in charge of the gifted program."

"Good. He'll make a good teacher."

"Pigeon goes on to med school, and he's going to be a gerontologist. He marries the girl next door. Literally."

"What about Sarah?"

"She just won a Tony for Best New Play. It's called *Big Fish*."

"No kidding?"

"I thought you'd like that."

"Sean?"

"It worked. A minute ago all the numbers changed."

"For the better?"

"Yeah. He stays legit. Puts his business sense to use running a company right here in Penworth, making video equip-

273

ment. He employs half the county. It's the only American company that makes most of this stuff.''

"And Chrissi?"

"Still no data."

"I don't get it."

"I don't eith—"

Al stopped talking abruptly when a small figure leaned through him, her face appearing through his green tie. She put her hands on Sam's shoulders, and leaned down to kiss his cheek. Al stepped aside to get a better look at her. He paled. "Is this Chrissi?"

"My father's going to work at the paper tonight," Chrissi said. "Some honeymoon. Jenny's pissed. She's taking me out for dessert. We're going to bond."

She leaned back, and in Sam's vision she was standing beside Al, a wide smile on her face.

(*Just like the smile on her face when he invited her to go back to Vegas with him.*)

The last piece of the puzzle fell into place.

Sam laughed.

"What's so funny?" she asked.

"This is not funny," Al said, but he was addressing the air, and Sam thought he was talking to Ziggy. "Is this your idea of a joke?"

A red car squealed out of the parking lot and pulled up in front of the town hall. There were two brief horn bursts, then the driver's side window was rolled down. Chrissi's stepmother leaned out. "Step on it, Christina!" she called. "I'm not waiting all night for you, either."

Chrissi shook her head and tousled Sam's hair, then ran to Jenny's car. She stopped halfway and blew a kiss at them. "Later, babe!" she called.

Al started to say something, thought better of it, started to say something else, thought better of that, too, and finally just watched, gape-mouthed, as the car peeled away from them.

Sam was still laughing when he Leaped.

ALL-NEW, ORIGINAL NOVELS BASED ON THE POPULAR TV SERIES

:QUANTUM LEAP:

__ODYSSEY 1-57297-092-8/$5.99
1983: Sam Leaps into troubled but gifted Sean O'Connor.
1999: Al Calavicci has the real Sean O'Connor in "detention"
in the Waiting Room—and he's determined to escape.

__TOO CLOSE FOR COMFORT 1-57297-157-6/$4.99
Sam Leaps into a 1990s men's encounter group, only to
encounter Al on a mission that could alter the fate of the
Quantum Leap project for all time.

__THE WALL 0-441-00015-0/$4.99
Sam Leaps into a child whose destiny is linked to the rise—
and fall—of the Berlin Wall.

__PRELUDE 1-57297-134-7/$4.99
The untold story of how Dr. Sam Beckett met Admiral Al
Calavicci; and with the help of a machine called Ziggy, the
Quantum Leap project was born.

__KNIGHTS OF THE MORNINGSTAR 1-57297-171-1/$4.99
When the blue light fades, Sam finds himself in full armor,
facing a man with a broadsword—and another Leaper.

__SEARCH AND RESCUE 0-441-00122-X/$4.99
Sam Leaps into a doctor searching for a downed plane in British
Columbia. But Al has also Leapt—into a passenger on the plane.

__PULITZER 1-57297-022-7/$5.99
When Sam Leaps into a psychiatrist in 1975, he must
evaluate a POW just back from Vietnam—a Lieutenant John
Doe with the face of Al Calavicci.

Based on the Universal Television series created by Donald P. Bellisario

Payable in U.S. funds. No cash orders accepted. Postage & handling: $1.75 for one book, 75¢
for each additional. Maximum postage $5.50. Prices, postage and handling charges may
change without notice. Visa, Amex, MasterCard call 1-800-788-6262, ext. 1, refer to ad #530

Or, check above books	Bill my: ☐ Visa ☐ MasterCard ☐ Amex	
and send this order form to:		(expires)
The Berkley Publishing Group	Card#_____	
390 Murray Hill Pkwy., Dept. B		($15 minimum)
East Rutherford, NJ 07073	Signature_____	
Please allow 6 weeks for delivery.	Or enclosed is my: ☐ check ☐ money order	
Name_____	Book Total $_____	
Address_____	Postage & Handling $_____	
City_____	Applicable Sales Tax $_____ (NY, NJ, PA, CA, GST Can.)	
State/ZIP_____	Total Amount Due $_____	

An all-new, original novel based on the smash hit TV series

sliders:
the novel

What if...it's Earth, it's 1995,
      but Newt Gingrich is President of the United States?

What if...it's Earth, it's 1995,
      but Elvis is still alive and performing in Las Vegas?

What if...it's Earth, it's 1995,
      but your father hadn't met or married your mother?

Quinn Mallory and his friends are about to find out—by taking the ultimate "slide" through parallel dimensions of Earth. Each time they step through the strange portals Quinn opens, a new present-day San Francisco awaits. Sometimes fascinating. Sometimes frightening. Always dangerous....

___1-57297-098-7/$5.50 (Available April 1996)

Payable in U.S. funds. No cash orders accepted. Postage & handling: $1.75 for one book, 75¢ for each additional. Maximum postage $5.50. Prices, postage and handling charges may change without notice. Visa, Amex, MasterCard call 1-800-788-6262, ext. 1, refer to ad # 623a

Or, check above books	Bill my:	☐ Visa	☐ MasterCard	☐ Amex	
and send this order form to:					(expires)
The Berkley Publishing Group	Card#				
390 Murray Hill Pkwy., Dept. B					($15 minimum)
East Rutherford, NJ 07073	Signature				
Please allow 6 weeks for delivery.	Or enclosed is my:	☐ check	☐ money order		

Name_____   Book Total $_____

Address_____   Postage & Handling $_____

City_____   Applicable Sales Tax $_____
                                (NY, NJ, PA, CA, GST Can.)

State/ZIP_____   Total Amount Due $_____

"Fast-paced...realistic detail and subtle humor. It will be good news if
Shatner decides to go on writing."—<u>Chicago Sun-Times</u>

— WILLIAM SHATNER —

___TEK POWER 0-441-00289-7/$5.99

Jake Cardigan must stop the Teklords from abducting the president, a man
addicted to Tek, and replacing him with an android which is programmed to
throw the country—and the world—into chaos.

___TEK SECRET 0-441-00119-X/$5.99

What began as a routine missing-persons case gives Jake Cardigan a chilling
glimpse into the world of super-industry growing more corrupt–and more
lethal–each day he manages to stay alive.

___TEKWAR 0-441-80208-7/$5.99

Ex-cop Jake Cardigan was framed for dealing the addictive brain stimulant
Tek. Now mysteriously released from prison, Jake must find the anti-Tek
device carried off by a prominent scientist.

___TEKLORDS 0-441-80010-6/$5.99

When a synthetic plague sweeps the city and a top drug-control agent is
brutally murdered by a human "zombie," all roads lead Jake Cardigan to the
heart of a vast computerized drug ring.

___TEKLAB 0-441-80011-4/$5.99

Teklord Bennett Sands's daughter and Jake's son are missing, and Jake must
enter the ruins of twenty-first- century London and survive a showdown with
a deranged serial killer...

___TEK VENGEANCE 0-441-80012-2/$5.50

Jake is lured away from his girlfriend before she testifies against the
Teklords. It is the biggest mistake of his life—one that sparks an act of
vengeance so powerful, that no human or android is safe.

Payable in U.S. funds. No cash orders accepted. Postage & handling: $1.75 for one book, 75¢
for each additional. Maximum postage $5.50. Prices, postage and handling charges may
change without notice. Visa, Amex, MasterCard call 1-800-788-6262, ext. 1, refer to ad # 394

Or, check above books   Bill my: ☐ Visa ☐ MasterCard ☐ Amex
and send this order form to: (expires)
The Berkley Publishing Group   Card#_____
390 Murray Hill Pkwy., Dept. B   ($15 minimum)
East Rutherford, NJ 07073   Signature_____
Please allow 6 weeks for delivery.   Or enclosed is my: ☐ check ☐ money order

Name_____   Book Total $_____

Address_____   Postage & Handling $_____

City_____   Applicable Sales Tax $_____
                                      (NY, NJ, PA, CA, GST Can.)
State/ZIP_____   Total Amount Due $_____